W9-ARQ-747

Also by Carolyn Hart

Death on Demand

Death on Demand

Design for Murder

Something Wicked

Honeymoon with Murder

A Little Class on Murder

Deadly Valentine

The Christie Caper

Southern Ghost

Mint Julep Murder

Yankee Doodle Dead

White Elephant Dead

Sugarplum Dead

April Fool Dead

Engaged to Die

Murder Walks the Plank

Death of the Party

Dead Days of Summer

Henrie O

Dead Man's Island

Scandal in Fair Haven

Death in Lovers' Lane

Death in Paradise

Death on the River Walk

Resort to Murder

Set Sail for Murder

Death Walked In

A Death on Demand Mystery

CAROLYN HART

WILLIAM MORROW
An Imprint of HarperCollins*Publishers*

HarperCollins books may be purchased for educational, business, or sales promotional use. For information please write: Special Markets Department, HarperCollins Publishers, 10 East 53rd Street, New York, NY 10022.

FIRST EDITION

Designed by Daniel Lagin

Library of Congress Cataloging-in-Publication Data

Hart, Carolyn G.

Death walked in : a death on demand mystery / Carolyn Hart.—1st ed.

p. cm.

ISBN 978-0-06-072405-4 (hc)

1. Darling, Annie Laurance (Fictitous character)—Fiction. 2. Darling, Max (Fictitious character)—Fiction. 3. Booksellers and bookselling—Fiction. 4. South Carolina—Fiction. I. Title.

PS3558.A676D46 2008

813'54—dc22 2007043589

---

08 09 10 11 12 OV/RRD 10 9 8 7 6 5 4 3 2 1

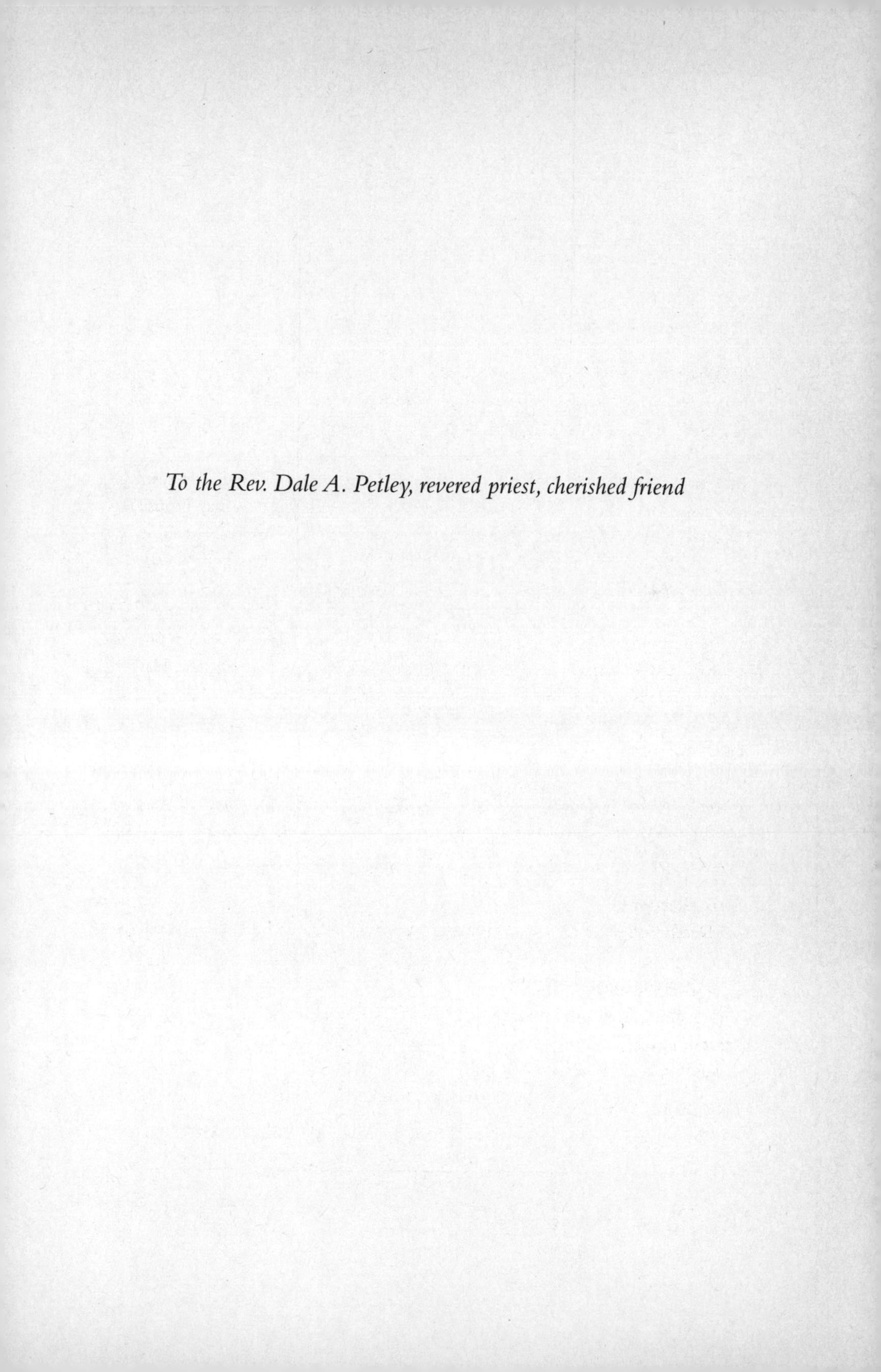

To the Rev. Dale A. Petley, revered priest, cherished friend

Prologue

The single-unit air conditioner wheezed in its never-ending battle against the Singapore humidity. Thunder rumbled in the distance. The store was in an unremarkable two-story white stucco building on a narrow street off Lor Liput in Holland Village. In the corner of the plate-glass window, small gilt letters spelled CURIOS. At the rear of the cluttered room, a man of indeterminate age sat behind a teak desk. He was possibly forty, possibly sixty, with a thin, impassive face, hooded dark eyes, and pencil mustache. One of his passports—this one UK—was in the name of Felix Fogg. It wasn't his real name. He would carry this passport when he flew to Atlanta for a rendezvous at the High Museum. He always transacted business in public places. He and his client would meet on the sculpture terrace outside the Wieland Pavilion. He would exchange a hollowed-out book with a sheaf of thousand-dollar bills in the sealed center for a small package.

Of course, he would first make a careful check of the goods. He knew his field. He would then travel to Fort Worth to meet a collector who cared only for the beauty of the pieces in his collection and was indifferent if their unknown history included theft, deception, or murder.

Chapter 1

Ben Travis-Grant wished he'd brought his ski jacket. He hated cold weather. Too bad Geoff's birthday was in February. It was more fun to come home to the island in July than in winter. He grinned as he thought of women on the beach in bikinis. However, despite Broward's Rock's chilly breezes, not one of them would miss Geoff's annual weeklong birthday bash. The entire family rallied round for cake and ice cream and champagne toasts to Geoff's longevity. Still, February was the pits. A damp chill oozed through a crack in the top of his classic '74 MGB convertible.

The house would be warm and cheerful, and Geoff's parties were always fun. Without exception, they all wished him a long life. When Geoff knocked at the pearly gates, the good times would grind to a halt. Geoff had unveiled his testamentary intentions several years ago. Everything went to Chastain College. The college had already repaid the expected boon with a position on the board of trustees and a distinguished-graduate award. Fortunately Geoff wasn't really old, though almost fifty seemed ancient compared to Ben's exuberant twenty-five. Ben brightened. Geoff had married Rhoda a couple of years ago. Sex was good for people. He'd seen a story the other day that even old folks enjoyed sex. He grinned. Why not?

None of them had any right to grouse. Geoff had been generous to one and all, adopting the offspring of his first two wives, giving them his name and helping them through college. He also had a real instinct for what mattered to kids. He'd insisted each kid add his birth dad's name to Grant. It bothered Geoff that Ben hadn't graduated, but Ben was in no hurry. As for the party, Geoff could always be counted on for a thousand bucks at his birthday gathering and a cool five thousand every Christmas.

Ben raised an imaginary glass. "Long live Geoff!"

Slowly his hand fell and his face furrowed. Could he touch Geoff for an extra ten thou this week? He thought of Joey in the hospital in Bangkok. He wanted to help Joey if he could—no money and sick as a dog.

He moved restlessly, almost opened the door to plunge out on the deck of the ferry and pace. He hated being confined, but he also hated the cold wind on the open deck. Earlier, he'd scanned the half-dozen cars waiting to come aboard and hadn't spotted any of the family. He'd hoped to see Kerry, but likely she was already at the house, seated on an ottoman near the fire, watching and listening, dark hair swirling to her shoulders, grave eyes attentive, sweet lips ready to curve into a smile.

Kerry. Kerry. Kerry. Lovely as a dream, elusive as a wisp of cloud, beyond his reach. Of all the women for him to want . . . It made no sense. He'd always rocketed along having fun, but deep inside he couldn't deny his hunger for Kerry. Yet, even if he somehow captured her heart, Geoff would make good his threat. Geoff had always been protective of Kerry. But who wasn't? She was goodness wrapped in beauty. Geoff was tough about some things. He wanted everyone in the family to set a good example to the world. That's what he'd told Ben on a grim day six years ago.

There was one way to forestall Geoff's revelations to Kerry.

Ben's hands clenched on the steering wheel. If he told the truth, he'd be safe. But he couldn't do that. What else could he do?

Rhoda Grant hurried through the statuary garden. She'd felt choked in the overly warm house. The misty February day was chilly, the temperature in the forties. She welcomed the brisk air, the sense of escape.

She stopped at the far end on the lowest terrace, hidden from view behind a reproduction of a nude Aphrodite kneeling. The white marble statue was a favorite of Geoff's. Her eyes flashed, but she pushed away the clamor of angry thoughts that threatened to envelop her. She had only a moment. Rhoda lifted her cell phone, punched a number. It rang without answer. She left no message, clicked off. If he'd answered, what would she have said? She had to make up her mind.

It was all Geoff's fault. If he hadn't sold the plane, she would have been happy. She loved to fly, going up into blueness, far from the earth, exhilarated and free. Would she ever be free again?

Hyla Harrison worked at a table in her room. She welcomed the warmth from the fireplace. She gave the .40-caliber semi-automatic Glock pistol a final swipe with the cloth. The steel-polymer gun gleamed, dark as midnight. She balanced it in her hand. Without warning, the nightmare vision returned, blotting out the dancing flames in the fireplace, wrapping her in shaking horror:

George called in. "Two-adam-seven." Dispatch responded, "Two-adam-seven, go ahead." "We'll be out of the unit checking a suspicious light in apartment construction at Market and Halliday." "Ten-four, two-adam-seven." George touched the screen, pinpointing their location. They grabbed their nightsticks and, flashlights shining, approached the entrance on opposite sides to avoid being silhouetted. After that, the details were hazy. Shots. George spun around, blood splotching his khaki uniform shirt. She called in. "Two-adam-seven, officer down! Officer down! Market and Halliday." Dispatch: "Confirm Market and Halliday?" "Affirm." As the sound of running steps dwindled in the distance, she knelt beside George. "Jessie . . ." His wife's name ended in a bubble of blood.

A black-clad figure in thick-soled running shoes slipped down the broad shallow steps of the main stairway. No one else stirred in the silent house. The grandfather clock in the main entryway tolled the hour, once, twice, marking the depth of night when sleep is heaviest, consciousness lost in the labyrinth of dreams and imaginings.

Once in the hallway, cautious steps led to the heavy oak door of the library. The recently oiled—think ahead, avoid trouble—

hinges made no sound as the panel swung in. With the red velvet curtains drawn against the night, the room was black as pooled oil. The hall door closed behind the silent figure. A pencil-thin shaft of light danced around the room, touching a basket of potpourri, a dingy suit of armor, settling on the glass display case.

Heart thudding, the figure reached the case. If this were successful, the future would be bright. The plan was foolproof, the contact made with the dealer, a huge sum of money the prize.

Eight quick steps reached the French window to the terrace. A pull and the heavy drapes parted. The pale rays of the February moon fell in a faint path across the room, turning the furniture ghostly. A click and the door opened. The figure stepped outside, eyes nervously scanning crushed-oyster-shell paths, moon-touched sculptures, a trellis covered by winter-browned vines, a dark row of cedars.

The garden should be empty at two o'clock in the morning. There was no movement, only the rustle of magnolia leaves fluttering in a sharp breeze.

The gloved hand reached inside, closed the drapes. It was important that faint splinters of glass be found embedded in the velvet. A thick cloth pad was pressed against the pane nearest the handle. Three sharp blows of a small hammer and the glass cracked, showering inward. The gloved hand yanked the drape out of the way, hurried back to the case. Several more blows, muffled by the pad, and the plate glass shattered.

The gray fox paused at the clearing. Head lifted, the vixen sniffed into the cool February breeze. She caught a hot, moist, rich scent. She waited, wary for movement or danger, but no sound broke the night calm and her sensitive nostrils detected no trace of dogs.

Satisfied, the fox veered left, padded noiselessly, nostrils quivering. The succulent scent grew stronger, more enticing. The chicken coop lay silent at the back of the modest yard.

The fox's sharp eyes studied the gray wooden structure in a pale wash of moonlight. She circled, nose close to the earth. At the rear of the coop, she found a broken slat and hooked it with a paw. The wood was old and rotten. The slat crackled as it split. The hens began to murmur and stir. The board ripped free. The fox nosed inside.

Frantic squawks clamored against the night silence.

A slight breeze stirred the curtains. Gwen Jamison slept with her windows raised, welcoming cool fresh air. She moved restlessly in her bed, her sleep fitful. A mother's heart grieves, going back over years and time, wondering what she could have done to make things better. She'd tried, but he wouldn't listen. Robert had been such a beautiful baby—

The shrill cries of the hens woke her. That loose board at the back of the henhouse! She'd asked Charlie to put in a new two-by-four. He'd promised but he hadn't been by yet. He was working so hard to fix up a nursery for the baby. Dear Charlie, such a good son.

She slipped into her house shoes, but didn't take time to get a jacket. As she ran through the kitchen, she grabbed a broom. No fox was going to get her hens. She could count on Buster, the cock, to fight with beak and spurs. Dust and feathers and straw would be whirling about the roost as the terrified hens sought escape.

She plunged out the back door and ran down the path. By the time she reached the henhouse, the hens were quieting. She saw a gray shadow running fast toward the woods. Buster likely had bloody spurs. She doubted the fox would return, but she tugged and pulled an empty rain barrel against the broken slat.

Gwen rested for a moment, breathing heavily. Her back ached. She shivered in her nightgown. She felt cold as frost on a windowpane. She'd fix herself a cup of hot chamomile tea, let her pounding heart slow. As she turned to go back to the house, she heard the squeak of the iron gate at the small, private cemetery nestled among the willows.

Gwen strained to see through the night. Willows screened the cemetery, but she glimpsed a flash of light. Someone with a flashlight had entered the old family cemetery. The burial ground dated back to plantation days in the late seventeen hundreds. Her mama and daddy's people were buried there. Nobody but her people had any business in that cemetery.

Kids up to no good, that's what it had to be. She'd make short work of them. She walked swiftly toward the willows. When she reached the gate, she stopped and stared.

A figure knelt by Grandpa Wilson's grave. The faint glow from a flashlight illuminated a face she knew. She watched as a hole was swiftly dug, a small packet thrust into it, the dirt replaced.

Gwen stepped deep into the shadows of a willow, held her breath as the figure moved past her and the gate squeaked shut. She stood until there was no trace of the flashlight, no sound, and she was alone with a mournful hooting owl amid old headstones silvered by moonlight.

Gwen didn't need a flashlight to move unerringly in the

cemetery. She weeded around the stones, wiped rain-spattered streaks from markers, always knelt by her mama and daddy's graves, remembering laughter and love and long-ago sunny days. She skirted Cousin Amelia's grave and Aunt Thomasina's to Grandpa Wilson's marker. She bent down and moved the bricks that had been placed above soft earth. She scraped away softened earth until her fingers touched the slick surface of a small package securely wrapped in a waterproof trash bag.

Annie Darling rolled over, still in that delicious floating world midway between slumber and wakefulness, eyes closed, one hand reaching for Max. The sheet felt cool to her fingers. She opened one eye. Max was already up. Her smile was sleepy, but content. He was always in a rush these days with so many plans for the remodeling of the old Franklin house. Something special was arriving on the ferry today. She didn't remember what shipment was scheduled to arrive, but Max was excited. Construction and remodeling on a sea island had challenges, not least of which was arranging for delivery of materials. However, she loved their remoteness. To her, Broward's Rock was the loveliest of the South Carolina sea islands, even if it wasn't a hub of commerce and the nearest Home Depot was across the sound in Chastain.

Both eyes opened even though she didn't hurry to wake up. February might not be the island's loveliest month, but the slow, hassle-free pace was welcome after the hubbub of Christmas. She had to handle the store by herself since Ingrid, her stalwart assistant, was out of town for two weeks. She and Duane were visiting her sister in Florida. Going solo wasn't a problem. Tourists were rare in February and she felt comfortable slapping up her BACK SOON sign whenever she needed to run an errand. Fellow islanders understood about February.

She sniffed. Mmm. Max was obviously fixing something special for breakfast. She popped up and shivered in her mid-thigh-length cotton sleepshirt from Victoria's Secret. Max always approved of lingerie from Victoria's Secret. She slipped into a soft fleece robe and pink fluff flip-flops, gave her tangled curls a quick brush, and ran lightly down the stairs and into the kitchen, the wonderful aromas enticing as an embrace.

Max was lifting a casserole from the oven. He turned, blond hair tousled. She loved his slightly disheveled morning appearance, the stubble of beard on his cheeks.

He grinned. "Why am I not surprised that you arrive at the same time breakfast is ready and the coffee brewing?"

Annie laughed. "Timing is everything."

Max slid the casserole onto the tile table, reached out to pull her close. "Good morning, Mrs. Darling."

Their morning ritual never varied, a smile, a hug, a cheerful beginning to the day. Ever since August, when Max had been jailed for a murder he didn't commit, they held each other extra tight.

Annie pulled out her chair, dropped into it, and looked at him expectantly.

"Just a trifle I put together early this morning. Baked apples stuffed with sausage and cranberries." Max delighted in cooking. All the finest chefs were men, he often exclaimed.

Annie would have pointed out the sexist-pig tenor of the comment, but she wasn't going to discourage creativity. Max's cooking was to die for. She lifted a succulent rose-red apple with its mound of stuffing onto her red Fiesta plate, caught a faint scent of thyme along with the rich aroma of browned sausage.

Max poured coffee. Their newest enthusiasm was Tanzanian Peaberry, strong, brisk, and delicious.

Annie heaped apple and stuffing on her fork. She took a bite. Her eyes widened. "Max! This is the best yet."

Max smiled modestly and served himself.

Annie reached for the paper. Except on Sundays, the *Gazette* was an afternoon paper. They saved each issue to read over breakfast the next day. This morning they looked at the Tuesday-afternoon edition. She slid sports and business to Max, kept the front section.

Annie unfolded the paper, glanced at the front page. "Wow."

Max looked over the top of the sports section.

"We had a million-dollar heist Monday night right here on our sleepy island. Marian wrote the lead story." She began to read:

BURGLARY NETS DOUBLE EAGLES
VALUED AT 2 MIL
by Marian Kenyon

Annie grinned. "I expect Marian came up with the headline. It's too jazzy for Vince." Vince Ellis, the editor and publisher, was much more formal. Marian's lively personality added spice to the *Gazette*.

"What happened?" Max added a dollop of butter to his stuffed apple.

Annie rustled the paper and read aloud:

> Eight twenty-dollar gold coins, including an extremely rare 1861 Philadelphia Mint Reverse Double Eagle, were stolen Monday night from the home of island civic leader Geoffrey Grant, Police Officer Hyla Harrison said Tuesday.

Annie raised an eyebrow. "I guess with Billy and his family on a holiday and Lou in the hospital, Sergeant Harrison's in charge." Lou Pirelli was recuperating from an infection following an appendectomy.

> Sgt. Harrison said Grant estimated the value of the 1861 Double Eagle at more than six hundred thousand dollars. According to Grant's report, the stolen coins total almost two million in value and include a rare Mint State (MS–65) 1850 Double Eagle valued at $200,000.
>
> Sgt. Harrison said Grant called police Tuesday morning when he found the glass display case containing the collection smashed and the coins gone.
>
> Sgt. Harrison said the display case stood in Grant's library. Grant told police he last saw the coins when he locked them into the case around ten-thirty p.m. Monday night. Grant told police he discovered the theft shortly after seven a.m. Tuesday.
>
> The officer said investigation revealed a broken pane in a French window leading into the study from the terrace.
>
> No one in the house reported hearing a disturbance,

> Harrison said. The officer declined to say whether any suspects had been identified.
>
> Grant served three terms on the town council. He is a past president of several service organizations and has worked with the Chamber of Commerce to publicize the island as a vacation destination. He is an adjunct faculty member at Chastain College and is an authority on Victorian literature. Grant said, "The stolen coins represent some of the finest American coins. I hope the thief can be found and the coins returned without damage."

Annie turned the front page for Max to see. "Two pix. One of Geoff Grant." Grant wore his black hair a little long. He looked genial and a trifle smug, a man sure of his position in the world. "And a shot of a gorgeous gold coin." Even in a newspaper reproduction, the coin had unmistakable glory. Annie said casually, "Maybe Grant will hire you to find out what happened."

Max retrieved another apple. "I'm too busy to run around looking for a small-time thief."

She was startled. "Since when is two million dollars small-time?"

Max added a dollop of orange marmalade to the stuffing. "The thief is small-time even if the theft isn't. It's too risky for a sophisticated crook. The only access to the island is by ferry or private boat or plane. You can bet Harrison's already got a line on arrivals and departures. I'll bet she already has a list of every car, truck, bike, or boat that left the island Tuesday morning. Strangers stand out like a sore thumb this time of year. A thief with any savvy would wait until July, maybe July Fourth when the island is packed with visitors, and it would be easy to come and go without notice. Here's my prediction: When the police find out why the theft occurred in February, they'll know the whole story."

Tendrils of fog drifted across the island, turning the marina ghostly, trailing over the boardwalk to hover near the plate-glass windows of the shops and stores. Snug in the inner office of Confidential Commissions, Max Darling reclined in his red leather desk chair, head resting comfortably, feet slightly elevated, and gazed at his favorite portrait of Annie in the ornate silver frame provided by his mother.

Come to think of it, he'd never paused to wonder at Laurel's selection. The intricate silver swirls of the frame were dramatic. A no-nonsense, plain silver frame, something on the Art Deco line, would better suit his delightful and delightfully predictable wife, honest, open, genuine, unpretentious, adorable Annie.

Was Laurel suggesting that the inner Annie—his mother was ever attuned to the subconscious—might not be quite so predictable? Certainly Annie was often impulsive. She'd been known to explode when provoked. Sometimes when she plunged directly toward her objective, she was unaware of possible repercussions. Max gave a thumbs-up to the portrait.

Annie's gray eyes gazed steadily toward him. Flyaway honey-bright curls framed an open and generous countenance. Her kissable lips were slightly parted, ready to smile.

Whatever, predictable or possibly possessing depths perceptible only to his perspicacious mother, he was one lucky man and he knew it.

Max's smile faded. He drew in a sharp breath as he grappled

with the sudden tightening in his chest that still came, though not so often now. He gripped the edge of the gleaming Renaissance refectory table that served as his desk. The table was one of the few furnishings that hadn't been replaced. Last summer, not long after a last-minute case embroiled him in a murder charge, he'd totally redecorated his office, cypress walls and bookcases, huge framed black-and-white photographs instead of paintings, spare Danish furniture, carpet in squares of black and white.

He'd never said why. The day the office was done, Annie stood on tiptoe to kiss him. She held him tight. "Don't you think a new desk would be better?" The table had been a Christmas gift from Annie when he first opened the office. "Something in chrome and glass?" That would leave the room completely transformed with nothing to remind him of the day when a sultry, hot-eyed young woman walked through that door and asked for help, all the while knowing that a shadowy figure behind her request intended no good for Max.

Max had touched Annie's lips with a finger. "I only think of you when I see my table." He smiled at the memory, and the tightness eased. He gave a final glance at Annie's portrait and was still smiling as he rose and moved quickly toward the door. He should have left a few minutes ago to meet the finish carpenter at the Franklin house. Hopefully, he was ready to put in new cypress paneling in the library. Next stop would be the ferry landing to pick up a shipment of solid bronze sash window fasteners.

Max was eager to get to the house. Yesterday the locksmith had been scheduled to install solid bronze doorknobs with a star pattern in the front and back doors as well as matching plates with upper keyholes which any old skeleton key would open, common to most antique locks, and lower covered keyholes that controlled newly installed interior dead bolts. Of course, there were often delays and complications in getting tasks accomplished. The first shipment of window fasteners had been lost in transit. Stained-glass windows with matching peacocks were overdue. If all went well—his grin was wry, the knowing resignation of a householder involved in renovations—they might move in by April. The house had been his salvation throughout the fall and early winter, always a decision to be made, a workman to hire, an elusive purchase needed. The memory of August blurred beneath happy days and nights.

The door to his office swung open. His tall blond secretary, Barb of the bouffant hairdo, culinary talents, and generous heart, beamed at him. She held the portable phone tightly to her chest, the speaker covered. "Max, a lady needs to talk to you. She says it's urgent."

Barb's voice lifted with delight. To her, urgent spelled trouble and trouble meant Max might soon have an interesting case and Barb could use her Internet skills to come up with information. Max understood her elation. Barb was high energy, and though she'd enjoyed helping choose swatches for the office furniture and dealing with the frame shop about the photographs, she often had nothing to do. She blamed Max for the fourteen pounds she'd gained since summer because she said she cooked too much when she was bored. Despite the limitations of a two-burner stove with a temperamental oven tucked into a dark corner of the storeroom, she created succulent triumphs. Yesterday's dish had been mustard fried rice seasoned with blackstrap molasses and garlic. It had been . . . interesting.

Ever since August, he'd turned down almost all who came to

Confidential Commissions. He'd helped a schoolteacher struggling with identity theft, found a missing gray cat, and failed to authenticate a pitcher's mitt alleged to have belonged to Babe Ruth though he and Annie had had a swell time in Boston checking out records.

He always insisted he wasn't a private detective, explaining that Confidential Commissions was devoted to assisting clients in solving problems. If in the past Confidential Commissions at times appeared to resemble a private detective agency, Max was determined that confusion would no longer arise. Problems he would deal with. But if anyone came to him with a tale of crime, he would remember the lesson that had been seared into his soul: People lie.

"Max?" Barb's whisper was piercing. "She sounds scared."

. . . sounds scared.

Max's face hardened. Last summer a sexy young woman had pretended to be afraid to go to the police. He'd fallen for her story, hook, line, and sinker, and he'd almost been sunk. If the caller was scared, she could be scared on her own time or ask a cop for help.

He sidestepped Barb and flung over his shoulder, "Got to go. Man waiting on me. Tell her to call the cops." He plunged toward the front door. On the boardwalk, he gave another thumbs-up as he passed Death on Demand, the finest mystery bookstore north of Miami. He didn't give another thought to Barb's disappointed face or to the caller who sounded scared. He strained to see through the fog and hoped the carpenter showed up and the ferry was running on time.

Chapter 2

Agatha, the elegant black cat who owned Annie Laurance Darling, stretched luxuriously on her red silk cushion atop the coffee bar in the Death on Demand mystery bookstore. She rolled over on her back.

Annie bent near to nuzzle a soft, sweet-smelling tummy. "Isn't this fun, sweetheart?" Annie was usually gregarious, eager for excitement and people and action, but occasionally she gloried in a quiet day. Today had been sheer delight, she and Agatha alone in the store, catching up on correspondence, packing up books to return, unpacking shipments, including books by Nancy Atherton, Carolyn Haines, and Aaron Elkins. Her faithful clerk Ingrid and husband Duane were sitting in the sun in Florida, no doubt sipping rum coladas. February was a slow month for tourists on the out-of-the-way South Carolina sea island of Broward's Rock, and the bell signaling a customer hadn't rung today, so

Agatha's cushion resided atop the coffee bar in splendor with no concerns about health department directives.

Agatha clamped her front paws to either side of Annie's face. Tiny pressure points hinted at sheathed claws.

Annie remained in a crouch. Agatha was simply being playful. Of course she was. Silky fur muffled Annie's voice. "Let go now, honey."

Did Agatha's claws seem infinitesimally sharper, just this side of embedded? Was there a suggestion of movement by her back paws? With enormous caution, Annie carefully gripped taut front paws to free her head. She pulled away just in time to avoid a rabbit thump from Agatha's back paws.

Annie looked reproachfully into gleaming green eyes. "That wasn't nice." Annie's tone was rueful, not angry. Agatha was what she was, captivating and capricious, loving when it suited her, unencumbered by even a shred of conscience. In short, she was a cat.

Agatha rolled to her feet and strolled on the coffee bar. She leaped to the heart pine floor, moved toward the fire. She looked up at the mantel.

Annie was poised to spring. There were replicas of two of the famous mystery awards, the ceramic teapot presented to winners of the Agatha Awards at the Malice Domestic convention and the rotund ceramic bust presented to winners of the Edgar Awards by the Mystery Writers of America.

Was Agatha getting ready to jump? Instead, Agatha stretched out on the hearth and gazed into the flickering flames.

Annie relaxed and admired the watercolors ranged above the mantel. Every month a local artist created five watercolor paintings, each representing a famous mystery. The first customer to correctly identify the books and authors received a free new book and coffee for a month. This month's offerings were by authors with utterly different and distinctive styles, each a personal favorite of Annie's.

In the first watercolor, a blond woman in a ski parka was trapped between icy dark water in a pumphouse reservoir and a man moving toward her with murder in his eyes and a gun stuck in his belt. His face was deeply tanned, his collar-length sandy hair streaked with gray. Behind him, a dark-haired girl stood on one booted foot. A curly-haired, athletic teenage boy with a fixed look of determination on his face moved forward, a girl's sharp-heeled ski boot clutched in one hand.

In the second painting, a neatly dressed young man, eyes burning in a bloodless face, pulled a younger girl toward the railing of an old brick bridge above a canal behind an abandoned factory. Sunlight glittered on the blade of the knife he clutched in one hand. Police moved toward them. On the towpath near the filthy water, a beautiful dark-haired woman stared upward in horror.

In the third painting, an attractive dark-haired woman in a long cotton dress balanced on wooden boxes stacked beneath a barred window. The alleyway was dim and quiet. She clung to the sill and stared inside the building. Another woman stood watch where the alley opened to the dusty street.

In the fourth painting, a big red pompom bounced on the soiled white stocking cap of a disheveled old woman hunched over the steering wheel of a pickup truck. In the passenger seat, a strikingly pretty slender blonde with hazel eyes held on tight as the truck swung into a snow-crusted drive.

In the fifth painting, guests elegantly attired in nineteen-thirties evening dress stared in horror toward a black piano on a small stage in a ship's saloon that gleamed with mahogany and teak. Half a dozen waiters stood between the guests and the piano. A too-thin, auburn-haired woman in a white satin gown spoke urgently to an angular woman in a black crepe dress who shook her head in refusal.

No entry had yet been received this month. A tiny frown tugged at Annie's face. It was absurd how many times Henny Brawley had won. Henny was Death on Demand's best customer and a cherished friend, but enough was enough.

When Henny didn't win, island mystery author Emma Clyde was likely to swirl into the bookstore in a multicolored caftan, lift a stubby finger, and whip off the answers in her gruff voice, all the while with a hint of disdain as if none of the books could possibly match any of hers. That premise was unspoken but clear.

Annie gave a little jig, carefully avoiding Agatha's tail. This month was going to be different. Henny and Emma were enjoying a sun-drenched sailing trip aboard *Marigold's Pleasure,* the luxurious yacht named after Emma's sleuth. In Annie's view, Marigold Rembrandt was about as charming as a tarantula, but several million readers found her enchanting.

Best of all possible worlds—Annie permitted herself a truly blinding flash of pleasure—Max's mother, Laurel, was also on board *Marigold's Pleasure,* far, far away.

Annie glanced guiltily toward the front door. Max loved to pop in unexpectedly and sometimes he had the same uncanny ability to read her mind as his mother seemed to possess. Annie wouldn't hurt Max's feelings for the world.

Laurel was—Annie searched for the appropriate designation.

Several adjectives hovered in her mind. Dizzy, ditzy, and daring occurred. Laurel in the past had sometimes gently chided Annie for a perceived lack of tact. Annie now made it a point to exercise tact as well as self-control in her mother-in-law's presence. A tactful description of Laurel? Easy as pie. Certainly she could describe Laurel with both tact and accuracy. Laurel was an AMAZING mother-in-law. That summed up Laurel as nicely as Annie knew how.

Laurel seemed—usually—to have Annie's best interests at heart. Max thought his mother hung the moon. Annie forbore to suggest perhaps she resided on it.

In any event, it would be lovely if Max popped in. However, she'd better be sure his surprise was well hidden. Annie skirted the espionage section, stopped in front of the collectible shelves. Max enjoyed mysteries too, especially those by Robert Crais, Ridley Pearson, and Les Roberts, but he wasn't likely to browse among titles by John Dickson Carr, Baroness Orczy, Melville Davisson Post, or Mabel Seely. Annie checked the fourth row. A slight volume with a dull pebbled gray spine was tucked between *The Old Man in the Corner* and *Lady Molly of Scotland Yard*.

Annie gently touched the book. The night she and Max moved into the Franklin house, Max planned to cook a special Low Country dinner of baked scallops, dirty rice, and a steamed vegetable medley with almond cake for dessert. Her gift to him would be the bound monograph: *A History of the Franklin House*.

Until then her surprise would be safe among the rare books, but, just in case he dropped in, she'd better not bring attention to this aisle. She smiled in anticipation as if the wish would magically produce him, thick blond curls damp from the fog, vivid blue eyes filled with love and laughter. To her, he was always the handsomest man in the room with straight firm features and a generous mouth. He was tall, strong, unflappable, and good-humored. For a time, his eyes had reflected the dark days when their life together seemed ended. Slowly, his natural ebullience was returning though he often pulled her near in the night and held her hard as if a rogue wave, unheralded, unexpected, unheard, might pull them apart.

Annie gave a last pleased glance at the book she'd hidden after the manner made famous by Edgar Allan Poe, then walked to the coffee bar. She looked up at shelves filled with white mugs. She never tired of scanning the titles emblazoned on the mugs. Each mug celebrated a wonderful mystery and its author. Which to pick today? Thinking of Max and the lie which had wrapped itself around him, almost destroyed him, she chose *The Franchise Affair* by Josephine Tey.

She reached for the carafe, full to the brim with newly brewed Tanzanian Peaberry. It was a shame to drink coffee alone. She'd give Max a ring and no doubt they'd close their businesses early and slip home for love and laughter on this foggy Wednesday morning. She was reaching for the phone when she remembered. He was going to be at the Franklin house, conferring with the carpenter about new cypress paneling in the library, then swinging by the ferry. They would meet at noon at Parotti's, the island's best and oldest and most down-home eatery. It was a perfect day for a fried oyster sandwich. And an afternoon frolic. . .

The telephone rang.

Annie grinned when she saw caller ID and the familiar number of Confidential Commissions. Sure, she believed in ESP. She lifted the receiver.

Barb's breathless voice started without preamble. "Annie, you know how it is. Max keeps his cell in the car pocket and I don't think he turns it on much. I called him twice."

Annie considered her cell phone a necessity. She wouldn't dream of turning it off. Who knew what she might miss? Abruptly she realized Barb was still talking. ". . . he didn't want to fool with anyone this morning because he was going out to the house. I didn't tell her that, of course. I just said Max wasn't here and she kept on talking. I should have told her he'd refused to take the call, because she asked me to have him call as soon as possible. She said she had to get— Then she stopped and stumbled a bit and went on kind of desperately, saying she couldn't explain it over the phone but the Franklin house was the only place she could hide something and know it would be safe and she'd used her key to get in Tuesday morning but when she went back this morning, her key didn't work. She had to get it—whatever it is—as soon as possible. She said everything would be all right and nobody would be in trouble, but she had to get the package. Max would be doing her a big favor and she promised it was the best way to handle everything. She asked me to please tell Max she was sorry she'd gone inside the Franklin house. Then she gasped, said she had to go, and hung up. I called Max twice and left messages, then I called her back. She picked up the phone but didn't say a word. I hung up and called again and the line was busy. I wouldn't bother you, but I can't catch Max. If this woman hid something in the Franklin house, maybe you should go talk to her."

Annie hunched over the wheel of her Volvo. The farther she drove on Bay Street, the more impenetrable the fog became. Nearly opaque patches were occasionally interspersed with swirling eddies that gave hope only to be snatched away as she plunged into thicker belts. She felt alone in a gray universe, familiar landmarks obliterated. She rolled down the driver's window. It seemed a long time ago that she'd glimpsed the white sign with the arrow pointing to the Sea Side Inn. Had she already passed the road that wound to the Franklin house? Who knew?

She slowed to a stop, studied her island map. Once she passed Sea Side Inn, it was another half mile to the drive to the Franklin house. A quarter mile past their entrance, Bay Street ended. If she turned right on Calliope Lane, she would be nearing her goal. Calliope Lane cut back to the northeast. It was a tiny squiggle on the map, running from Bay Street to Palmetto Drive. Barb had used the caller ID number to find the address. Barb said it was the only house on the lane and it belonged to Gwen Jamison and she supposed the woman on the phone was Gwen Jamison.

The fog thinned momentarily. Annie recognized a lightning-split oak near the drive to the Franklin house. Encouraged, she continued to the dead end and turned right. She encountered another thick patch and drove with white-knuckled determination, praying no one else was on the road.

The fog abruptly shifted, allowing a clear view. She followed a jog in the road. Once around the curve, she saw a neat white picket fence and a mailbox to her right. If the only house on Calliope Lane belonged to Gwen Jamison, Annie had arrived.

She turned into a crushed-oyster-shell drive. A small white house loomed ahead. Lights shone in a front window, a cheerful beacon. Annie parked and walked the short distance to steps and climbed to the porch. The white porch swing looked recently painted. A green pottery frog with a rollicking smile sat by the doormat. She lifted the heavy brass knocker on the front door. She knocked once, twice, a third time. No response. Annie was abruptly aware of heavy silence, made more oppressive by the muffling fog.

She glanced at the lighted window. Had Mrs. Jamison gone out but left the lights on? The curtains were open. Annie walked a few steps and looked inside at a modest living room, a tan and black sofa, a rocking chair with a gay red cushion, an oval braided rug, a portion of an upright piano . . .

Annie felt breath bunch in her throat. A trail of blood began on the floor near the piano bench. She followed it to a slender, work-worn hand that lay palm up near the base of a floor lamp. The fingers jerked. Annie stood frozen for an instant, then plunged toward the front door. She yanked open the screen, turned the knob and the door swung in.

A slender black woman lay on her back near the piano. Blood stained the front of her white blouse, spread in a slow pool to one side. Her eyes were open. The fingers of one hand moved feebly.

A portable phone lay nearby. A mechanical voice announced a phone off the hook. Annie felt frantic. Should she go out to the car, get her cell phone from her purse? The injured woman needed help as quickly as Annie could get it. As visions of fingerprints whirled in her mind, she ran to the phone, dropped to one knee, picked it up. She pushed end, talk, 911.

"Broward's Rock emergency center." In a corner of her mind, Annie wondered who was answering. She didn't recognize the voice. Mavis Cameron, wife of Police Chief Billy Cameron, served in turn as dispatcher for the police department and first responder to emergency calls, but Mavis and Billy and their children were on vacation this week at Disney World. "Please send help." Annie didn't recognize her own voice, high, thin, and wavering. "A woman's been shot."

The responder sounded shocked. "Where are you?"

Annie tried desperately to remember the house number. Barb had given her the number, she'd written it on her map, but the map lay on the front seat of the car. "Calliope Lane. It's the only house. I can't remember the number. One something."

"Who has been shot?" The question was urgent.

"I don't know for sure. It's probably Mrs. Jamison. Please. You've got to hurry. Send help. She's still alive but she's bleeding and—"

A guttural sound came from the woman on the floor.

Annie jumped up and hurried to the wounded woman. She knelt beside her. In her ear, the voice continued, "Please stay calm. An ambulance is on its way. I need to know more—"

"Not now. She needs help. Please hurry."

A whisper of sound came from that still form. Dark eyes blinked. The fingers of one hand moved again. Annie put the phone down, took that seeking hand in her own. "Mrs. Jamison, who did this?"

The gravely injured woman gave no indication she'd heard. Her desperate gaze beckoned Annie.

Annie leaned so near she could feel the faint thread of breath, smell a sweet scent of violet, and, hideously, the rank muskiness of blood, blood that continued to well, turning the starched white cotton blouse sodden and limp.

The voice was louder now from the discarded telephone. "Who is speaking, please?"

The wounded woman's eyes closed, reopened. With enormous effort, her lips parted. She spoke, but the faint sound was lost in noise from the telephone.

Annie reached out, closed the connection. "Mrs. Jamison?"

The dying woman—Annie knew she was dying, there was the smell and feel of death—seemed to steel herself. From deep inside, she drew on a last vestige of strength. Her dark eyes locked with Annie's. ". . . griff . . ." She gave a convulsive jerk. Her body sagged against the floor. Her gaze was fixed and staring. The hand Annie held was at one moment living flesh, the next it was limp, the husk left behind.

The telephone shrilled.

Annie grabbed it up.

A worried voice demanded, "Did you initiate a nine-one-one call? I'm trying to help you but I must know who you are."

Annie managed a choked answer. "She was dying. Now she's dead." Annie tried to stop shaking. "Someone shot her. Please come."

"Ma'am, it is imperative that you remain on the line. An officer is en route and emergency vehicles. Stay calm. I need your name."

"Annie Darling."

"Annie?" There was a change in tone. "Oh, my heavens.

Annie, this is Lana Edwards. I'm trying to take care of the desk for Mavis, but I've never done it before and seeing that red flash for nine-one-one has me all upset. How did you find the lady?"

Annie felt a surge of thankfulness. Speaking to someone she knew made her feel better and safer. Lana Edwards was a retired teacher. Annie had met her in Friends of the Library. "I'll tell them when they get here. It's very complicated. I'll explain to Billy"—she stopped. Billy was in Orlando—"to the officer when she gets here. I'll wait on the front porch." She broke the connection. Quickly, she dialed Confidential Commissions.

With sudden capriciousness, the fog lifted. Max picked up speed. A quarter mile later, he turned the Corvette into the drive to the Franklin house. At the end of the drive, he looked in vain for a bright red pickup with a gun rack in the cab. The drive was empty. Troy Hudman had his pick of jobs on the island and was known to walk out in the middle of a job if he didn't like the owner's attitude. Surely he would understand Max being delayed by fog. Perhaps Troy too was late.

Max parked and strolled up the front steps. The new doorknob had a bright shine. A white sheet poked from the screen door.

Max pulled out the note: "Had to take the early ferry to the mainland. Chance to pick up a '47 Packard. Catch you tomorrow. Troy."

Max crumpled the scrap of paper into a ball, jammed it in his pocket. Hudman collected vintage cars. He could indulge his passion because he earned a great deal of money as the best finish carpenter on Broward's Rock. He was one of many artisans Max had wooed and cajoled to work on the Franklin house.

Max's irritation was momentary. He'd learned in a hard school what mattered and what didn't. What difference did a day make? Max was relaxed as he walked down the broad front steps. He turned and looked back at the two-story tabby house with piazzas both downstairs and up. The majestic white columns had Ionic capitals on the first level and Corinthian on the second. The house sat high on tabby foundations. Tabby was the Low Country's original building material, oyster shells mixed with lime and sand. The support was as firm today as when built in 1805. The front faced southeast to catch prevailing summer breezes.

He took great pleasure in the transformation he and Annie had wrought. The Franklin house had been a sagging ruin, windows broken and boarded over, the stately live oak avenue leading to the house rutted and choked by encroaching ferns and untended shrubbery. The road had been bulldozed level and covered with crushed oyster shells, the trees trimmed, the woods cleared of excess undergrowth.

Max almost climbed into his new black Corvette, but he was in no hurry to see Barb. She wouldn't say a word, but she would be brooding over the client he had turned away. After lunch with Annie, he'd drop by the island bakery and pick up a happy face cookie. Barb would try to hold on to her frown, but she was too good-humored to be grumpy for long. He'd be extra appreciative of today's cooking effort, sweet potato pudding.

He walked to the back of the house, looked down on the garden. The azaleas they'd planted in the fall would create a fairy tale of delicate color next month along with japonica, anemone, daffodils, wisteria, and dogwoods. Patches of fog still shrouded the plants and shrubs. He could barely make out the fish pond. It had been dredged, the surrounding retaining wall rebuilt. In summer, he and Annie would sit in rocking chairs on the back piazza, listen to the grunts, snores, whangs, and wheezes of male frogs serenading their lady loves. Man, did he understand. Guys and frogs did whatever worked, Godiva chocolates, wheezes, whatever. He grinned as he climbed the back steps.

He enjoyed entering the house. The unfurnished rooms were like stages waiting for players, the ceilings immensely high, the doorways wide and tall, the windows huge. Empty, there was nothing to distract the eye from the recently painted or papered walls, spectacular crystal chandeliers, intricate pilasters framing doorways, elaborate cornices throughout, and, Max's favorite, the coved ceiling of the drawing room.

He pulled one of the new keys from his pocket. He was reaching to insert it in the lock when he realized the back door was ajar. Somebody had been careless. He shrugged. No harm done. Many houses on the island were never locked.

A shaft of sunlight pierced the fog, the light emphasizing the rich glow of the refinished floor of the porch. If the floor had been less shiny, he might not have seen a sprinkle of glass near the first window to his right, a window that opened into the back of the main hall.

In two quick steps, he reached the window. The pane in the top frame nearest the interior lock was broken out. How easy to reach inside, undo the lock, push up the bottom sash, and step over the sill. His eyes swung back to the unlocked kitchen door. An intruder would be smart to open an avenue for escape.

Max strode back to the door. He eased the panel wide and

stepped into the kitchen, dim and shadowy despite the array of gleaming new appliances.

A muffled creak sounded above him, followed by dull thumps.

Someone was in the small study upstairs. Max moved to the butcher's block and grabbed a mallet for pounding meat. He stepped out of his loafers and ran soft-footed toward the narrow back stairs.

The interior back stairs were narrow, uncarpeted, and blacker than Arthur Conan Doyle's ghost-hound. Max took a tighter grip on the mallet, which suddenly seemed small. He thought, not for the first time, that the arcane mystery knowledge he'd gleaned from Annie was not always reassuring. Creeping up unlighted back stairs in search of an intruder in a house remote from neighbors could land him in a fight. He wished he'd taken time to grab a log from the woodpile as a possible weapon. Better still, he should have returned to his car and used his cell to call the police. He pictured the cell, resting in the glove compartment. He didn't like to be tethered. Cell phones and BlackBerries were great but he avoided them. He would be the one to order his life, not electronic pings. At this moment, he would have welcomed a tether to the outside world.

The back stairs seemed cocooned in silence. He tried to hurry, stumbled, crashed on all fours in the darkness. No hope now to arrive unannounced. He came to his feet, raced up the steps, flung open the door.

Pounding steps sounded on the main staircase.

By the time Max reached the upper landing, the door to the kitchen banged. Max went down the steps three at a time. He burst into the kitchen. The kitchen door was ajar. He hurried out onto the back piazza. Fog still clung to the trees, drifted across the garden, bunched thick as cotton candy in the lower garden near the pond. Crushed oyster shells popped under running feet.

Max thudded toward the steps.

A shot rang out and then another.

Chapter 3

Annie's voice was high and shaky. "Barb, somebody shot the woman who called. She was still alive when I got here. She died." Annie remembered dark desperate eyes, the warmth of a slender hand.

A siren shrilled, drowning out Barb's reply. Dust rose in a cloud as a police cruiser swung into the drive. The car jolted to a stop, red light whirling.

"The police are here. Find Max and tell him where I am." Annie ended the call. She looked up and came face-to-face with Hyla Harrison, the newest member of the island's police force. Behind her was a man in a crumpled gray suit. He was slightly over six feet tall and probably weighed two hundred and fifty pounds. Cold brown eyes in a seamed face scanned Annie, the porch, and the yard.

Annie remembered Officer Harrison as a tall, somber woman

with lank red hair who wore no makeup. Today there was a difference in the officer's appearance: freshly waved hair that shone, blush, and lipstick. She was the officer who had arrested Max last summer, training a gun on him and treating him like a dangerous felon. Annie fought a rush of dislike even though she knew she wasn't being fair. Still, Annie avoided her at any social gathering, the ice cream and cake social at the club for kids where Officer Harrison and Max both volunteered, Friends of the Library meetings, wherever their paths crossed.

Officer Harrison kept one hand on her holstered gun. She glanced at Annie, swiftly looked around before demanding, "Did you report a gunshot victim?" There was a tiny flicker of recognition in her eyes, but she gave no other indication she'd ever had contact with Annie.

"The woman's dead now. I was holding her hand and she died. I kept asking for help." Annie knew her tone was accusatory even though likely no one could have arrived in time to make a difference. "She's inside."

An ambulance swung into the yard, light flashing, siren wailing. The sound ended abruptly. Two EMTs jumped out, a middle-aged woman with a bush of gray hair and a muscular dark-haired young man with a coral snake tattoo crawling up one arm.

When they reached the porch, Officer Harrison used a pen from her uniform blouse pocket to open the screen door. "Victim inside. Check for life. Don't touch anything. Watch where you step."

Annie almost objected. She'd told her that Mrs. Jamison—if it was Mrs. Jamison—was dead. But procedure had to be followed. Before an investigating officer could touch the body, death had to be officially established.

Officer Harrison gestured toward her companion. "Interview the witness." She disappeared into the living room.

He walked up to Annie. "Officer Douglas Thorpe." His voice was surprisingly soft for such a big man. He flipped open a notebook. "Your name?"

He was polite, but he was a moon-faced stranger. "I know Billy's out of town. Who are you?"

His eyes narrowed. Maybe in his experience, innocent residents weren't on a first-name basis with the police chief and his staff and certainly he hadn't seen any evidence of a relationship with Officer Harrison. "Officer Pirelli isn't available at the moment. I'm working for the department on a temporary basis. Now, miss, what's your name?"

Annie answered questions and tried to decipher the mutter of voices in the living room.

Max crawled to the end of the porch. He took a chance, hoping the fog was thick enough to hide him. He rose and went over the railing and dropped to the ground. In an instant, he was running low to reach the cover of pines. He took his time, darting from pine to pine. He eased his way to the front of the house. The Corvette was within twenty feet, but there was no more cover. He was almost certain his assailant was long gone.

Almost.

He bent, picked up several pinecones. He threw one hard toward the front piazza. It landed with a resounding smack. Max lobbed another and another.

A crow squawked. Magnolia leaves rustled in a gentle breeze. Nothing else broke the silence.

Running in a crouch, Max plunged into the open, raced to the car, slammed inside. As he opened the car pocket, his eyes scanned the surroundings. He yanked out the cell phone, saw the signal for missed messages, punched 911.

"Broward's Rock emergency center." The woman's voice sounded oddly breathless.

"This is Max Darling. I'm at the Franklin house. Nine Bay Street. I surprised an intruder in the house. When I gave chase, someone shot at me. I'd like for an officer to come and check out the house with me."

There was an instant of shocked silence. "Oh, golly, Max, this is Lana Edwards."

Max had a swift memory of a plump retired teacher whom he knew from the Haven. She taught chess.

"I'm helping out while Mavis is gone. There's nobody available right now." Her voice was hurried and excited. "We already have an emergency—a lady shot—and the department is shorthanded. Lou had an emergency appendectomy and he got an infection and he's still in the hospital. They just called in for the crime van and I tracked down Frank Saulter and he's on his way to drive the van . . ."

Max knew the former chief, now retired, didn't mind being called on. Odd to have a woman shot and another shooting in the same morning and the department short-handed. When Billy headed off to Disney World, he would never have expected a rash of crime in sleepy February.

". . . so you can see we're stretched pretty thin. I'll send someone out as soon as I can. Oh, dear" —her voice climbed—"are you hurt? I can come and get you."

Max was confident now that his attacker was gone. Probably

the gunshots had been intended to prevent pursuit, not harm him. "I'm fine. I don't think the shots came near me. I'll drop by the station and make a report after I take a look inside the house." He was already distancing himself from that shocking moment when shots exploded. He was puzzled by the attack. Bringing a gun when breaking into an empty house seemed extreme and shooting it when discovered even more extreme.

"Let me see . . . Yes, that's what I thought," Lana continued artlessly, very likely unaware as a substitute that dispatchers never revealed details of investigations or police response. "I checked the map and the house with the shooting is very close to you. If someone shot at you, maybe it's connected, especially since the call came in from Annie."

Max felt as though a giant hand had grabbed his heart and squeezed. A woman shot? A call to 911 from Annie? Annie should be at the store.

Max fought disbelief. "Annie?"

Lana Edwards was quick to answer. "She called a little while ago. She found a lady shot in a house on Calliope Lane. It runs northeast from the Bay Street dead end. The woman died while Annie was on the phone, but the ambulance and police—"

Max turned on the motor, gunned the car, and careened down the drive.

Officer Thorpe wrote with painstaking slowness. "So your husband's secretary called you and you came over here?" He frowned. "Why?"

Annie pointed at the house. "A woman from this house telephoned my husband's office this morning and asked to speak to him. He was on his way out and didn't take the call. She continued to talk to my husband's secretary and finally she said she'd put something in our house—"

He glanced at his pad. "You live on Scarlet King Lagoon."

Annie felt that she was advancing into a swamp and the muddy bottom sucked at her feet. "Right now we do. But we are redoing an old house—the Franklin house—and it's about a half mile from here." As she spoke, she realized it might be much less as crows flew.

Thorpe looked bewildered.

"Anyway," Annie kept going, "that's why Barb called me. She thought if Mrs. Jamison had hidden something in the Franklin house, we should find out about it."

"What could she have hidden there?" He sounded skeptical.

"I don't know. I hoped to find out."

"Did you?"

"She'd been shot. She tried to speak, but she couldn't."

His eyes narrowed. "She didn't let you inside?"

"No. When no one answered the door and I saw the lights on in the living room, I looked in through the window. She was lying where she is now. I saw"—Annie's voice wavered—"her fingers move. The front door wasn't locked and I went right in. I called nine-one-one. She tried to speak and I couldn't hear her so I ended the call."

"What did she say?" The pen was poised over the pad.

Annie remembered a whisper of sound, scarcely heard and ended mid-breath. ". . . griff . . ." "It sounded like 'griff.' "

" 'Griff'?"

"I think so." She strained to remember. Definitely a *gr* and surely she'd heard an *ffff* sound.

"Maybe a name. Griffin? Or maybe 'grifter'?"

"I don't know." Annie wondered if anyone today ever used that old-fashioned name for a petty crook.

Thorpe glanced toward the living room. "Any cops in her family?"

"I know nothing about her, Officer."

His glance was speculative. "Yeah. That's what you say."

Annie almost made a sharp reply, but cautioned herself to be patient. The officer didn't know her.

The crime van pulled up behind the cruiser.

Dust rose as Max's Corvette arrived at the same time and skirted both the cruiser and the van to slide to a stop in the front yard right by the porch. Max piled out of the car and ran toward the porch.

Officer Thorpe reached for his gun.

Annie grabbed to catch his arm. He jumped away to avoid her touch. "Keep your hands away, lady. Don't touch anything." Now his gun was free and trained between Annie and Max.

"What the hell's going on?" Max kept on coming.

"Max, stop!" Annie yelled.

Thorpe held the gun steady. "Hold it, buddy. This is a crime scene. The lady's hands have to be tested."

Frank Saulter reached the steps. "It's okay, Doug. I'll take over." He casually stepped between Thorpe and Max. "Come on out to the van, Annie. It will just take a second. I'll run the GSR test." Frank was lean and wiry with sharp features and a sallow complexion. He was a little grayer and more stooped than when he had been the island's chief cop.

Thorpe looked at Frank. "You know these people?"

"Small town, Doug. Sure. They're okay, but Annie won't mind if we follow procedure."

As they walked to the van under Thorpe's guard, Annie realized Frank intended to test her hands for gunshot residue. Thorpe was just doing his job.

Max ignored Thorpe. "Frank, listen, I need to tell you—"

Thorpe broke in, "Stow it for now, buddy. Let's get her hands done then you can chitchat."

Max looked thunderous.

Annie gave a tiny head shake, murmured, "Hey, it's okay."

Max frowned. "I'd say nothing's okay right now. What's going on? What are you doing here? Who's the dead woman?"

Thorpe didn't interrupt this time. Instead, he listened intently as Annie explained about Barb's call. She realized he was making sure her account to Max agreed with what she'd told him. As she talked, she held out one hand, then the second for the swabs.

Max looked bewildered. "She hid something in the Franklin house?"

Annie felt bewildered, too. Was the house chosen because it was unoccupied? "That's what she told Barb."

As Frank finished testing, two more cars arrived, Dr. Burford's shabby mud-spattered black sedan and Barb's bright yellow Neon.

Dr. Burford stalked past them, shaggy gray hair uncombed as usual, face drawn in a dark frown. He was the island's revered general practitioner, chief of staff at the hospital, and medical examiner. He worked seven days a week, fighting death with the tenacity of a cornered tiger. He loved babies and hated murder.

He gave them a short nod, his mind focused on the body that awaited him.

Barb skidded to a stop beside them, her eyes bright and excited.

Thorpe glared at her. "Ma'am, this is a crime scene. No loitering permitted."

Max ignored him. "Thanks for coming, Barb."

Barb looked indignant. "Of course I came. The minute Annie called, I tried your cell. I left a message, then headed here. I couldn't let Annie be here all by herself. It's all my fault she's here. Maybe I shouldn't have told her about the call." Barb turned huge, anxious eyes toward the small frame house.

Thorpe stepped nearer, spoke to Barb. "You the secretary?" At her nod, he began with name and address, led her through the morning call missed by Max, the gist of the conversation, and Barb's decision to contact Annie. He wrote fast. "Yeah, I got it now."

Dr. Burford thumped down the front steps, face grim. He stopped beside them. "Death by gunshot. No weapon found. Victim is Gwen Jamison. Apparent murder. They asked if it could be suicide. Sure, if she ate the gun or somebody took it away, but suicides aim for the head, not the chest. Besides, Gwen would never have killed herself. She beat cancer five years ago. She wanted to see her grandbaby born. Fine woman." His voice was weary. "Been a patient of mine since she was a little girl."

Frank Saulter looked grim. "I recognized the address, hoped it wasn't Gwen."

Now the identification was official: Gwen Jamison, dead by an unknown hand on a foggy February morning.

Frank sealed the samples. He closed the test kit and handed Annie a wipe to clean her fingers. As he turned to head for the house, he said softly to Annie, "Thorpe is okay. He's a big-city cop. Cut him some slack," and he was striding toward the porch.

Thorpe stepped closer to Dr. Burford. "You the dead woman's doctor?"

Dr. Burford nodded.

"Who's next of kin?"

"Two sons. Charlie and Robert. Charlie's held a steady job ever since he was in junior high. Robert"—Dr. Burford looked bleak—"well, it will be easier to find Charlie."

Thorpe picked up on Burford's tone. "What's with Robert?"

"Robert's been a handful for Gwen. I don't think he has a steady job."

Thorpe looked like a dog with a scent. "In trouble?"

"Some. Nothing too bad. Drunk and disorderly. Stopped a few weeks ago and marijuana was found in his car. He swore he didn't know anything about it. He's eighteen now so he's charged as an adult. He's out on bail right now."

Thorpe reached for his cell. "I'll get out a pickup call."

Burford shook his head. "Robert wouldn't hurt his mama."

Thorpe wasn't impressed. "Maybe Mama got in his way. Maybe she got on him about something he'd done. Sounds like he's done plenty." He nodded toward Barb, "According to her story the woman was worried about something, maybe hid something in their house." He glanced at Annie and Max. "Their other house. Maybe her son stole something and she was going to try to return it."

Max hesitated, said abruptly, "If she hid something in the Franklin house, I may have interrupted somebody this morning who was hunting for it. I got shot at when I chased him."

Thorpe swung toward Max, his gaze suspicious. "Get a look at the perp?"

"No. I heard him running down the stairs. By the time I reached the back porch, he was out of sight in the fog. I heard oyster shells crunch. The sound came from the far end of our garden."

"You hear a car start up?"

Max blinked in surprise. "I didn't hear anything after the shots." He'd listened hard for the rustle of shrubbery, the crackle of a twig, anything to mark the approach of an armed adversary. "I'd have heard a car."

Thorpe looked around. "Is your place as off the beaten track"—Thorpe's tone as he scanned the ranks of pines, live oaks, magnolias, and thick underbrush equated the location with a far desert outpost in the Indian subcontinent—"as this house?"

"We have three acres. Mrs. Jamison's house may be the residence closest to us."

Thorpe tapped his pen on his notebook. "Kind of unusual for a thief to hike to a place to break in. Now"—he sounded patronizing—"if we had a bunch of homeless bums like in the city, a thief on foot would be no big surprise. Here, I don't think so." He slapped the notebook shut. "You the only one at your place when this happened?" He sounded skeptical.

Max was unruffled. "Yes."

Thorpe pursed his lips. He glanced at Max's hands, shrugged, and walked away.

Max managed a dour smile. "He's implying I can't prove anything and maybe I made it all up. I'm surprised he didn't call Frank out to give me a GSR test."

Annie wriggled her fingers. They still felt sticky. "No point in it. Whether a gun went off or not, you had plenty of time to wash your hands before you got here."

Max frowned. "You on his side?"

"Nope. Just seeing it the way he does. And"—she managed a wan smile— "you're in good company. He didn't believe a word I said, either."

The fog might never have been. The pale blue sky was clear, the air warming into the sixties. Annie parked her Volvo behind Max's Corvette near the front steps of the Franklin house. She jumped out and hurried to join him.

Max smiled as she neared, but his eyes were thoughtful. "Maybe you should go on back to the store. Or"—he sounded hopeful—"you can help Barb round up some facts." Barb had headed straight for Confidential Commissions with a list of questions Max wanted answered. He'd ticked them off in a no-nonsense voice, a wary expression in his eyes, proof that he was still suspicious of Mrs. Jamison's call to his office. "We need to know more about Mrs. Jamison. I'll look around inside."

She didn't bother to answer. She was not made of breakable crystal nor was she worried about a sniper. She'd already linked Gwen Jamison's death to the shots fired here.

Max was worried. "If the guy who shot at me hung around, he'd have heard me leave in a tearing hurry. If he's after something Mrs. Jamison hid here, he may have tried again to find it."

Annie glanced up at the lovely old plantation home and felt a ripple of fear. However, the prickle of uneasiness made her mad. She didn't want their beautiful house, the house Max loved, to be off limits because of something dark and dangerous that left death in its wake.

"I'll fix that." She turned and trotted back to her car. Quickly, she was behind the wheel and turning on the ignition. She pressed on the horn, let it blare.

Max strode toward her.

She stopped pushing and looked complacent.

Max bent to the window.

She nodded with satisfaction. "If there's a bogeyman, he knows we're here and he'll hotfoot it away. We'll give him a few minutes to disappear, then the coast should be—" Her eyes widened, her mouth formed an expressive O.

Max swung around.

A large man advanced around the corner of the house, a shiny shotgun cradled in one arm. He was ruggedly handsome with sun-bleached hair, brown eyes, and strong features. A sharp gaze raked them. He was likely in his forties and moved with easy grace as if he could walk for hours and never tire. A red-and-white-checked flannel shirt was tucked into faded jeans held up by a broad leather belt with a huge silver buckle. He walked silently on thick-soled running shoes. He was a man any woman would instantly notice. He had a faintly insolent air.

Max moved to shield Annie. One hand behind his back made turning motions.

Annie got it. Max wanted her to start the car. If he jumped out of the way, she could drive right at the man if he lifted the shotgun.

The stranger's voice was deep. "Are you Max Darling?"

Max's hand stopped turning, flared into a stop sign. "Yes. And you?"

Their visitor's pugnacious expression eased. "Hal Porter. Critters No More. You got an aggressive alligator, I'm your man."

Annie's fingers hovered near the key.

Porter, a good four inches taller than Max's six-one, stopped a few feet away. "I've been keeping an eye on things here. I was in the middle of putting up a bird feeder at the Grant place." He inclined his head toward the base of the garden. "I heard some shots. I had to get the pole set right in the concrete, then I decided to take a look. Nobody should be shooting a gun off in these woods. They're private. There's a bunch of company at the Grants' this week and somebody might go out for a stroll. I heard a noise in the bushes over by the old cemetery. I gave a shout. Nobody answered. That didn't seem right to me so I gave the cops a ring. Lady told me there'd been a shooting at the old Franklin house, but nobody could come right now. I gave her my name and said I'd check things out. I came up through your garden, but everything was quiet. Nobody's been around until you showed up."

Max stepped forward, hand outstretched. "Thanks, Mr. Porter. I appreciate your looking out for us."

A huge hand enveloped Max's, gave a firm shake. "Call me Hal."

Annie yanked open the door, slid out to stand near Max. "I'm Annie Darling."

He nodded toward her, his gaze admiring.

Annie wondered if Hal Porter was the man who'd corralled a ten-foot alligator last summer that had followed the smell of teriyaki sauce on a backyard grill, meandered onto the front porch, and flopped against the front door, looking for all the world like a dinner guest intent on ringing the bell.

Porter's gaze swung back to Max. "The dispatcher said there was trouble here. What happened?"

"I chased an intruder out of the house and got a couple of shots in return. That's what you heard. It was too foggy for me to see, but I heard noise in the garden. I searched but didn't have any luck, then I had to leave. I appreciate your coming over to see about the shots. That took time away from your job."

Hal shook his head. "No problem. It's the off season. Gators are hunkered down for winter. Snakes, too. I'm doing some handyman stuff for the Grants, but there's no hurry."

Max studied Porter, gave an abrupt nod. "If you've got some free time, I'd like to hire you to watch the Franklin house. We haven't moved in yet, but we think something hidden inside may be linked to a murder."

"Murder?" Porter's eyes narrowed.

"Gwen Jamison was shot and killed this morning." Annie found it hard to say. "She lived on Calliope Lane."

Porter rubbed a thumb against the shotgun barrel. "So she was shot a little ways from here and somebody"—he glanced at Max— "shot at you. What's the connection?"

Annie pointed at the house. "Mrs. Jamison hid something here Tuesday."

Porter's eyes narrowed. "Drugs?"

Max shrugged. "We don't have any idea what she hid."

Annie grabbed his arm. "Max, it's got to be the coins." She turned toward Hal Porter. "You said you're working for the Grants. Geoff Grant?"

Porter nodded. Sudden understanding gleamed in his eyes. "You think those stolen Double Eagles were hidden in your place." He shot a puzzled look at the Franklin house. "Funny place to stash stuff, but I'll be glad to stand guard for you. Fifty bucks a day, if that works for you." He slid his hand along the shiny barrel of the shotgun. "I'm working just up the path. I'll mosey over every little while, though I expect your trespasser won't come back in the daytime anymore. Too much going on here. Tonight I'll bring my camping gear and set up by the back porch. I sleep light. Nobody'll get past me."

Chapter 4

On the back porch, Annie watched as Porter strode to the end of the garden and was lost to view in the pines. "I'm glad he'll stand guard for us."

"Let's hope there's still something here to guard." Max held the back door for her. "Maybe the thief came back. If Mrs. Jamison hid the coins, they may be long gone."

Annie was thoughtful. "Nobody tried to get into the Franklin house until Mrs. Jamison used it for a hiding place. I think the murderer shot her and came over here on foot."

Max rattled off sharp questions. "Why did she hide something here? Assuming she had the coins, did she steal them? How did she have a key? How did the murderer know she hid something here? Why was he on foot? Where did he go?"

"Old locks open to almost any skeleton key. It's the new ones that kept her out today." Annie turned toward the back door. "Anyway, we know she came here early Tuesday and got in without any trouble. The new locks were installed later in the day. When she came back this morning, she couldn't get in so she called you. I think the murderer heard her talking on the phone to Barb. Mrs. Jamison told Barb she'd hidden something here, then suddenly she said she had to go and hung up. That's when the murderer walked in. I'll bet anything the killer came in the back way—most people don't lock their doors in the daytime—and heard her talking."

Max looked grim. "Why shoot her?"

"Whatever she hid, the murderer couldn't afford for anyone to know about it. Maybe it was the coins or maybe a confession of some sort." Annie had a quick memory of the telephone box in *The Confession* by Mary Roberts Rinehart. "Or proof of a crime. As for walking to her house"—Annie looked excited—"we need to find out who lives nearby."

"Isn't that guilt by association?" Max's tone was wry. "I don't think that narrows the suspect list much. Downtown's a mile that way." He gestured to the northeast. "Sea Side Inn's a half mile east of us."

"I don't care." Annie was stubborn. "If somebody walked to her house then walked over here, he—or she—walked away from here and I'll bet the destination wasn't far away."

"Whoever shot at me ran toward the pond." Max gestured at the garden. "Once through the stand of pines, there's a path. It heads north. Another path to the left winds past that old cemetery to her house. I'll bet the murderer hid a car on Calliope Lane."

Annie remembered Calliope Lane. "We can check it out. It was too foggy for me to be sure, but I think the woods come right up to the lane. Besides, by the time someone shot at you, I must have been at Mrs. Jamison's house. I didn't hear a car go past." In her mind, a shadowy figure disappeared into their foggy garden. On foot. Annie pointed outside. "Let's check out the lane, see what we find."

Max held up a hand. "A map would be easier. We'll find out who lives where and whether any of them had a connection to Mrs. Jamison. Right now, we need to see if we can find what she hid or some trace of a hiding place."

In the kitchen, Max looked up at the ceiling. "I heard a creak directly above me, then thumps."

Annie was ready for action. "I'll go up and walk around and knock on the walls. See if that sounds like what you heard." Her footsteps echoed on the heart-pine flooring of the hall. She gazed about, seeking anything odd, anything different, but the empty hallway and rooms were just as she'd last seen them, lovely with the application of fresh paint and new wallpaper.

Annie carried with her the memory of Mrs. Jamison lying on her living room floor, hand seeking help, life draining away. Mrs. Jamison had slipped into the Franklin house yesterday, leaving a package behind.

At the stairs, Annie brushed the wing of the ornate carving atop the newel post, a habit she'd begun on her first visit inside the Franklin house. As she climbed, she looked for any hint of Mrs. Jamison's presence. She gave another pat to an ornate carving on the second-floor newel post and crossed the landing to the study. There was no sign of a search, nothing out of place.

The study was exactly as she'd last seen it, the freshly stuccoed walls a pale lime, cheerful white curtains at the windows, a cozy room with just enough space for their favorite sumptuously comfortable love seat opposite a wall-mounted TV set. Max liked love seats.

"Annie?"

Max's faint call brought her back from her decorating daydream to the uncomfortable memory of a woman dead too soon. Annie set to work. She thumped along a head-high line around the perimeter of the room, circled again thumping waist-high.

The hall stairs creaked. Max burst into the study, face eager. "That sounded like what I heard. That's encouraging."

Annie's face crinkled in a puzzled frown. Had she missed something here? Why should Max be encouraged?

Max claimed to be able to read her like a book, not a pronouncement she found especially flattering. He immediately looked smug. "It's obvious, my dear Watson."

Annie's eyes narrowed. Sherlock Holmes had never been her detective of choice. "What's obvious?"

"The guy who broke in was pounding on the walls. That means he was looking for a hiding place, and if he was looking for it, he doesn't have any idea where it is. I interrupted his search and he got away. So, whatever Mrs. Jamison hid must still be here. Come on, Annie."

They started in the basement. Everything was fresh, the stucco walls painted gleaming white, extensive pine shelving installed and empty of contents, new heating system mounted on a cement block.

Max made a circuit of the basement, knocking on the walls. The resounding thump never varied in pitch. "Nothing hollow." He glanced at the heating system, shook his head. "Can't be anything there. It's all new."

They checked the rooms on the first floor, thumping as they went. The heart-pine floors were solid, the freshly painted woodwork unmarred. By the time they reached the library, Max was discouraged. "Either the walls are solid or hidden compartments don't sound hollow."

The library was the only room still needing repair. At some point, its cypress paneling had been removed and replaced with red bamboo. At the moment, the room was down to its original tabby walls. At the end of a fifteen-minute survey, Max shook his head. He tried moving the panels on either side of the fireplace. They didn't budge.

They checked every room on the second floor. Max once again poked and prodded near the fireplace. Finally they reached the attic. Max stood on tiptoe to grab a ring that pulled down a suspended stairway. He climbed up the steps.

Annie didn't follow. If Mrs. Jamison indeed had hidden something in the Franklin house as she claimed, they hadn't found it. Maybe they could discover something in the last few days or hours of Mrs. Jamison's life that would explain her decision to put something in a house that didn't belong to her.

Max dropped the last few feet from the suspended stairway that led to the attic. "No cobwebs. No boxes. I opened the windows and hung out to be sure nothing was taped to a gutter. I ran my hand along the rafters as high as I could reach. I didn't find a thing."

Annie studied the suspended stairway. To pull down the steps required grabbing a recessed ring and tugging hard. Max had stood on tiptoe to reach it. Annie remembered the slight form lying on the floor. "Mrs. Jamison wasn't tall enough to reach the pull cord handle."

"So she couldn't have climbed up to the attic." Max shoved the hanging steps up and the opening to the attic closed. "We've checked every room. We scoured the cellar. We knocked on walls looking for hidden recesses or fake panels. As far as I can tell, the Franklin house is as solid as a rock. Where could she have put it?"

Stepping into Parotti's Bar and Grill and bait house usually made Annie, true to her Amarillo upbringing, happy as a Texan with a mess of lamb fries and cold beer. The unpretentious restaurant across from the ferry landing was owned by Ben Parotti, who also ran the ferry and was the canny landlord of most of the small downtown merchants. When Annie had first come to the island, Parotti's had been dimly lighted and down-at-heel with a rank smell of bait in open barrels and old hot grease. A few years ago, overall-wearing, beard-stubbled, diminutive Ben met the refined, ladylike owner of a tea shop on the mainland. Each saw more than appearance and romance blossomed. Now Miss Jolene, as Ben reverently addressed his wife, held sway over the kitchen at Parotti's. A clean-shaven, smiling Ben, snazzy in a white polo, blue blazer, and chinos, welcomed diners when he wasn't piloting the ferry (renamed the *Miss Jolene*) between the island and the mainland. The café had new lighting and blue-and-white-checkered cloths on the tables. The menu offered salads and quiche in addition to fried oysters, pulled-pork sandwiches, fried catfish, hush puppies, and beer on tap, but Ben had drawn a line in the sawdust on the bait-shop floor and the old familiar fishy smells wafted from bait barrels teeming with live eels, fish, and squid.

Since it was February and fishing limited to channel bass, croaker, grouper, sheepshead, red snapper, and spotted sea trout, there were few fishermen and no charter parties, so the café held only a few diners.

Annie took a deep breath of the heady scent of bait, sawdust, and beer and automatically headed for their favorite table near the nineteen-forties jukebox, but without her usual sense of delight and happiness.

Barb waggled rolled-up blueprints as they approached. "Annie, I ordered you a fried-oyster sandwich heavy on tartar sauce with fries. Max, I got the special for you, poached grouper with clams. Sides of cole slaw and hush puppies." Barb always ordered a cheeseburger with sweet potato fries. "I've got a slew of stuff for you and Annie and here are the blueprints for the Franklin house."

As they sat down, Ben neared with a serving tray, his gnome-like face filled with welcome. "Miss Jolene's got fresh Key lime pie today."

Annie wished it were an ordinary, everyday lunch at Parotti's. Usually she'd hold up two fingers, ordering for herself and Max. Max would grumble that she had a sweet tooth the size of a *Tyrannosaurus rex* molar and Annie would assure him she was simply doing her part to applaud the island's finest chef. It would be a crime to hurt Miss Jolene's feelings, and if Max didn't feel up to doing his part, she'd eat both pieces, thank you very much.

Today she looked down at the tablecloth and didn't say a word.

"Key limes all around the table, Ben." Max's voice was firm.

She looked up into Max's grave blue eyes and blinked back tears.

When Ben turned away, Max reached across the table, grabbed her hand. "I'm sorry you were there. It's my fault."

"There's no fault." Her tone was hot. He must not ever feel she blamed him. He had reason enough to be suspicious of callers who claimed to be scared.

Barb whopped the blueprints on the tabletop. "Cut it out. Both of you. Sure, she called and asked for help, but you have to remember she got herself in a pickle. She's the one who used your place for a hidey-hole. If she'd been able to slip back into the Franklin house and get her stash, you'd never have known about any of this and Annie wouldn't have found her dying. Now"—she spread open the blueprint—"I didn't find anything that looks like a secret compartment. . . ."

Ben served their meals with a flourish. "You got a line on who killed Gwen Jamison and shot at Max?"

Annie didn't feel the slightest quiver of surprise. Ben saw all, heard all, knew all.

Max grinned. "We're counting on you helping us. You didn't think we came for the food, did you?"

Ben's eye glinted. "Want to cancel the order?"

Their chorus of nos satisfied him. He rocked back on his heels, face squeezed in thought. "Looks like all of a sudden there's trouble in the neighborhood. The Grant coins stolen Monday night, Gwen Jamison shot this morning, then a shooting at the Franklin house a little while later. Everything happened close together." Ben leaned forward, arranged the salt and pepper shakers and slender hot pepper bottle in an isosceles triangle tipped to one side. "The salt shaker at the tip of the triangle is Gwen's house." He tapped the pepper shaker, which sat down and to the right. "The Franklin house." Ben's gnarled finger moved straight up to touch the hot pepper bottle. "Grant place."

He left the triangle in place, said mildly, "Kind of interesting, especially since Gwen was housekeeper for the Grants." Ben's nose wriggled. "I hear the cops are looking for her son Robert. Lana Edwards called a while ago to order in a mess of food. They're working so hard nobody had time for lunch and she said they think Robert stole the Grant coins and somehow Gwen found out and hid 'em at the Franklin house." He tipped his head toward Max. "That's how I knew you'd had a spot of trouble there this morning. They think Robert shot his mama when she wouldn't give them back. Guess that's what city cops might think. Some pretty mean kids in big cities. Me, I'd be surprised if Robert knew a double eagle from that squinty foulmouthed parrot that lives in Lessie Bassett's antique shop. Besides, Robert may have got himself in trouble here and there, but he wouldn't hurt his mama." Ben turned and walked away, shoulders squared.

Annie knew they'd heard the judgment of the island. When both Doc Burford and Ben Parotti spoke, they should listen.

As the kitchen door swung shut behind him, Annie put down her fried-oyster sandwich. "That makes it pretty certain the coins are hidden in the Franklin house. She was the housekeeper at the Grant place."

Max pushed capers atop a piece of grouper. "Did Mrs. Jamison get the coins from her son? Or did she steal them?"

Annie shook her head. "If she was a thief, she wouldn't have called to apologize for hiding something in the house and said she was sorry." Annie turned to Barb. "Didn't you get the idea she was hoping Max would let her in to retrieve whatever it was?"

Barb's face crinkled in thought. "I think so. She didn't have time to finish. I think she'd promised someone she'd get it back."

Max looked sardonic. "Okay, let's say she wasn't a thief. Why was she going to cooperate with a thief? That's called conspiracy. Why didn't she call the cops? I keep going back to that."

Annie finished her oyster sandwich. "It looks to me like she had to be innocent of any crime since she was shot."

Max shrugged. "Crooks fall out. Or maybe the police are on the right track. Her son stole the coins. Somehow she found out and hid them to keep them out of his reach and he shot her when she wouldn't hand them over."

Annie believed in community judgment. "Doc Burford said he wouldn't. So did Ben."

"She was strict with her sons. I've got that here." Barb shifted several folders, opened one. A glossy sheet slipped out. Barb caught it before it fell from the table. "Here's a picture taken last Easter. It ran in the *Gazette* and I got a color print off the Web site."

Annie took the eight-by-ten sheet. Sunlight had fallen across Gwen Jamison as she turned in the doorway of a small white wooden church. Her eyes seemed to glow with delight. She was smiling, her light tan face elegant with deep-set eyes, high cheekbones, and a rounded chin. She wore a softly swirling violet silk dress. Her hat was a gossamer thing of beauty, delicate white straw with curved brims that looked like butterfly wings in flight.

Barb ran a finger down a printed sheet. "She's been active in Shady Lane Baptist Church all her life, sung in the choir, taught Sunday school, worked in the thrift store. She was forty-seven." Barb cleared her throat, read aloud: "'She was born on the island. Her parents were Mattie and David Kingston. Mattie was a homemaker. David was a tile layer. Three children in addition to Gwen. Only Gwen still lives on the island. Gwen married Prentice Jamison when she was nineteen. He was a bricklayer. He died in a car wreck five years ago. Two children, Charlie, twenty-three, and Robert, eighteen. Charlie is assistant manager of the Stop 'N Go. His wife, Judith, is a schoolteacher. They're expecting their first baby. Robert dropped out of school last year. He was working for a landscape design company, but was laid off at the end of summer. He's done odd jobs here and there. Gwen always made the boys toe the line. Charlie never gave her any trouble. Robert moved out when he quit school. She told him he could come home when he was ready to do right. Sometimes he lives with friends. He got a job over Christmas at the video store, worked long enough to get the money to rent a cheap apartment.

" 'Gwen cleaned rooms at Sea Side Inn after she graduated from high school, then she worked for several families as a maid. Eighteen years ago, she became the housekeeper at the Franklin house—' "

Max nodded. "So she had a key."

" '—and stayed there until old Miss Truscott died ten years ago. The house was in poor repair and heavily mortgaged. The bank took it over but had no luck selling it. It fell into ruin and sold recently.' "

Annie smiled at Max, who'd known the old house could be restored and made beautiful again.

Barb turned the page. " 'After Miss Truscott died, Gwen went to work as housekeeper for Geoff Grant. She's been there ever since.' "

Max's gaze was cool. "Clearly she could be mixed up in the Grant theft. The coins were taken Monday night. She used her old key to the Franklin house Tuesday morning. This morning she told Barb she hid something there and it makes sense that she left the coins. The question is, how did she get them?"

Annie took a bite of Key lime pie. "We need to know more about Gwen Jamison." As she spoke, she knew she'd made a decision. She intended to respond to Gwen's last pleading breath of a word. She looked at Max.

He felt her gaze, met it directly. "Maybe she stole the coins and was going to try and sweet-talk me into letting her look for a package she'd hidden, claim it contained old family pictures that a crazy aunt threatened to destroy. Anything's possible. Maybe she was a good woman caught up in something she hadn't started. I don't know the answer. I'll try to find out." His expression was somber.

Annie saw wariness in his eyes, the distrust of a man whose happiness had almost been stolen by a lie, and she saw sadness, a good man's concern that he'd walked by on the other side of the road, leaving a helpless woman in jeopardy.

"There wasn't time for you to save her." Annie was insistent. "I went straight there and it was already too late."

"If I'd agreed to meet her at the Franklin house, maybe she would have left before her murderer arrived. I'll never know. But whatever involved her involves our house. So we're going to find out who she was and what she did." He looked at Annie. "See what you can find out about her. I'm going to talk to Ben about the ferry. And I have some questions for Robert Jamison."

Barb glanced at the clock. "The press has rolled at the *Gazette*. I'll take Marian a slice of Key lime pie and a double mocha delight."

Annie almost bent to nuzzle Agatha's silky tummy. Remembering the unsheathed claws that had threatened to ensnare her earlier, she resisted the impulse. Cautiously, she curved her hand behind Agatha's head, yanked it away as Agatha flipped over and tried to clamp her paws on Annie's arm. "You're in a mood, aren't you?"

Agatha's green eyes glittered.

"Not enough attention? February doldrums? Be patient, sweetie, spring will come and customers who adore you. Respectfully, of course." Annie poured out fresh dry food for Agatha then checked the telephone for messages. There were three:

> 12:40 p.m.—*"You switch on your Geiger counter for bodies this morning?" Marian Kenyon rattled on, her gravelly voice impatient. "What's your connection to the deceased? On deadline, give me a call."*

Annie clicked delete. Barb would pick up whatever Marian knew and Marian always knew more than appeared in the *Gazette*.

> 12:47 p.m.—*"Been thinking about what you heard . . . griff . . ." Frank Saulter was circumspect. "Don't want to suggest anything, but could she have made a sound like* a *in 'at,' not* i *as in 'lift'? People who are hurt go off on tangents sometimes. Don't push it. Let your memory play out when you're rested."*

Annie clicked save. What did Frank have in mind? She murmured, "Gra . . ." Was he asking if Gwen Jamison had tried to say

"Grant"? Slowly Annie shook her head. The faint sound seemed long ago, hard to recall now with accuracy, but memory held to . . . *gri* . . . *ff* . . . with the faintest *ff* sound.

> 1:05 p.m.—*"Mrs. Darling, this is Jessamine Holbrook. We met at the last AAUW luncheon. Could you help me find a book I've been looking for forever? There's a woman who's in a coffee shop or it might have been a restaurant in Greece or it might have been Italy and somebody comes up to her and hands her the keys to a car and says it's a matter of life and death and he leaves and disappears in the crowd and she wanted to go up in the mountains anyway . . ."*

Annie clicked save.

Actually, she had a good idea which mystery Jessamine wanted, the breathtakingly suspenseful *My Brother Michael* by Mary Stewart, but Jessamine would have to wait.

Annie found the phone book, got an address, then burrowed in her desk for an island map. When she spread it on a table near the coffee bar, Agatha jumped up and plopped in the center. Annie peered over a paw.

The map made crystal clear the nearness of the Franklin house to Gwen Jamison's house and the Grant house. Annie drew lines from the Jamison house to Franklin house and from the Jamison house to the Grant house. She added the vertical line from the Grant house to the Franklin house and had as pretty an isosceles triangle as anyone would wish. Ben Parotti knew his island.

Ben Parotti stood outside the bar and grill with Max. He pointed toward the harbor. "Like I told that Officer Harrison, I knew every man, woman, and child that took the ferry Tuesday morning. Same for Tuesday night and this morning. I only run the *Miss Jolene* four times daily in winter during the week, six crossings on Saturday, two on Sunday. I'll add to the schedule come April. Like I told her, no stranger took those coins off island Tuesday. I don't think Mayor Cosgrove, Mrs. Stanley from the Baptist Mission Society, the Purdy family going in to Savannah for their little boy's birthday, or Tony Hassam on his way to get his wife at the airport had those coins in a pocket. Same thing Tuesday afternoon. Only two passengers, Mary Peters who'd been here to visit her mom and Carson Howell who drives the UPS truck out of Chastain. This morning the passengers were all locals. Troy Hudman after a car, Emily Bishop going in to see her aunt in Savannah, Joe Bob Morris off on a business trip, and Kayla Lester with a box of homemade cookies for her son at that design school in Savannah. She gave me one. Pineapple macadamia nut. The fog came in before I started back. I had to wait for it to lift. The only passengers coming back were regulars."

Max watched a sailboat scud into the Sound, sails full. "Maybe the thief came and went in a motorboat." In that event, what had Mrs. Jamison hidden in the Franklin house?

Ben was judicious. "Could be. Lots of solitary places a boat can land. It would probably take lights at night to find your way and people have a way of noticing. I haven't heard of anybody seeing lights in a funny place. Like I told Officer Harrison"—his successful-businessman's face was shrewd—"somebody had to know about those coins to take them. I'd lay odds the coins and the thief are still on the island."

Marian Kenyon was stretched out on the saggy brown sofa in the *Gazette* coffee room. At the sound of brisk steps, she opened one eye a slit. "Vince, I need a Coke and a bag of peanuts." When she recognized the visitor, both eyes popped wide and she pulled herself upright, expression intense. "Hey, Barb, give me the skinny. What was Annie doing at the Jamison house? Does the Jamison murder have any connection to the gunshots at the Franklin house?" She looked aggrieved. "Had to dig that one out of a police report."

Barb held up a brown bag. "Miss Jolene's Key lime pie. A double mocha. Bet you haven't had lunch."

Marian shoved a hand through wiry black hair peppered with silver. "Let's cut a deal. Give me the grub bag and the low-down on Annie and Max and I'll give you what I've got."

They settled at the Formica-topped table scarred with long-ago cigarette burns. Marian ate, her monkey face intent as Barb related what she knew. Slurping the last of the double mocha, Marian tilted back her chair. "I picked up the report on the shooting at the Franklin house but nobody anted about the possibility something was hidden there. Something, hell. Jamison worked for the Grants, two mil's worth of coins disappear, so what do you think she was hiding?" Clearly the question was rhetorical. "Got to be the Grant coins. So"—Marian's face furrowed—"that's why they got an APB out for Robert. Harrison must figure Robert got the coins, hid them at his mom's place, and she found them. They figure he came home, they quarreled, and he shot her. 'Course, I don't figure they've got it right. You got a couple of bucks?"

Barb fished in her purse, handed Marian two bills.

Marian carefully straightened out the crumpled bills, fed them slowly into the vending machine, hit two buttons. She returned to the table with a Coke and a bag of Planters peanuts. She dribbled peanuts into the Coke, took a big mouthful, crunched. "I raise iris. So did Gwen. She was one tough mama. If Robert stole those coins, she would have kicked his butt all the way to the cop shop. Nobody's asking me, but I can tell you what happened."

Barb scarcely breathed she listened so hard.

Marian munched and took another swallow. "Gwen found those coins on her property, but Robert didn't steal them. She hid them because she knew the police would immediately jump on her kid and this time he wasn't the bad dude. So"—her eyes slitted—"that means Gwen knew who took the coins. That means she saw something—hell, someone—Monday night." Marian pressed fingers to her temples, eyes closed in the best fortune-teller fashion. "Yeah, that's how it had to be. Gwen saw somebody she recognized putting something—a small package maybe—on her property and it was funny enough and strange enough she checked it out. She waited until the coast was clear and got the package. When she opened it, she knew what she had. She probably dusted that display case every day." Marian's eyes popped wide. "Okay, she's got the coins. No way does she want that kind of stolen goods anywhere near her house, so she hikes over to the Franklin place, puts the package somewhere. She must have been scared Robert would be blamed even though she knows who took the stuff. She didn't call the cops because she thought nobody'd believe her. Instead, she tries to put everything back to square one, give the coins to the perp with the understanding they'll be returned. She thought wrong. Here's what we've got to find out." She flipped up one finger. "Who did she see that she knew well enough to contact and say I've got the swag, let's talk? The cops'll claim it had to be Robert. That, I don't believe. But"—Marian's dark eyes glowed with intensity—"she was covering for somebody. So here's the biggie. Why the hell would she?"

Chapter 5

Gwen Jamison's drive was empty. No police cars. No ambulance. Yellow crime-scene tape crisscrossed on the front door. The house had a deserted air. Or was that Annie's perception because she knew the slender woman would never again sweep her front porch, polish the shiny brass knocker, sit in her swing in the spring and take joy in the purple glory of iris?

Thoughts darted like minnows . . . private property . . . the drive wasn't blocked . . . for sure Officer Harrison wouldn't want her nosing around . . . what harm could it do . . . maybe now or never . . .

With a final check to be sure she was unobserved, Annie turned the Volvo into the drive, eased past the side of the house. She parked behind the garage, knew her car was hidden from the road. Chickens cackled in a pen as she followed a well-defined dusty gray path. About twenty yards beyond the chicken coop, she reached a small, very old cemetery. It was well kept. Azaleas grew next to the wire fence. The gate was ajar.

Annie passed the cemetery. The path wound around a clump of willows and into a grove of pines. Annie stepped into dimness. Birds chittered. Pine boughs rustled softly in a gentle breeze. The path from the Jamison house ended as it met a north-south path. She turned right and moved warily into thick woods. Abruptly the way was rough. Weeds clumped underfoot and tendrils of vines snared her ankles. Palmetto fronds and ferns poked against her. The inland forest thinned and she entered another pine grove. Here the path was barely discernible. She reached the end of the pines and saw a cypress-rimmed pond at the foot of the Franklin house garden. Their house lay beyond the garden beds on a slight rise.

It had taken her no more than five minutes to walk from Gwen Jamison's house. How easily the murderer could have moved silently through fog-wreathed trees to the Franklin house.

Annie turned and retraced her steps. She ignored the path to Mrs. Jamison's house and continued north. This path was well tended, the underbrush trimmed back. A thick bed of oyster shells crunched underfoot. She wished the shells didn't make so much noise. She was a trespasser, but she kept going, straining to hear over the crackle of breaking shells and the occasional *tick-tick-tick* of an unseen clapper rail in the nearby salt marsh. She'd gone perhaps fifty yards when she reached the Grant garden with banks of azaleas, beds of rosebushes, a white wooden gazebo, and almost a dozen marble statues, replicas of famous classic sculptures.

The two-story Beaufort-style frame house sat high on a

brick foundation. Black shutters accented white wood. A small tabby cottage stood about twenty yards from the main house. It would be easy to slip between the cottage and house, reach the road beyond. A half-dozen black rocking chairs sat on the wide back porch, but none would likely have been occupied on a cool, foggy morning. In spring, the porch would afford a breathtaking view of azaleas blooming in shades of rose and salmon, scarlet and pink. The path looped around a fountain then ran straight to the back porch. A partially constructed wooden bench was placed equidistant between the fountain and a fresh bed of concrete that held a metal pole.

Annie wondered if Gwen Jamison had come to work this morning. If so, she must have slipped away and hurried to the Franklin house to retrieve whatever she'd hidden.

Annie shook her head impatiently. It was clear enough that somehow Gwen had come into possession of the stolen coins, hidden them, promised to give them to someone. This morning when she found the Franklin house locked, she went home, called Max's office, talked to Barb. All the while, the sands of her life were dwindling to a trickle and then to nothing.

A tinny rendition of the opening bars of "Wake Up Call" startled Annie. She yanked open her purse, pulled out her cell. "Hello." She knew she sounded as though she were in a cellar. That's what trespassing did to her.

"Annie, that you? You sound funny." Barb barreled on. "I talked to Marian. Here's what she thinks . . ."

Annie listened. Marian's ideas made lots of sense. "We have to find out who Gwen would have been willing to protect."

"I'll get on it." Barb clicked off.

Annie took a final look at the house where Gwen Jamison

had worked, then turned and strode swiftly back toward the dead woman's home. She'd written down Charlie Jamison's address. Maybe Charlie would know who his mother would try to protect.

Flamingo Arms sat at the end of a dusty road that angled to the northeast shore. It had a view of eroded beach which could no longer be reached because the wooden walkway had tumbled into the dunes. At one time, Flamingo Arms had been a cheaply built motel next to a miniature golf course built around a lagoon. The lagoon became infested with a horde of cottonmouths that sometimes slithered unexpectedly from water hazards, discouraging play. The course was ultimately abandoned. The motel went bankrupt and was bought and refashioned into one-room efficiency apartments.

Max avoided a broken step as he climbed the exterior stairs to the second-floor units. He stepped over sticky goo that had oozed from a rusted car battery tipped to one side. Bait coolers, bicycles locked to the iron railing, a six-wheeler tire, a folded beach umbrella, and piled boogie boards narrowed the walkway.

He stopped at No. 16, knocked. He waited a moment, knocked again, rapping his knuckles hard against the smudged once-white door.

The door to 18 opened. A young woman with a tired face and uncombed bleached hair poked her head out. "He's not there. Like I told the cop, he slammed out of here early this morning. He woke the baby up. As usual. If he isn't slamming doors, he's playing rap music that keeps us all up. Please don't knock again. I just got her down for—"

A shrill cry erupted behind her.

The weary blonde gave an exasperated sigh and slammed the door.

Max looked at the broad window to 16. Chocolate-brown drapes were tightly shut. Max turned away, hurried down the steps. He found the manager's office in unit 1.

The room was thick with cigarette smoke. A wiry man in his fifties looked up with a frown. "Yeah?"

"I'm looking for Robert— "

"No bill collectors, vendors, or peddlers." The manager yanked a fist with his stubby thumb pointing outside. "Beat it."

Max took out his billfold, retrieved a card, wrote a message on the back. He took two steps, dropped it on the littered desktop. "If he returns, tell him to get in touch with me. I'll make it worth his time."

Max refrained from slamming the door on his way out. Manager he glanced at a nameplate—Manager C. T. Burke didn't owe him the time of day and likely he had no information as to Robert Jamison's whereabouts, so the surly encounter didn't matter. Who on the island might know something of Robert's friends? Max turned over names in his mind, abruptly nodded. He walked briskly toward the Corvette.

A police car came around a clump of bamboo, slid to a stop behind the Corvette, blocking it. Officer Harrison got out.

Max felt a bristle of irritation. He reached the Corvette and gestured at the cruiser. "I'm ready to leave."

She stopped a few feet from him, unsmiling, her light eyes speculative. "This morning you said you didn't know Mrs. Jamison, had never had any contact with her."

"Right." Max pulled his keys from his pocket.

She glanced toward the second floor of the apartment building. "Do you know Robert Jamison?"

"No."

"Why are you attempting to contact him?"

"Who says I was?"

"You knocked on his door."

Obviously Manager Burke had been primed to let the police know if anyone came around the place searching for Robert. Probably he kept a close eye on the place and had called when Max first arrived and knocked on the door to 16. Max's stop in his office had provided plenty of time for Officer Harrison to arrive.

Max rocked back on his heels. His mother's variation on honey and vinegar floated in his mind: People like pats, not punches. He wasn't sure it would work with Hyla Harrison, but it was time to try. He spoke pleasantly. "Mrs. Jamison needed help today. I wasn't able to respond." Wasn't able? He'd walked away, avoiding any chance of entanglement in lies. Had she lied? Was she a liar and a thief and the victim of a quarrel over stolen goods? He needed to know. "I want to find out what happened to her."

"That's our job." Officer Harrison's stare was cold. "Robert Jamison is a person of interest to this investigation. Should you speak with him, I suggest you recommend he get in touch with us."

She marched with stiff precision to the cruiser. She backed out of his way. Max turned left out of the Flamingo Arms parking lot. The police cruiser loomed in his rearview mirror. Max drove at a slower pace than usual, aware that the cruiser remained a steady twenty feet behind his Corvette. Was she going to fol low him?

The cruiser turned off on Main Street.

Max felt a flash of triumph. He picked up speed, took a familiar road that curved to the northeast tip of the island.

A few blocks farther on, a motorcycle turned onto the road from an intersecting side street. His thoughts on his destination, Max scarcely noticed the helmeted rider.

Cars were lined up on both sides of the dusty unpaved street. Several were parked in the front yard at 219 Katydid Lane. Annie nosed the Volvo off the road between a palmetto and a live oak.

As she walked in the soft gray dirt toward the house, the front door opened to admit several women carrying foil-wrapped dishes. Soft voices carried back to her. "... so terrible ... talked to Gwen yesterday ... I never thought something like this could—" The door closed.

It took all of Annie's courage to walk up the crushed-oyster-shell drive and mount the steps. She came empty-handed. She had no comfort to offer Charlie Jamison. She stood at the door.

Shells popped behind her. Someone was coming. She lifted her hand and knocked as steps sounded on the wooden porch.

The door opened. A middle-aged black woman looked at Annie with surprise. "Yes?"

"Hello. I'm Annie Darling." Annie wondered wildly what she could say to gain admittance to a house of mourning for a woman she'd never known. Then it was surprisingly easy as the truth often is. "I found Mrs. Jamison and I thought I should come and tell Charlie."

"Oh." There was a soft-drawn breath. Dark eyes widened. She held the door and stepped back, making room for Annie. "Please come in."

From the living room came the sound of a deep voice. ". . . let us pray for our Sister Gwendolyn as she is surrounded by the glory of Our Lord Jesus Christ. May—"

The woman who'd answered the door held cautionary fingers to her lips.

"—He welcome her to the company of saints and may He reach down to us and give peace to hearts stricken by sorrow, hearts hurt and bewildered by the violence that has wrested away the soul of our sister. May He make His light to shine upon us now and forevermore. Amen."

A soft chorus of amens followed.

A tremulous silence was broken as a rich contralto slowly began to sing "Swing Low, Sweet Chariot." The one haunting voice carried the melody and then slowly other voices joined, and there was a glory of music rising to the Heaven now open to Gwen Jamison.

Annie felt surrounded by sorrow.

A knock sounded on the front door. Annie stepped out of the way. The woman who had welcomed Annie once again opened the door. A tall, dark-haired white woman in a turtleneck sweater and gray slacks stepped inside.

A stocky young man with a broad face and stricken eyes came through the crowded living room toward the front hall.

The black woman gestured toward Annie. "She wants to talk to you."

He gave Annie a puzzled glance, then looked past her with quick recognition to the newcomer. "Mrs. Grant." His voice was husky.

"I just found out." Her voice was shaken. She reached out to take Charlie's hand. "The paper came and I carried it into the study. I opened it and it said Gwen had been found shot. I thought maybe there was a mistake. The paper said she was killed this morning. I called her house several times when I couldn't find her today. She came to work this morning but I couldn't find her after breakfast. I knew something must have happened to take her away. But murder—" She looked past Charlie at the people crowded in the small living room. "It's true, isn't it?" She spread her hand at the women with dolorous faces.

Charlie's face squeezed in misery. A young woman in a pink maternity smock came to his side, held his hand tight as she struggled to hold back tears.

Annie stepped forward. "I found your mother." Annie's voice was thin, but steady.

Everyone looked at her.

Charlie took a step toward her. "Who are you?"

"Annie Darling."

"Hello, Annie." A slender woman with dark hair pulled back in a bun pushed gold-rimmed glasses higher on her nose.

Annie recognized Inez Willis, a librarian who specialized in genealogy. "Hello, Inez."

Inez touched Charlie's arm. "Annie has the mystery bookstore at the marina."

Charlie continued to look puzzled.

"This morning your mother called my husband's office." Annie described the call to Barb. As soon as she spoke of something hidden at the Franklin house, it was as if everyone stepped back even though no one moved. Dark eyes gazed at her suspiciously. Mourning faces turned impassive. Even Inez looked wary.

Charlie's face tightened in anger. "Wait a minute. That's what the police are saying. They're saying Mama hid those coins that somebody stole Monday night from the Grants. They said maybe Robert or Mama took them."

Indignant voices rose. "No call to talk like that." "Gwen never touched a penny that wasn't hers." "That's a lie . . ."

Mrs. Grant turned on Annie, too. "Not Gwen. Never. Not in a million years. Gwen wouldn't."

Annie's fists clenched. "You aren't hearing me. I'm telling you what Mrs. Jamison told my husband's secretary. She said she'd hidden something in our house and when she came to get it this morning—"

Mrs. Grant looked startled. "She went somewhere. I couldn't find her."

"—the locks had been changed and she couldn't get in. But here's what's important." She looked from one hostile face to another. "Please listen. Mrs. Jamison told Barb that she didn't want to cause trouble for anyone. She wouldn't have said that if she'd taken the coins. I don't think she did. In fact"—Annie banked on Marian Kenyon's knowledge of Gwen Jamison and pulled together all she'd learned and what she guessed—"we think she saw someone hide the stolen coins on her property. She put them in the Franklin house and arranged to meet the person who'd taken them, intending for the coins to be returned. Instead the person who came to get the coins shot her. Now, who did she see? Not Robert. If it were Robert, she'd have said she wanted to keep someone from being in trouble, not that she didn't want to make trouble for someone. If it were Robert"—Annie had confidence in the judgment of Doc Burford and Ben Parotti—"she'd have made him do the right thing and return the coins. Besides, everyone says he'd never have hurt his mother. But she knew who took those coins. It had to be someone she knew well, someone she felt she could persuade to return the coins. Who?"

Charlie was angry. "You come here with this big story about Mama. I can tell you she never took anything in her life that didn't belong to her and she would have whipped Robert hard and marched him over to the Grant house and made him give the coins back even if he had to go to jail. Besides, it's crazy to think Robert would have had any idea how much that kind of stuff was worth, and what would he do with them if he got them? Take them to a pawnshop? Robert doesn't have good sense, but he's not a crook. Mama didn't raise a crook. I don't know anybody she would have seen do a crime and kept quiet about it."

In her mind, Annie heard Barb's imitation of Marian's husky voice: "That's the biggie. Why the hell would she?"

Annie understood what Charlie and his mother's friends were saying. Their Gwen was a good woman. To them, Gwen hiding stolen coins didn't make sense. Yet it had happened.

Annie looked at the circle of closed faces. Nobody here was going to give her any help at all.

Max liked the way basketball courts smelled of sweat and hard wood. He loved the thump of the ball and the dance of feet, the coach's shouts, the shrill of whistles. He looked along the sidelines, saw the familiar face he sought.

Gerald Allensworth, the high school principal, rarely missed after-school practices, football in the fall, basketball in winter, baseball in the spring. He knew his students and he cared for all of them, no matter their race or background or athletic ability. He knew those who failed as well as those who succeeded and he never stopped trying to reach the ones who needed help. Always impeccably dressed in a gray suit, white shirt, and red tie, the slender black man stood with his arms folded, his sometimes remote face softened by a smile. He saw Max, looked surprised, then walked toward him.

They shook hands. Max had grown to know the educator well at the Haven. Max spoke loudly to be heard over the thud of the ball and the squeak of athletic shoes. "I'm trying to find Robert Jamison. I'm hoping you might be able to help me."

The principal nodded toward the exit. When the gym door closed behind them, the quiet was almost startling. The late afternoon sunlight slanted across the empty football field. Allensworth led the way to the bleachers, spread his hand to invite Max to sit with him. Allensworth studied Max's face. "I saw in the *Gazette* that his mother was shot."

Max wasn't surprised that the principal received the afternoon newspaper at school and had already read it. There would be few on the island now who would be unaware of Gwen Jamison's murder.

Max described their day, the call to his office, something hidden in the Franklin house, Annie's discovery of the dying woman, the shots at the Franklin house. "I've been looking for Robert.

The police think he stole the coins and his mother found them and put them in the Franklin house and he shot her."

"No." The principal's response was almost curt. "Not Robert." His expression was sad. "He was in eighth grade when his dad died in a car wreck. He was on his way to watch Robert's soccer game. Robert went from a cheerful, bouncy kid to a thin, haunted-looking boy. We tried to tell him—everyone tried to tell him—it wasn't his fault his dad died. But he looked at us with empty eyes and you knew he kept thinking if his dad hadn't been coming to the game, he wouldn't have been on that road. Robert's grades slipped, he started skipping school. He hung around a rowdy crowd, sneaking beer out to the beach, drinking, getting sick, keeping on drinking. But"—he took a deep breath—"he's not mean. He's not a thug. He's locked up inside with pain he doesn't know how to handle."

"He doesn't have a job." Max looked at the pines standing like sentinels across the field. "Hard to buy beer"—or maybe speed or crack—"if you don't have a job. Maybe he was desperate for money."

Allensworth took a moment to answer, a man who reviewed the facts, marshaled his thoughts before he spoke. "I don't believe Robert would steal, but even if I granted theft by Robert, he would never harm his mother."

"What if he was drunk? Or strung out?" Drugs and alcohol can roil minds, induce acts of incalculable violence.

Allensworth turned his hands palms up. "To my knowledge he's never been involved in any kind of violence."

"I want to talk to him." Max felt an urgency to see Gwen Jamison's son. Maybe he wouldn't learn much, but maybe he'd find a piece of the puzzle that would explain Gwen Jamison's actions. Was she a good woman in trouble, trying to deal with danger? Or was she involved in a big-time theft from the house where she worked? Or had she found her son culpable and tried to protect him?

Deep inside, Max understood that he was looking for release from a sense of responsibility even though he might very well not have been able to prevent her death. If he found Robert hungover, bleary, ridden with guilt, Max would mark the incident closed and urge Annie to leave the investigation of Gwen Jamison's murder to the police. "Do you know how I can find him?"

The principal stared unseeing at the pines, the sun now slipping behind the crowns. "If Robert doesn't know about his mother, he needs to be found. If he knows . . ." Allensworth took a deep breath, faced Max. "He could be anywhere. His best friend used to be Terry Phillips. Terry's going to Armstrong State, but he's home on spring break. Terry might be able to help."

Max thanked Allensworth for the address and strode quickly to his car. He knew Terry Phillips, a great kid who'd always made everyone laugh at the Haven. He loved to joke and tease but always in a generous fashion. Max revved up the Corvette.

The road into the school complex was a dead end. Max drove to the through street, turned right. As he curved around a bend, a motorcycle pulled out from behind the dangling brown fronds of a weeping willow.

Annie fixed a cappuccino, adding an extra dollop from the whipped cream can. She needed a pick-me-up. She felt restless and dissatisfied. She paced uneasily near the coffee bar, oblivious to the watercolors hanging over the fireplace. Usually she took such pleasure in being at Death on Demand.

She hadn't accomplished anything by going to Charlie Jamison's house. Those who knew and loved Gwen Jamison had closed ranks. Maybe Max had found Robert and learned something that would point them in the right direction.

She glanced at the clock. She'd head home after she caught up on e-mails. Max had fixed meat loaf yesterday. They'd have thick slices between crusty French bread and a bowl of Manhattan clam chowder for dinner. Which reminded her . . . She fixed Agatha a fresh bowl of water and another of dry food, her favorite seafood combo.

Annie carried her cappuccino to the storeroom. She settled at her computer and was soon absorbed, responding to orders, deleting spam, and saving for last a series of e-mails beamed from *Marigold's Pleasure* in the sunny Caribbean.

Chapter 6

Max parked in front of Matilda Phillips's house. Likely she was still at work at the Wash 'N Fold Laundromat near the harbor. A tiny woman with gold-rimmed glasses, hair tucked back in a granny bun, and regal posture, she had a bright smile. Terry's smile was a mirror image of his grandmother's. She had reared Terry after his mother's death. Matilda could always be counted on when the Haven had a potluck supper. Her cashew pie was famous on the island. The modest yellow frame house glistened with fresh paint. Terry and his friends had repainted it before he left for school in the fall. Two cars were parked in the drive, a red Chevy pickup faded by time but polished to a glitter and a mud-spattered green Gremlin with a battered back fender and no bumper. A rope tied the Gremlin's trunk lid to the tilted license plate holder.

Max walked toward the porch, then veered right when he heard male voices rising in staccato bursts and the muffled thud of a basketball pounding on hard-packed dirt. He came around the side of the house. Two young men, faces sweaty, totally absorbed, wove back and forth, the much bigger Terry with the ball, now dribbling, now sidestepping, his skinny opponent rushing close, arms waving. Terry jumped. His shot thumped into the basket.

Panting, the thin young man shook his head. He wore his hair in a bushy Afro. His sweatshirt was oversized, reaching almost to the knees of baggy dungarees. "You got me again. Twenty-one to six. That sucks."

Terry cuffed him on the arm. "You got to stay in shape, Robert. I've been doing intramurals twice a week." Terry looked trim and muscular in basketball jersey and jeans.

Max felt as jolted as when he'd tripped charging up the interior stairs of the Franklin house. He'd pictured Robert Jamison in his mind, a sullen dropout on his way to big-time trouble, drinking too much, caught with marijuana, out on bail. He'd pictured a big, tough guy, who might shoot his mother if she caught him with stolen goods.

Instead he looked at a weedy, unprepossessing teenager, skinny as an eel, who was embarrassed he hadn't played better with an old friend. Would that matter to a kid if he'd shot his mother that morning, watched her crash to the floor mortally wounded?

Max called out. "Hey, Terry."

Terry turned his way, began to smile, then looked beyond Max. Terry's smile slid into blankness.

Officers Harrison and Thorpe moved swiftly past Max. Officer Harrison gave him a sidelong sharp glance as she passed. "Police." Her voice was crisp. She held up her right hand, badge showing. Officer Thorpe stayed with her, eyes wary, face hard, hands loose at his sides.

Officer Harrison stopped two feet from the skinny boy. "Robert Jamison."

He stared at her with wide eyes. He took a step back.

"Don't move." The command was harsh. "Robert Jamison, I am taking you to the police station for interrogation concerning the murder of your mother."

Robert made an inarticulate sound like a puppy's cry. His face contorted. He choked out words. "Mama? Somebody hurt Mama? No. Please. Mama?" He shook his head back and forth as if denial would make the awful words go away.

Max felt sick. Harrison's cold voice had slammed Robert's heart and gut, ripped him from a world of commonplace to unthinkable emptiness.

Robert struggled for breath. His words came in irregular hiccuping bursts. "You made a mistake. Mama's all right. She phoned this morning, left a message for me. I called her back but I didn't get an answer. My mama's Gwen Jamison. She works for Mrs. Grant. She be there now. You made a mistake."

Officer Harrison's bony face was stolid. "Gwendolyn Jamison. Fatally shot this morning at 14 Calliope Lane. You can make a statement when we get to the station. You can call a lawyer at any time. Come this way."

"Shot?" Robert hunched his shoulders as if he'd been struck.

Max stepped forward. "Robert"—his voice was kind—"your mother called me this morning—"

Officer Harrison snapped, "Mr. Darling, I'll ask you not to interfere with a police investigation."

Max fought a surge of anger. Couldn't she see that this stricken teenager had only now learned of his mother's death? He ignored her, looked at Robert. "I'll arrange for a lawyer to come to the station."

Robert didn't seem to hear. He trembled, his face slack and empty.

The officers came up on either side of him.

Robert stumbled toward the front yard between them.

As they reached the drive, Officer Harrison glanced at the pickup and the Gremlin. "Jamison, is one of these cars yours?"

Robert looked at her dully. "That one." He pointed at the battered old Gremlin.

"Do you have any objections if we search it?"

"No." His voice was dull. He wrapped his arms across his chest and rocked back and forth, tears streaming down his face.

Terry came up and hugged his friend, his face tear-streaked, too.

Harrison nodded to Thorpe. He walked to the police cruiser, opened the trunk, reached inside. A black motorcycle leaned on its kick stand next to the cruiser.

Max stared at the motorcycle. He'd heard one after Harrison turned off on Main when he was on his way to the high school. She'd sent Thorpe to follow him and he'd led them right to Robert Jamison.

Thorpe pulled on latex gloves, walked to the Gremlin. He yanked the rope loose, lifted the trunk lid. He stood still as stone for an instant, staring down, then whirled to look at Robert. He walked toward the grieving boy. "Let's see your gun permit."

Thorpe and Harrison had eyes for no one but Robert. Max

edged nearer the Gremlin, looked inside the trunk. A .45 pistol lay next to a tire tool.

"Gun permit?" Robert shook his head. "I don't have a gun." There was a touch of hysteria in his voice. He looked from Thorpe to Harrison. "I didn't do anything. I don't know about a gun or what happened to my mom. Who shot my mom? What happened to her?"

Thorpe ignored him. He nodded to Harrison. "A forty-five. The doc said the wound was from a big-caliber gun. I'll bag it. Looks like we got him."

Annie grinned as she read Laurel's salutation: "Dearest Annie." Had absence made her mother-in-law's heart grow fonder or was Laurel simply being even more splendidly ebullient than usual?

> Edith Cummings sends us the *Gazette* by e-mail.
> The coin theft is amazing!

Edith, the island's canny research librarian, was an online whiz. Annie always pictured an octopus slapping at a keyboard, no fact beyond her reach.

> We were shocked to learn of Gwen Jamison's death. She often volunteered at the hospital on the weekends. She was a kind and caring woman. We're sorry you suffered the distress of discovering her body. The *Gazette* story gave no hint as to how that occurred. Are you and Max involved, possibly because

> of the coins? You must know by now that Gwen worked for the Grants. Emma at once pounced upon that fact. I'm passably acquainted with the romantic saga of Double Eagles. Rupert, a dear friend—

Annie grinned. For "friend" read "lover." Laurel of the Grecian features and white-gold hair attracted men from nineteen to ninety. They flocked to her flame with the alacrity of hedonistic moths. She loved and moved on, leaving behind her men forever enchanted.

> —was simply mad about Double Eagles. Of course, he couldn't spend all his time holding coins and he once told me that I surpassed—Oh well, that was before we parted. I bid Rupert farewell when he spent an entire evening absorbed in an 1868 Proof-66 Double Eagle. I was wearing a Christian Dior and had a garland of tiny rosebuds in my hair. He was such a handsome man. However, I will cut to the chase as Emma is impatient to send her instructions. Dear Emma has—

Annie wondered if close quarters might possibly be inducing strain among the travelers, madcap Laurel, imperious Emma, and no-nonsense Henny.

> —such decided opinions. In any event, be sure to find out how many coins were in the collection. If coins of much lesser value were left behind, that would suggest a sophisticated thief. To the untrained eye all Double

> Eagles look very much alike, gloriously golden, but, as I once observed to Rupert, "Full head or flowing robes, does it really matter?" Our relations were never quite the same after that.
>
> Much love to Max and more anon.
>
> Your most devoted servant—Laurel

Annie clicked print. Max would enjoy his mother's missive. The next e-mail was vintage Emma:

> Was the collection insured? For how much? Who gets the money? Was the collection widely known? Who was in the house when the theft occurred? What is their financial situation? As Marigold always reminds Inspector Houlihan, *cherchez* the bucks.

To Annie, Marigold Rembrandt was one of the most supercilious sleuths of all time. Emma spoke of her sleuth as if she were in the next room instructing the hapless inspector. Annie wanted to shout, "Emma, she isn't real!" but resisted the temptation.

Annie reread the crisp questions. They were very good questions, indeed. Could insurance fraud be involved? Annie clicked print.

The final e-mail was from Henny:

> Wish I were in the thick of things. I could be a great help.

Of course Henny Brawley wished she were involved. She fancied herself a modern-day Miss Marple with the humor of

Anne George's Patricia Anne Hollowell, the observing eye of Elaine Viets's Helen Hawthorne, and the small-town know-how of Patricia Sprinkle's MacLaren Yarbrough.

> I had no idea those coins were worth so much. I knew they were $20 gold pieces but even so! Rhoda had a tea last year for the 99ers. She was very active in our group but—

Henny was a longtime pilot and member of the women's flying group founded long ago by Amelia Earhart and still thriving today. Henny had served as a pilot in the Women's Air Force Service during World War II, flying bombers across the country. She was one of the first jet pilots, testing YP59 twin turbine jet fighters at Wright Field in Dayton. She still flew a vintage plane to Confederate air force rallies in the southeast. She insisted that as long as she passed her flight physical, she intended to fly.

> —they sold their plane a few months ago and I haven't seen much of her lately. She was excited to join the 99ers. I think she met her husband out at the field. It always surprised me to think of him as a pilot. He seems too absentminded to be a good pilot. He paints watercolors and teaches literature and has a dreamy expression. Maybe that's how he looks when he's thinking. Maybe I shouldn't buy into stereotypes. Rhoda's his third wife. Widowed twice, I think. Anyway, someone asked Rhoda about the display. The coins were arranged in rows against black velvet in a glass showcase in their library. She said Geoff had

an almost complete collection from the first Double
Eagle in 1849 to the last in 1933 when Roosevelt
called in all gold and ended production of gold coins.
But there was nothing said to indicate the collection
was so valuable.

Annie went online and discovered some Double Eagles could be purchased for less than a thousand dollars each with cost dependent upon quality. She jotted down some years. If the Grant collection had contained both rare and less valuable coins and only the valuable Double Eagles were stolen, then the thief had indeed known what to take. That didn't sound like the work of a high school dropout.

When you have time, send us the details.
Stay safe. H.

It was unlike Henny to urge caution. She was always the first to take a challenge. Fingers flying, Annie sent Henny a succinct summary of what she knew.

Annie looked at the kitchen table, bright with yellow place mats and Fiesta pottery. They were in cheerful contrast to the February grayness. She always chose a red bowl, gave blue to Max. He should be home soon.

The phone rang. Annie snatched it up, smiling as she recognized his cell number on the caller ID. She spoke without preamble. "Soup's on. I've got—"

Max broke in, his words hurried. "Robert Jamison's being

held. They found a forty-five in the trunk of his car, but I swear he didn't know his mom was dead until Harrison told him. I led the police right to him. Ever since, I've been trying to chase down Handler Jones."

Annie's eyes widened. Handler Jones was a famed Low Country criminal lawyer who took on high-profile criminal and civil cases. Last summer he'd defended Max.

"Handler just called. He's on his way to catch the last ferry. Go ahead and eat. I grabbed some food for Handler and me from Parotti's. Listen, Annie, here's what I want you to do . . ."

Annie knew the way now. She nosed the Volvo off the road and snubbed the front bumper up to a palmetto. When there is heartbreak in a house, all the rooms are lighted and cars clog the drive. For the second time that day, she walked up on Charlie Jamison's porch. When she knocked, a different woman opened the door. Again there was a look of surprise, quickly overlaid with a subdued smile.

Annie stepped inside. In the small living room, voices were mournful. An elderly woman faced Charlie Jamison. "I don't care what the police say, Robert never hurt his mama. Have you been able to talk to him?"

Charlie sounded scared. "Only for a few minutes. Robert said a lawyer was coming to help him. He said the lawyer would call and talk to me tonight. Terry Phillips told me a man he knows at the Haven hired the lawyer. They found a gun in Robert's car trunk. Robert swears he never saw it before."

Annie forced herself forward. Curious faces turned toward her. Slowly the room fell silent. Annie focused on Charlie. Once again she was an unwelcome outsider. This time she had something to offer that might give some comfort. "Charlie, I'm Annie Darling. I was here earlier." She looked at a circle of closed faces. "My husband, Max, asked me to come and see you. Max was at Terry Phillips's house when the police found the gun. Now Max is waiting at the police station to meet with the lawyer who will help Robert."

Charlie looked at her with suspicion. "This afternoon you said the police thought Mama or Robert stole those coins."

"I'm afraid that is what the police believe. I didn't come about the coins." She spoke faster, trying to reach this anguished, frightened young man. "I came to tell you Robert is innocent. He didn't know your mother was dead until the police told him. My husband was there and he swears Robert had no idea. Max wanted you to know."

Charlie lifted a trembling hand. Suddenly his face convulsed in tears.

His wife hurried across the room and put her arms around him.

The elderly woman moved toward Annie. She folded bony arms, her gaze demanding. "I heard about you. You found Gwen. How come you went to her house?"

Annie recounted the events of the morning, stressing as she had earlier what she felt had to be true. ". . . think Gwen found the coins and knew who had taken them. For some reason she tried to persuade the thief to return them. Instead, the thief shot her. We know it wasn't Robert. Max is positive he's innocent. All of you"—Annie reached out a seeking hand—"can help. If anyone knows who Gwen saw, please call and tell us."

Handler Jones stepped out into the anteroom of the police station, quietly closing the door to the hallway that led to offices and the interrogation room. In his mid-forties, he was still boyishly attractive with crystal-bright blue eyes, chestnut hair streaked with silver, and handsome features. He moved with the grace of an athlete. His gray tweed suit was well cut, his black shoes glossy with polish. He looked intelligent, prosperous, pleasant, and curiously unaffected by the utilitarian surroundings of a police station where many entered or left with grim foreboding.

Max was sure Jones had perfected a bland expression to avoid ever tipping his hand to the police or to a client. Last summer Max had taken great comfort in the criminal lawyer's confidence that Max was innocent, but Max wasn't his client now and Jones would never repeat what Robert had told him in confidence.

Max understood that. He had a law degree though he'd never practiced. Any exchange between a lawyer and client was privileged and confidential. Max hoped that Handler had learned something that would help prove Robert's innocence.

Handler headed for the door. "I'm staying at the inn."

Outside, Max welcomed the cool moist night air. The street was deserted. Not many walk for pleasure on a dark February evening when a chill mist haloes streetlamps. The waiting room had seemed oppressive, too warm and weighted with futile what-ifs. What if he had taken Gwen Jamison's call and asked her to meet him at the Franklin house?

Oyster shells crunched beneath their feet as they walked toward the parking lot. Max said it aloud. "Maybe I would have saved her life if I'd talked to her, agreed to meet her."

Handler's response was immediate. "Or lost your life, too. She was shot shortly after she spoke with your secretary. What if you'd talked to her and she'd explained that she'd put something in the house? Whoever shot her had to be nearby. If she'd gone to the Franklin house to meet you, she'd have been followed."

Max pictured himself and a woman—he remembered the elegance of Gwen Jamison in her Easter finery—walking together into the Franklin house. Once the hidden package was recovered, what then?

When they reached the parking lot, Handler gestured toward his red Mercedes. "I'll spend the night at the inn. I'm going back to the mainland on the early ferry. Robert's under arrest and will be arraigned tomorrow. I'll see if I can get bail set. They've moved fast. They're keeping a tight lid on what they've got, but an arrest has to mean the gun matched."

Max had known a match was likely. Why else would the gun be in Robert's trunk? He understood the arrest: the Grant coins stolen, Gwen Jamison hiding something in the Franklin house, Gwen hunting for her son, the murder weapon found in Robert's car.

Handler used his remote to unlock his car. "I'll see what I can get from the circuit solicitor tomorrow. If the ballistics match, we have to find out how the gun got in the trunk of Robert's car." Handler quirked an eyebrow. "Who's the best private eye on the island?"

Max looked at him blankly.

Handler's voice was smooth. "I often use a private eye to find out facts for me. Are you available?"

Max's grin was wide. He'd hired Handler. Handler could hire him. Sure, Max would be paying his own fees, but he would be an official part of the lawyer's team. Handler couldn't divulge what his client had told him, but he could tell Max what he needed to know to defend the case and, as any *Jeopardy!* fan understands, knowing the answers makes the questions explicit.

"I'm your man. What do you need to know?"

"Robert's fuzzy about times this morning." Handler's tone expressed neither acceptance nor rejection. "Harrison kept after him. Robert said he wasn't doing anything special in the morning. He drove around for a while—"

Max looked at the lawyer sharply. So where did a teenager drive on a foggy February morning? It wasn't a beach day or a fishing day. He drove around?

"—but he stumbled all over himself when she wanted to know where and when. He kept saying he was here and there, wasn't paying any attention, didn't know exactly where he'd been. Then he remembered he needed some food and he went to the grocery. When he came back to his apartment, there was a message from his mother on his answering machine. She wanted to see him. He didn't know why. He called her and when he didn't get an answer, he dropped by the Grant house. He thought it was around eleven-thirty, but she wasn't in the kitchen. He hung around for a while out in the garden. When she didn't come, he went to Buddy's Pool Hall and had lunch and played snooker for a couple of hours, then he went over to see Terry Phillips. He claimed he didn't go by her house because she wouldn't be home on a work day. Trace Robert's activities today. Figure out times. We need to know where he was from ten o'clock on. We need to know where his car was every minute after the murder and the shots at the Franklin house."

Max understood. If Robert was innocent, another hand had placed the gun in the trunk of the Gremlin. Where was Robert's car after Gwen Jamison was killed and the intruder shot at Max?

Max put another log on the fire. He eased onto the downy couch, careful not to disturb Dorothy L. The fluffy white cat opened one eye, gave a tiny cat sigh, and sank back into slumber. Max reached over her and took Annie's hand.

Annie gave his hand a squeeze. They often ended their evenings here, enjoying the crackle of a fire on cool nights. They'd talk about their day and often he'd lift her hand, hold it to his lips.

Tonight he stared into the fire as if seeking answers. "Why didn't Robert say where he was when his mother was shot? I keep coming back to that."

Annie remembered being a teenager. "He was doing something he shouldn't have been doing. Or something that embarrassed him. Or he promised someone he wouldn't say he'd been someplace. Or maybe he was selling pot to somebody on a back road. If so, his timing's lousy."

"Handler said Harrison got up and walked to a chalkboard and fixed a grid with the time in half hours. She asked Robert to fill it in and he wrote down 'driving around' from ten to eleven. Handler wants me to try and pinpoint where he was this morning."

Annie's heart gave a glad leap. Max hadn't made a big deal out of signing on to help clear Robert. But it was a big deal. He wasn't backing away from involvement anymore. He was putting last summer behind him. If he was able to trace Robert's meanderings, show that he was at a specific place when Gwen was shot, it could make all the difference. The time . . . Annie concentrated. Gwen Jamison called Confidential Commissions around twenty minutes after ten. Annie found her dying less than half an hour later.

Annie let go of Max's hand, stroked Dorothy L.'s back. "It doesn't take more than twelve minutes to drive from one end of the island to the other. If Robert was on the back roads on the north end, he could cover every one of them in an hour. But why would he? He must struggle to put gas in his car. Max, I don't think he's telling the truth."

"I don't, either." Max sounded grim "Yet I'd swear he didn't know his mother was dead. Maybe Handler can get him to open up. Tomorrow I'm going to canvass the north end of the island. He had to be somewhere."

The phone rang.

Annie picked up the portable receiver. She glanced at caller ID. It was not a number she knew. "Hello."

"Mrs. Darling?" The voice was a low whisper. It could be either a man or woman.

Annie was wary. "This is Annie Darling."

"Gwen told me what happened Monday night." The whisper was faint, hard to hear.

Annie sat bolt upright. She frantically waggled her left hand, then tapped the phone and pointed toward the kitchen and the extension.

Max was on his feet and moving swiftly.

As he picked up the extension, Annie spoke loudly, hoping to mask the click. "Who are you?" It wasn't polite, but neither were whispers.

The husky voice—a man, a woman?—was quick. "If you want to know what Gwen saw, come to the end of Fish Haul pier. Come now. Come alone. No flashlight." The connection ended.

"Wait." There was no answer. She looked at Max. "Can we trace that call?"

"Hold on. I've got the number." He hurried to the den, turned on the computer, clicked several times. "It's the pay phone on the ferry landing."

As Annie came up behind him, she pictured the pay phone, one of three left on the island. A streetlamp stood about ten feet away. "Whoever it was didn't want to stand there very long and take a chance on being seen and remembered. I'll have to go and find out."

He looked up at her, his face pulled into a frown. "To the end of the pier? Alone? Without any light? No way."

She brushed the top of his head with a kiss. "Chill, Max. Nobody's threatening me. Whoever called is desperate not to be seen and identified. Here's what we'll do . . ."

Chapter 7

The ferry office was dark, the *Miss Jolene* at her berth. Occasional lights on the boat docks glimmered through the mist. Past the docks, near the end of the harbor's curve, Fish Haul pier jutted five hundred feet into the sound. The pier was open to the public and a favorite place to fish for king mackerel and black drum in the summer. There was always a crowd during the day, but plenty of nighttime anglers enjoyed it, too. On a bleak February night, the pier was deserted and shrouded in darkness.

Annie walked slowly onto the wooden pier. The sound of her shoes seemed loud. She squinted, trying to make out the end of the pier, uncertain whether a faraway dark shape was a pile or possibly a bench.

The wood was slick beneath her feet from the mist. She felt cold despite the warmth of a navy peacoat, pullover sweater, and wool slacks. One hundred feet. Two hundred. Soon she felt far from shore and Max standing in the shadows of a gnarled live oak near the boardwalk. Three hundred feet. Four hundred. In one hand she held her cell phone, open and connected to Max's cell. He'd be listening. She hoped the greenish glow of the phone wasn't visible if her caller watched. She wondered if the caller could hear the clap of her shoes and the slap of water against the pilings.

The sound of surging water was louder at pier's end. The dark sweep of the sound seemed immense. Annie reached the cross railing. No one waited for her. She was alone on Fish Haul pier.

She was lifting the cell phone to talk to Max when a voice called out, "Walk to the ladder." The call was muffled, yet magnified.

Annie looked back and forth. She was alone at the end of the pier. She walked to the ladder, gripped the railing, looked down.

"Climb over. Come halfway down," the husky voice called from the impenetrable shadow beneath the pier.

Annie hesitated. If the hidden speaker hadn't harmed Gwen Jamison, Annie shouldn't be in danger. Still, and it came to her with a blinding clarity, she knew one fact that might be of compelling interest to the murderer. Annie had heard Gwen's dying effort: ". . . gri . . . ff."

"I want to be sure you don't have a flashlight." The voice was louder, impatient. "Hurry, girl. I've got to get home." A woman spoke. Her voice was tense and nervous, but without any hint of threat. There was a thunk as an oar hit a piling, no doubt keeping a boat steady beneath the pier.

Annie tucked the cell phone in her coat pocket. Max

wouldn't be pleased but she felt reassured. The woman who'd made such an effort to see her was much more nervous than Annie. Clearly Annie couldn't hold a flashlight and cling to the ladder, which indicated careful thought and intelligence in planning this rendezvous.

Annie climbed cautiously over the railing, uneasily aware of the deep water beneath her. She wasn't dressed for swimming. She wished she'd worn gloves because the wood was damp and slick. She moved down the ladder until she could see beneath the pier. The darkness there was inky. She didn't have any idea where the boat might be.

"Thank you, girl." There was no longer an attempt to whisper though the voice was low and hurried. "I got to tell somebody, but I got to tell you now that I won't go to the police. I talked to Gwen Tuesday morning. A fox got into her henhouse Monday night. When she ran out to see, she heard the clang of the gate to their old cemetery. She was worried it might be kids going to mess things up. When she got there, she saw someone burying something behind her grandpa Wilson's grave. She had a clear view because there was a flashlight propped up. She saw who it was, clear as day. She said she was scared, but she waited until the person left and then she dug up a small package wrapped in a plastic trash bag. She took it in the house and opened it. She found the coins inside. She knew what it was. She'd worked for the Grants for years."

Annie strained to see but the shadow was too dark. "Why didn't she call the police?"

"Oh, girl." The voice sounded weary. "Who would believe she'd seen someone from the Grant house coming in the middle of the night to hide a fortune in her cemetery?"

"Someone from the Grant house?" Annie held tight to the ladder. "She said the thief was someone from the Grant house?" Not Robert. Not a wayward teenager. If the thief came from the house, then the robbery had been staged to make it appear someone had broken in. The thief had known very well indeed which coins to pick.

"It's gospel, girl. 'One of the family.' That's what Gwen told me. She didn't know what to do. She said she couldn't call the police, give them the coins without telling them who she'd seen. She was afraid the police wouldn't believe her, that they'd think she had taken the coins, or that Robert had. She hated to do it anyway. The Grants have been good to her. She didn't want to hurt the family. She said she walked the floor all night, trying to decide. She said she was so tired her head pounded and her bones ached, but she knew she had to get the package away from her property. As soon as it was light, she went to the Franklin house. She told me, 'I put the coins in a safe place and I wrote down exactly what I saw and who and when.' After she got home, she kept figuring and decided the best thing to do was get the thief to take the coins back and return them and then no one would be in trouble."

"Why did she care if the thief got caught?" This would be the sticking point for the police. Why would Gwen Jamison take a chance of being involved in a major theft, perhaps accused of committing it, to protect a family she worked for? The Grants had been nice to her, but was that reason enough to shield a thief?

There was a long silence, then a sigh. "Mr. Grant put up bail for Robert. Gwen felt beholden." There was anguish in the woman's voice. "I told her she should have rung up the police right that minute. Or leave the coins somewhere, call Crime Stoppers. But Gwen was afraid the same thing would happen all over again and that wouldn't be right. If it did, she'd know who was responsible and nothing would be solved, and if she didn't do anything to stop it, she was making a crime possible. Instead, she decided to ask the thief to return the coins and everything would be back the way it should be. She said she was going to leave a note and set up a meeting at her house Wednesday morning. She was going to write it so it would be clear she'd never tell anyone. She planned to get the coins from the Franklin house but I hear the locks were changed and she wasn't able to get hold of them when the time came for her to meet the thief."

When the time came. . .

The mist seemed heavier or possibly it was the memory of life running down which made Annie feel stiff and cold. "Did she say where she put them in the Franklin house?"

"She said they were safe as in a vault."

Annie pictured the freshly repainted, empty rooms, the pristine basement, the clean attic. Somewhere in that unfurnished house a fortune in coins was hidden along with a damning description of the thief.

Even if the coins were never found, this information was enough to save Robert. Annie spoke fast. "You've got to come with me. We can go to the police—"

"No, girl." The voice rose high. "Gwen saw too much. She's dead. I don't want to die."

Abruptly Annie understood why this meeting was so carefully arranged. The woman in the boat was terrified that she might become known and the murderer would come to kill her.

Annie spoke before she thought. "Gwen told you who she saw."

Oars splashed on water. A scrape on the opposite side of the pier signaled the boat's hasty departure out into the sound.

Annie cried out, "Wait. Please!"

No voice responded.

Annie climbed up the ladder, pulled herself over the railing. She ran to the end of the pier, looked out to see a faint glimmer of gray white in the darkness as the boat moved steadily away.

Officer Harrison sat ramrod stiff, her thin face empty of expression, her arms folded. An untouched legal pad lay on the desk before her. Her small windowless office scarcely afforded room for an old walnut desk that faced two metal straight chairs. The overhead light was starkly bright. Max's knees jammed against the desk. Annie felt cramped and hot and terribly afraid her words tumbled into an abyss of indifference. "It's clear Robert is innocent. The thief came from the Grant house. We wanted you to know in time to alert the DA and keep Robert from being arraigned tomorrow."

Officer Harrison balanced a pen between her index fingers. She glanced toward the clock, a reminder that it was nearly ten o'clock and she'd returned to the police station after-hours to meet them. A strand of red hair drooped across her forehead. Her uniform was wrinkled. She spoke politely. "Citizen cooperation is always appreciated. I will inform the circuit solicitor of the circumstances of your meeting with an informant and the content of that meeting."

The legs of Max's chair scraped on the cement floor as he leaned forward. "This information clears Robert."

Harrison's eyes glinted. "I think not. What Mrs. Darling offers is hearsay, what she claims was said to her by someone who claims"—the emphasis was distinct on the verbs—"to have spoken with Mrs. Jamison. There is no proof. We don't have this witness's name or—"

Annie broke in. "She was afraid. The thief killed Gwen Jamison. The woman who met me was terrified."

"Her actions suggest fear." An understanding nod. "They could also be the actions of a person who wishes to direct the focus of the investigation away from Robert Jamison and pretends fear as an excuse for remaining unidentified." Harrison placed the pencil squarely in the center of the unmarked pad. "Who is this woman? How credible is she? What proof do we have she knew Gwen Jamison?"

Annie kept her voice level. "If you had heard her, you would have believed her."

Harrison tapped the pad with her pen. "Obviously, you had an unnerving experience, going out in the darkness on the pier, hearing a disembodied voice. But"—and now she was crisp—"clearly the meeting was contrived to produce precisely the effect it did." Implicit was the suggestion that Annie was both naïve and credulous and possibly frightened of the dark. "You rushed here with accusations against the Grant family. Have you thought how interesting it is that the unknown informer claims the thief came from the Grant house?"

"Interesting?" Annie frowned.

Harrison's tone was patient. "Robert Jamison's family obviously understands an explanation must be produced for the presence of the murder weapon in Robert's car. So, presto, we have a dramatic rendezvous tonight in which a disembodied voice assures you Gwen Jamison recognized the thief as someone from the Grant house. That diverts suspicion from Robert and it suggests the murder weapon could have been placed in the trunk of Robert's car when he went by the Grant house late this morning."

Max's response was quick. "It could have happened exactly that way."

Harrison leaned back in her chair. "Why would members of the Grant household know Robert's car?"

Annie could imagine a half-dozen ways that might be true. "Perhaps the murderer saw Robert arrive."

Impatience edged the officer's voice. "You are making quite a few assumptions. However, I will give this information to the circuit solicitor." Harrison pushed back her chair and stood, the interview at an end.

Max came to his feet, his face somber. "You saw Robert when he learned his mother was dead. Couldn't you tell that he didn't know? He was a kid hurt about as bad as a kid can be hurt." Max's voice was gruff. "Didn't you look at him?"

A dull flush reddened Harrison's sallow cheeks. "I looked at him. I saw a punk, a good-for-nothing, weasel-faced punk who'd kill his mother or anybody else as quick as he'd step on a palmetto bug. I know about punks. A punk shot down my partner on his last patrol before he retired. You know why? The punk stole some copper plumbing from an apartment building. We saw a light there and got out to check. The lawyers dressed the punk in a blue blazer and white shirt and khakis for his trial and he got eight years. A first offense. Not premeditated. Eight years and less with good time. The punk's going to live a long time. George is dead and buried and he never got to go fishing like he'd planned. Don't tell me about punks."

Annie paced back and forth, her steps clipping against the stone floor of the kitchen. "What good did that do? Harrison isn't going to investigate. She didn't even ask me what the woman looked like." Annie stopped, hands on her hips. "All right. If that's the way she wants it, I'll stir things up for her." She glanced at the clock, made a quick decision, and grabbed the portable phone.

She punched a familiar number. She was relieved when an obviously wide-awake Marian Kenyon answered. Marian sounded as frisky as a terrier with a cornered rat. "Yo, Annie. What's up?"

"Quid pro quo, Marian." Annie crossed to the counter, turned on the speaker phone, replaced the receiver. She found a pad and pen. "How would you like an exclusive interview with me about an unknown informant with shocking revelations about the theft of the Grant Double Eagles and the Jamison murder?"

"Who's the informant?" Marian always got right to the point.

"Anonymous friend of Gwen Jamison's. Gwen told her the thief came from the Grant house and was a member of the family. I'll give you a blow-by-blow, my rendezvous in the dark at the end of Fish Haul pier, a disembodied voice, a rowboat disappearing into the night."

"Woo-hoo." Marian's raspy shout filled the kitchen. "This'll frost the networks. Let me grab some paper."

Annie turned a thumbs-up to Max who was stirring hot chocolate. "Okay, Marian, your turn first. Who was in the house when the theft occurred?"

A satisfied chortle. "You pushed the right button, sweetie. I do news the old-fashioned way. No handouts for this old broad. I got the police report. In the house that night were—"

Annie wrote down the names.

"—Geoffrey Grant, fifty-three, home owner; Rhoda Grant, forty-four, wife; sons, Ben Travis-Grant, twenty-five, and Justin Foster-Grant, twenty-eight; daughters Barb Travis-Grant, twenty-five, and Kerry Foster-Grant, twenty-four. Geoff Grant adopted the kids when he married their mothers. One at a time, of course. Ben and Barb are fraternal twins. Also in the house was Justin's fiancée, Margaret Brown. Present in a cottage on the grounds was Denise Cramer, former sister-in-law."

Annie was perplexed. "Do they all live there?"

"Only Geoff and Rhoda plus the ex–sis-in-law in the cottage. The brood shows up every year for a house party to celebrate Geoff's birthday."

Annie nodded toward Max. He had predicted that when they knew why the coins were stolen during the winter doldrums, they'd know everything. They didn't know everything, but now there seemed to be a very good reason for the timing of the theft.

Paper crackled on the other end of the line. "Okay, kid. Now for the exclusive—"

Annie replied with gusto. Marian would milk every fact and supposition for maximum drama. When the story appeared in the *Gazette,* it would be garlanded with the gloom of night, the salty scent of the sea, the hollow thunk as the rowboat bumped the pilings, the slap of waves, the disembodied voice thinned by fear. ". . . so that's the story."

"Good story." Marian sounded thoughtful. "It's got big-time problems. I'll have to do a fancy dance with it, see what I can finesse."

Annie pictured Marian's monkey face creased in thought. "Finesse?"

Marian was crisp. "The boss isn't big on libel suits."

"Libel?" Annie felt like an echo machine.

"Quotes from the unseen informant aren't privileged, sweetie. Privileged is the holy grail in a news story, meaning the material is quoted from court or legislative proceedings or in a pronouncement from a public official. Maybe I can fish a quote from the cops that will open things up. I'll see what I can do." Her husky voice exuded enthusiasm. "As an old lawyer once told me: There are many different ways to tell the truth. Speaking of truth, what's in this for you besides the names of the house party?"

"Just between us?"

"Anything I may need?" Marian was prepared to do battle.

"Nope."

"Okay."

"Officer Harrison blew me off. I doubt if she checks with anybody at the Grant house. Somebody thinks they're sitting pretty. Maybe a story in tomorrow afternoon's *Gazette* will rock that boat."

"I imagine this story will be read with interest by everyone concerned." Marian's tone was dry. "Catch you later."

Annie hung up and reached out to take the mug of hot chocolate from Max. "I wonder if anyone in the family is suspicious?"

Annie welcomed the heat of the chocolate through the porcelain mug.

He looked at her sharply. "Sometimes you're damn clever."

Annie was torn between enjoying the compliment or taking offense. "How about," she demanded, " 'You're damn clever.' "

Max grinned. "I just said so."

Annie picked up a couch pillow and tossed it.

Max ducked. He was still grinning. "You are always clever, Mrs. Darling. Merely a slip of the tongue."

Annie wished she could be an unseen observer tonight in the Grant household. Families cut to the chase. They know who's greedy or selfish or dishonest or weak or—most frightening of all—coldly determined always to prevail no matter the cost.

Annie had a quick memory of the New Year's dance at the country club. "Grant's the good dancer, right?" Grant was a little pudgy but graceful. His rounded face always had a slightly bemused, professorial expression.

"He gets around a dance floor pretty well." Not as well, Max's tone implied, as one Maxwell Darling. "I've played golf with him a few times. Nice guy. Cheerful. I don't know much about his family except he's been widowed a couple of times, has the four kids."

"Do you know him well enough to call him up and—"

Max shook his head. "And say, 'Hey, old buddy, has it occurred to you that somebody in your family's a thief and a murderer?' " His eyes narrowed. "First I want to scare up everything I can about the family." Max replaced the poker. "Since Handler hired me, we're official."

He walked to the sofa and dropped down beside Annie, took her hands in his. "After last summer, I thought about closing down Confidential Commissions. I didn't do it. I don't like to be a quitter." He stared into the fire, his expression somber. "My father would have said I never finished anything. I went to law school but I didn't want to be a lawyer. I came to the island after you and I wanted you to be proud of me. You work hard. You've made Death on Demand a great store. So I opened Confidential Commissions and I put that ad in the paper."

Annie nodded. She knew it by heart:

Confidential Commissions
17 Harbor Walk
Curious, troubled, problems?
Ask Max.
Call today—321-HELP

"I've helped some people."

"A lot of people." She spoke with pride.

"I turned down almost everybody this fall. This morning I was too busy to take Gwen Jamison's phone call." He looked bleak. "Scratch that. I didn't want to take the call, not when Barb said the woman sounded scared. I'd been down that road. This time I was wrong. Gwen Jamison had good reason to be scared. Maybe I couldn't have made a difference for her, but I'm going to do my best to make a difference for Robert."

Annie saw resolve and determination and no trace of hesitation. She felt a surge of delight. Max was back, her Max, ready to help those in trouble. Yes, he'd be wary now, always and forever, but he would no longer walk away.

The shrill summons of the telephone exploded in the quiet bedroom, strident and menacing. Annie blinked awake but Max was already reaching for the receiver. She peered at the clock. A quarter after three.

Max punched on the bedside lamp, squinting against the glare. His thick blond hair was tousled, his cheeks bristly. "Yeah . . . I'll be right there. Hal?" Max frowned. "He clicked off." Max hung up. He moved fast, pulling sweats from a drawer.

Annie moved fast, too. She slipped into a red turtleneck and jeans, looked for her sneakers. "What's happened?"

"Somebody tried to get inside. Hal called nine-one-one." Max's voice was muffled as he pulled on the sweatshirt. His head poked through and he saw Annie tying her sneakers. "I'll go. You don't need to come."

She didn't bother to reply as she hurried to the closet. She found a dark hooded sweatshirt, yanked it on, and headed for the hall.

The Corvette's headlights were thin spears in the darkness of the tree-lined drive. "Hal didn't give me a chance to tell him to stay put."

Annie balanced as Max drove too fast up the narrow lane. "The police car's there." She felt a rush of relief at sighting the flash of the revolving red dome light.

The Corvette jolted to a stop next to the cruiser. Max left the lights on. "Wait till I check things out." He slid from the car, yelled, "Hal? Where are you?"

A Maglite's harsh beam settled on Max.

Annie hurried to catch up, squinting against the glare.

Max held up a hand to shield his eyes. "Who's there?"

"Officer Thorpe." He was brusque. "What's going on?" Thorpe was a dark shape behind the light.

Max and Annie reached the patrol car. Max looked around. "Where's Hal?"

"Nobody's here. We got the call somebody was trying to break in, but the caller hung up. I just got here. Who called? How come you two are here?" Thorpe sounded suspicious.

"This is our house. After somebody broke in this morning, then shot at me, I hired Hal Porter to keep a lookout. He called and said there was a prowler." Max stepped out of the Maglite's glare. "Hal?" His shout was echoed by the mournful hoot of an owl. "Hal?"

Only the rustle of shrubbery and the owl's wavering tremulous moan broke the heavy silence.

"I'll get a flashlight." Max hurried to the Corvette.

The three of them, Officer Thorpe in the lead, made a careful circuit of the house. On the back porch, glass shards once again gleamed on the flooring. The broken pane of the morning had been covered with a wooden board. The glass pane next to it was knocked out.

Max pointed. "The sash hasn't been raised. My guess is that Hal heard the glass breaking and got here before anyone got inside."

Thorpe swung his light out into the backyard. "After he called, he should have stayed put, left it to us to find the perp. All right. Let's take a look. Keep behind me."

Annie wondered if she would ever feel quite the same about the garden at the Franklin house. The newly planted shrubs and refurbished pool had enchanted her, but that was in daylight with the soft chirrup of birds in the trees and sunlight spangling the glossy magnolia leaves. Now the magnolias rattled in a vagrant breeze, sounding as lonely as ghostly steps in an abandoned house.

They made no attempt at stealth, shouting Hal's name, moving at a quick jog with leaves crackling underfoot, flashing the lights behind banks of shrubs. They stopped at the pond.

Annie darted unwilling glances at the dark water as Thorpe circled the pond.

Max poked a broken limb into the depths. "We dredged it. There shouldn't be anything here."

She scarcely breathed until Max shook his head and tossed the stick away.

Thorpe swung the Maglite toward the path that disappeared into the pines. "We'll have to wait until daylight—" He broke off, his right hand dropping to his holster.

In the distance, leaves crackled in the pine grove. Someone was coming, heavily and slowly, toward the pond.

Thorpe jerked a peremptory thumb. "Get out of sight." He clicked off the Maglite and disappeared in the sudden darkness.

Max grabbed Annie's hand and pulled her behind the trunk of an old live oak. She felt the warmth of his arm tight around her shoulders, his breath against her cheek. They waited, listening to the irregular, uneven progress as the unseen person came nearer.

Slowly Annie's eyes adjusted. Moonlight made the trees ghostly. She stared into blackness where the path plunged into the pines.

Chapter 8

A dark form emerged from blacker shadow.

The sudden brilliance of the Maglite brought into sharp clarity a big man in a blue down jacket with a hand clamped to his head. He stumbled to a stop. A portion of his sleeve jacket obscured his face.

"Police. Hands up. Police." Thorpe held his revolver in an attack stance.

Max shouted, "That's Hal. Man, what happened to you?"

Porter wavered unsteadily. His hand dropped, revealing a mud-crusted cheek and a bloody abrasion on the left side of his face. "A couple of guys slammed me."

Thorpe lowered his gun, nodded toward the path snaking into the pine grove. "Where are they?"

Porter started to shake his head, winced. "They're long gone." He blinked, focused on Max. "I called you." His gaze was bleary. "How long ago?"

"Twenty minutes."

"That long . . ." Porter sounded woozy. "I guess I was out of it for a while."

Thorpe looked impatient. "Who slugged you? Why?"

"A couple of black kids tried to get inside." Porter squinted toward the Franklin house.

A couple of black kids . . . Annie saw shock on Max's face. This changed everything. Max had been convinced of Robert's innocence.

Porter's bruised face was haggard. "I was in my tent. I heard glass break. I moved through the bushes and turned a flashlight on the back porch. A couple of teenagers were trying to shove the window up. I guess I should have called nine-one-one, but I thought I could handle them. They were just kids. I yelled for them to hold it, said I had them covered. Instead of stopping, they ran and jumped over the porch railing and headed this way. They had about twenty yards on me, but I followed the noise down through the garden and into the pine grove. I got to where the path splits and stopped to listen. I heard noise on the track to the cemetery. I hurried that way. About the time I realized I didn't hear any twigs breaking, something came out of nowhere and whacked me on the side of the head. I guess they'd gone off the path and were waiting for me with a thick branch. I went down. I don't think I was ever totally out, but I couldn't get up." He lifted his hand to gingerly touch his temple. "I was groggy long enough for them to get away. I think they took my shotgun and flashlight. I couldn't find them when I pawed around, but it was too dark to see so I don't know for sure."

"A missing shotgun?" Thorpe looked grim. "We'd better take a look."

Max frowned. "Shouldn't we get Hal to the emergency room? Annie and I can take him."

"I'm fine." Porter was gruff. "I'm more ticked off than hurt. I want to see about my shotgun. Later, if you've got a key handy, I'll use your washroom and clean up. I've got a first-aid kit in my truck."

Thorpe gave Hal a quick look, nodded. "If you're okay, let's look for the gun." The officer glanced at Max and Annie. "Stay here. When I get back, I'll search the house, see if I can find anything."

Annie waited until Thorpe and Porter disappeared into the pines. "This looks bad for Robert."

Max looked discouraged. "Thorpe will think Robert and a couple of guys planned the theft and Robert's buddies broke in tonight. Annie"—his voice was stubborn—"I'm sure Robert didn't know his mom was dead."

"Maybe he didn't know." Annie felt sad. "Maybe he was involved and he told the others and one of them shot her."

Max was crisp. "Maybe. Maybe not. By this time, everybody on the island knows about the coins and Mrs. Jamison's murder and Robert's arrest. What's to keep some guys from thinking they'd take a look in the house, see if they could find the coins? Or maybe these kids are Robert's friends and they thought if they staged a burglary while Robert was in jail, it would prove his innocence."

Annie knew how easily information traveled across the island. One of Max's scenarios could be right, but proof would be hard to find.

Max moved back and forth, casting impatient glances toward the pines. "In the morning, I'll announce a reward for information concerning tonight's attempted break-in. As for the house, Thorpe can look it over but if we couldn't find anything, neither will he."

The crackle of steps announced the return of Thorpe and Porter. Annie felt chilled as she watched the men walk toward them. Hal Porter was empty-handed.

Porter was angry. "We found where I went down. The grass was knocked flat. I guess I wallowed around some. We looked everywhere. There was a chunk of wood with some blood on it. Thorpe has it. We hunted behind trees and under logs. We didn't find my flashlight. Or my shotgun."

Faint tendrils of sunrise streaked gunmetal-gray stratus clouds as Max strode on the boardwalk toward Confidential Commissions. No one else stirred on the dark deserted harbor front. Many of the boats in the harbor were battened down for winter. Lights gleamed from the cabin of a big cruiser from Miami, *Lady Luck III*. Max hurried into his office, pushed up the thermostat. By the time he was in place behind his desk with a fresh legal pad and pens, the chilly room had warmed. He glanced over the e-mails from *Marigold's Pleasure* that Annie had forwarded and jotted down a series of questions:

Who needs money in the Grant family?

Were the coins insured?

Did the collection contain coins of varying value?

Who are Robert's buddies?

Where was Robert when his mom was shot?

Can Handler Jones persuade the circuit solicitor to hold off filing charges?

Max drew a squarish face topped by spiky hair. Emma Clyde's most recent dye job was mostly silver with bronze streaks to match a dressy caftan decorated with beaded chrysanthemums. He had to hand it to the island's brusque mystery writer. Her e-mail to Annie was on point. Who needed money and was a bundle of greenbacks due from insurance? Max looked thoughtful as he added a soaring vintage plane to his sketch. Henny Brawley's e-mail added another possibility. Rhoda Grant was no longer piloting a plane for pleasure. Did that hint at a money crunch in the Grant household? Or was there trouble in Geoff's third marriage? It would be important also to determine, as Laurel had recommended, whether the collection contained coins of lesser value. Had the thief been well acquainted with the collection?

Max glanced at the clock, waited until the minute hand moved past six. It was far too early to place most calls, but he was confident Matilda Phillips was up and bustling about her kitchen.

The phone was answered on the first ring. "Haven't you caused enough trouble? What right have you got to bring the police down on us?" Matilda's voice was shrill. "My Terry is a good boy and I told that ugly-faced policeman Terry was right here last night. He wasn't running around the island breaking into that old Franklin place and he would never hurt anyone. Never."

The phone slammed into the receiver.

Caller ID had announced him to Matilda. Max slowly replaced the receiver. Was Terry still at home or had Thorpe taken him to the police station? Max turned to his computer, clicked rapidly, found Terry's cell phone number. He punched in the numbers.

"Hello." Terry's young voice was strained and guarded.

Max spoke fast, hoping Terry would listen. "I didn't know the police were following me when Robert was arrested. I had nothing to do with the police coming after you about last night." Max quickly described the late-night call from Hal Parker and its aftermath.

Terry's voice was uneven. "It wasn't me. That cop accused me and Gramma told him she was up in the night with her arthritis and she knew I never left the house. I guess even a white cop knows my gramma doesn't lie. I don't know anything about what happened last night."

"I believe you. I never thought you were involved. I'm calling because I have to find out more about Robert's friends. It could be that Robert and a couple of other guys planned the robbery. Robert would never hurt his mom but maybe—"

"That's crazy." Terry was furious. "Do you think the guys Robert hangs out with are killers? Some of them get drunk or smoke pot, maybe steal a six-pack. But nobody's mean. Besides, Robert was getting things together. He wants to get married. He was looking for a job. He thought he had one lined up as a deckhand on the ferry. Mr. Parotti was going to give him a chance. Now Robert's in jail. That'll ruin everything with Serena's dad. He never liked Robert anyway."

"There's another possibility." Max spoke quietly, hoping to soothe Terry, keep him talking and maybe he'd give Max some names. "Everybody knows now about the coins being hidden in the Franklin house. Maybe some guys decided to take a look. Maybe they were trying to help Robert. If I find them, I'll listen to what they say."

"That won't help Robert. Nothing's going to help Robert. Who cares about a black kid?"

"I care." Max looked toward the doorway, remembering Barb's eager face and the phone she had held, a link to a woman with only a few hours left to live.

Terry's answer was slow in coming. "You got the lawyer for him."

"Handler Jones will do his best for Robert. I'm trying to do my best for him. Look at it, Terry, Robert was in jail last night. He wasn't breaking into the Franklin house. That could prove Robert's innocent. But I can really prove he is innocent if I can find out where he was yesterday morning when his mom was shot."

"I don't want to screw everything up for Robert." Terry drew a deep breath and Max could imagine his troubled face. "But if he doesn't get out of jail, everything's ruined anyway. If you go to Shady Grove Baptist Church . . ."

Annie yawned and stretched. She opened one eye. Seven forty-three. Her eyes popped wide. They usually got up at seven. She sniffed. No delectable scents beckoned her downstairs and the house was too still. "Max?" She was aware of a tired ache behind her eyes from too little sleep. She rose and slipped into her bathrobe and knew the house held only her. She stepped into flip-flops and hurried downstairs.

She found a note at the breakfast table.

Good morning, Mrs. Darling,

Max wasn't here to pull her near, but the salutation was almost as warming.

Thought you needed to sleep. I'm going by CC. I'll find out everything I can about the Grant family, then I want to round up kids who know Robert and see if I can pick up his trail yesterday morning.

I'll fax over what I get. I'll give Marian Kenyon a ring, let her know what happened at the Franklin house last night. Coffee's made. Blueberry muffins ready. Fresh cantaloupe. Dorothy L.'s eaten.

Love—Max

Annie poured steaming coffee into a mug, wished its warmth could lift away the cloud of fatigue. It took only a moment to microwave a muffin. Annie was liberal with the unsalted butter from an island creamery. She spooned fruit into a bowl, poured a glass of whole milk. She ate quickly, took an even quicker shower, selected a cream turtleneck, russet corduroy slacks, and matching loafers.

The sunlight was pale but cheerful as she drove. She loved the early-morning somnolence of the winter-quiet island and spared a moment of pity for drivers snarled in gridlock in major cities. She parked behind Death on Demand, her off-season commute down to six and a half minutes.

As soon as she opened the back door, a piercing meow announced Agatha's unhappiness. Agatha bounded toward her. As Annie hurried through the storeroom into the coffee area, Agatha nipped at Annie's ankles, not quite playfully.

"Stop it, Agatha." Annie high-stepped across the floor. "These are new socks and I'm only about an hour late. What's an hour?" She poured dry food into Agatha's bowl in record time, then retreated to the lavatory to check her ankles. She found only one real welt. She scrubbed the ankle with soap and water and dabbed it with hydrogen peroxide.

Agatha padded into the lavatory, jumped up to the sink to bat at the running water, splashing until her eyes were golden and her tail plumed.

Annie laughed, her good humor restored. "After all," she informed her imperious cat, "you are gorgeous and fun so a touch of temper is acceptable. I feel snarly if breakfast is late, too." She didn't resort to nipping the food server's ankles, but she wasn't a cat.

Agatha was in such a good humor, she joined Annie at the computer, insinuating herself onto Annie's lap. Annie petted cashmere-soft fur as she checked e-mails. As she'd expected, the traveling trio had more opinions to share.

> As Marigold once observed, any sleuth with a sliver of brains knows when a suspect simply isn't up to the job. Marigold says good people can do bad things, but a gentle heart won't kill except in defense of a loved one. You can tell that policewoman that she's

> wasting her time suspecting Robert. He did some yard work for me last summer, but he took time off at his own expense to help stand watch to protect the nesting area of a loggerhead sea turtle. You know we've had poachers the last couple of years who steal the eggs. Robert and some kids from the Shady Grove Baptist Church kept watch around the clock until the hatchlings made it safely into the sea. Murder his mother? I don't think so.
>
> Emma

Annie stroked Agatha's lifted chin, felt the vibrato of her purr. "We don't know about Robert's friends. Neither do Emma or Marigold."

Agatha assumed Annie spoke to her. The purr increased.

"But," Annie was quick to add, "Robert's friends aren't part of the Grant family." Last night's episode at the Franklin house might be important or might not. She was still convinced the truth would be found at the Grant house. Her unknown informant at the pier had radiated fear because she possessed knowledge too dangerous to reveal. Annie couldn't prove this was so, but she had no doubt that Gwen Jamison had told her friend the identity of the thief who had slipped from the Grant house to the old family cemetery, carrying a fortune in coins.

Annie felt a sudden deep wave of sadness. Robert protected sea turtle eggs. Max had described him as a gangly teenager. Was he still in one of the cells at the island police station or had he been taken to the county detention center? If he was innocent, he was struggling with heartsick grief made worse by fear of what the future held.

Annie glanced at the clock. The minutes were speeding past. She clicked on Henny's e-mail.

> I knew Helen Grant, Geoff's second wife. Nice woman. Too nice maybe. Besotted about her kids, Ben and Barb. That's not good for kids. They grow up thinking they are special and that spells trouble. Check out Ben. I think he got in some trouble when he was in college. Helen was a shadow of herself for a while with soulful murmurs about men not understanding the artistic temperament and boys always had a wild fling or so, it was part of growing up, and Geoff could be so stern and she'd told him it was a Christian's duty to forgive. Not to give a dog a bad name, but I'd look Ben over. Little lapses can be signposts. Keep us up to date.
>
> Henny

Annie's fingers hovered above the keyboard. The traveling trio would be fascinated by her surreptitious meeting at the pier and Hal Porter's encounter in the middle of the night at the Franklin house. Edith would send the holidayers this afternoon's *Gazette* with the dramatic tale of Annie's sojourn on the dark pier and, no doubt, Max's update about last night. Until then Emma, Henny, and Laurel knew nothing . . .

Annie's hands remained aloft. Was it fair that she immediately thought of Laurel when the words "knew nothing" bobbed in her mind? An imp in the back of her mind high-fived. Annie's rush of guilt was so intense she immediately clicked on the unopened e-mail from Laurel.

> Emma and adorable Marigold see the criminal as greedy, unscrupulous, and callous. Henny dwells upon weakness of character. I, my dear, with a passing acquaintance of love's power—

Passing? The imp sang a husky verse of "Always True to You in My Fashion." The old song was a favorite of Laurel's. Did that reflect an amazing self-awareness?

> —urge you and dear Max to seek the heart of the matter. Whatever the outward indications, I am confident that love or its lack will prove to be the cause of the theft and murder. Sad to say, love does not always turn a happy face to its seeker. Who has lost love? Who seeks love? Is love blocked or thwarted? Passion is ever a pointer.

If ever anyone knew the ins and outs of passion . . . Annie refrained from completing the thought. After all, Laurel was Max's mother. Annie welcomed the sudden ping of the fax machine. Good. The dossiers. That's what mattered. She appreciated Laurel's effort, but this time Annie was ready to embrace Emma and (with a grimace) Marigold's analysis. Greedy, unscrupulous, and callous—that described a thief and murderer.

Annie pushed away from the computer. E-mails would have to wait. Snugging Agatha over her shoulder, Annie stood and hurried toward the fax.

Max sketched a barred window. He spoke rapidly into the telephone receiver. "I talked to Hal Porter a few minutes ago. He's got a headache but insists he's fine. Workmen are scheduled every day for the rest of the week so that covers the Franklin house during the day. I'm going to set up a cot and stay at night. Hal insists he'll be on guard, too. He's mad as hell, wants to make somebody pay for whopping him."

Handler Jones spoke in his usual relaxed, honey-thick drawl. "I kind of wonder if the coins are still there."

Max drew an inch-tall question mark, underlined it three times. "Maybe not. After the murderer shot at me, Annie and I searched. Hal looked it over yesterday, too. Last night I gave Thorpe permission to search. Obviously he didn't have any success or I would have heard. I don't know that finding the coins will make any difference for Robert. Harrison thinks the informant at the pier was a put-up job to divert suspicion from him."

"That's not a bad theory from the police perspective." Handler was measured. "I expect the police attitude is similar about last night's excitement at the Franklin house."

Max felt stymied. "Maybe another murder would get the cops' attention."

"We'll hope it won't come to that." The lawyer's tone was dry.

Max's pencil flew, creating a caped figure fleeing into pines. "We need something that will persuade the circuit solicitor to hold off filing charges. Mud always sticks. If Robert's innocent, there will always be someone who whispers, 'He was arrested for murder once . . .'" Max's voice was harsh. There were still sidelong glances, quick appraisals, when he met someone who'd seen the news photos of a wan Max in handcuffs.

Handler didn't mince words. "Robert needs an alibi. I've talked to a lot of defendants and I can smell it when they're hiding something. I pick up that signal from Robert. Find out where he was yesterday morning. There's something going on there."

Max hesitated, then took the plunge. "I wasn't going to say anything because I promised my source I'd keep this quiet. But I may have a lead on where Robert went yesterday morning."

"Are you sure of your information?"

"Certain." Terry Phillips had been reluctant but definite.

The lawyer spoke slowly. "I've got a pretty good relationship with the solicitor. I'll ask him for twenty-four hours. That's the best we can hope for."

Chapter 9

Annie crawled on hands and knees to retrieve the faxed sheets sent flying by Agatha's skidding leap to the top of the coffee bar. As Annie reached for the last sheet, Agatha pounced, locking her front and back legs around Annie's arm.

First immobilize your prey . . .

Annie knew cat mores better than she wished. Next would come claws. Annie snatched a sheet with her free hand and waggled it. Agatha's head whipped toward the crackle. Eyes gleaming, she loosened her grip, and rolled over. Annie scooted backward. Agatha launched herself. At the last moment, Annie yanked the sheet away and popped to her feet.

Striving to breathe normally, she found a plastic spoon, tapped it on the counter to get Agatha's attention, then tossed it on the heart-pine floor. Agatha raced after it. Clicks sounded as

Agatha knocked the spoon with the skill of a field hockey star. That would entertain her until time for a nap.

Annie smoothed her tousled hair, brushed dust from her sleeve, and poured a mug of coffee. She carried the mug and the dossiers to the midsection of the store and settled in one of the wicker chairs with a bamboo table to one side.

Max's cover note was brief:

> *I checked the* Gazette*'s online archives for pix. I also made some phone calls and talked to some of Geoff's old friends. The personal stuff from them is confidential. I'm on my way to the Shady Grove Baptist Church and Buddy's Pool Hall.*

Annie picked up the first dossier:

> **Geoffrey Warren Grant, 53.** B. Broward's Rock. Father William, an inventor. Mother Louisa, homemaker, active in artistic circles. William ran a shoe repair shop to pay the bills. Awarded a patent on an early version of eight-track tapes. The technology is now obsolete. At one time the family enjoyed substantial income. Geoff has bachelor's and master's degrees in English literature, writes poetry, and has entered original plays in several area contests though he's never made the short list. He teaches nineteenth-century American literature as an adjunct at Chastain College. His specialty is Emily Dickinson. He handles the family investments. He married Nancy Blaine Foster, a divorcée, when he was in graduate school and adopted her children, Justin and Kerry. Nancy died in a car wreck. Several years later, Geoff married Helen Howard Travis, a widow, and adopted

her twins, Ben and Barb. Helen died from breast cancer. He married Rhoda Wickham three years ago. They have no children. Geoff is genial, friendly, and likable though he can be a little full of himself. He loves to quote Dickinson. One of his favorites is "Because I could not stop for Death." That can add a melancholy tinge to an evening. His take is that remembering our fate prompts appreciation of the moment.

Annie much preferred "Two butterflies went out at noon." She studied the sheet containing a montage of color photographs. Geoff Grant's face was just round enough to have a disarming quality. The lock of black hair that drooped over his forehead reminded her vaguely of Edgar Allan Poe although Grant was the picture of health with pink cheeks. On a golf green, Grant was elegant in a crimson polo and cream-colored knickers as he waited for his companion to putt. A shirtless Grant was flabby though tanned as he maneuvered the tiller of a sailboat. In a tuxedo, he smiled at a slender, laughing woman, his partner on a dance floor.

Annie put down the print, selected the next dossier.

Justin Foster-Grant, 28. Justin was born in Savannah. His mother moved to Broward's Rock with Justin and his sister Kerry after her divorce from Matthew Foster. She taught third grade. Geoff adopted Justin and Kerry. Justin worked for a local vet in high school. He was an Eagle Scout. He graduates from vet school this spring. Plays bass in an amateur rock group, the Spiny Dogfish. *Gazette* social notes at Christmas said: "Wedding bells may soon ring for Justin

Foster-Grant, whose houseguest this holiday is the lovely Margaret Brown from Mobile."

Annie smiled at the picture of a guitar-strumming redhead with a luxuriant handlebar mustache. In another picture, he was clad in a white lab coat, his face creased in concentration as he palpated a Lab's abdomen. A younger photo, premustache, captured him in full Scout regalia, standing tall and proud as he received an award.

Annie reached for the next sheet.

Kerry Foster-Grant, 24. Born in Savannah. Bachelor's degree in social work from Armstrong State. Employed as a caseworker by a social services agency in Atlanta. In her high school yearbook, she was described as "Kerry who looks past the here and now with an eye to Heaven." An accomplished pianist.

Annie studied Kerry's high school class picture. Lustrous dark hair framed a narrow face with grave blue eyes and a serene expression. A hint of a dimple and a slight smile saved the photograph from severity. No matter the circumstances of the photograph—Kerry with graceful hands above a keyboard or laughing with her brother or hoisting a two-by-four at a Habitat for Humanity construction site—there was a hint of otherworldliness.

Ben Travis-Grant's dossier was as different as the crashing chords of Chopin from the ethereal strains of Debussy.

Ben Travis-Grant, 25. Born on Broward's Rock. His father was the late Charles Travis, a geologist who died in an offshore drilling-rig accident. Ben and his twin sister Barb were adopted by Geoff Grant after his marriage to their mother Helen. Ben has been in and out of college but is currently enrolled at Armstrong State with a major in Spanish. He has traveled extensively in South America, Europe, and the Far East, backpacking and living off savings earned as a waiter. He has a blog with stories and pix of his travels. A few months ago he described the immensity and fascination of the night safari at the Singapore zoo. "It's wonderful and terrible. The animals appear to roam freely in their jungle surroundings, but they aren't really free. Is there any freedom left anywhere? I won't be trapped. I'll never settle for the illusion of freedom."

Ben's photographs from the Singapore zoo included both day and night scenes with zoom close-ups of a baby tapir nuzzling its mother, a prowling Malayan tiger, a lion devouring a chunk of bloody meat, and a sloe-eyed snow leopard. There were several personal photos from his world travels. Wearing crumpled khakis that looked slept in, Ben stood with a booted foot on a fallen tree in a jungle. He was big and burly with a ruddy complexion and thick chestnut curls. Other pictures showed him in front of a Moorish castle, face flushed, a bottle of wine lifted high, and in a kayak, plunging through hissing rapids, drenched but exhilarated.

Annie eyed the photos thoughtfully. Clearly, Ben was a risk taker and greedy for thrills. How far did his greed extend?

Barb Travis-Grant, 25. Dropped out of college after her freshman year. Aspiring actress. She's worked as a barmaid, waitress, nightclub hostess, and riverboat blackjack dealer with stays in Birmingham, Biloxi, Jacksonville, and Savannah. Currently she's a sales clerk in a high-fashion Savannah boutique. She's been engaged twice. She's had small roles in local theaters in Birmingham, Jacksonville, and Savannah. Lousy credit rating, often running up big bills on credit cards.

Golden-brown hair framed an expressive face with deep-set brown eyes, high cheekbones, and pointed chin. A quick glance at the photographs suggested Barb's life was as uncharted as the flight of a windblown leaf. The images reflected amusement, rebellion, and sensuality. The most revealing picture was a stagy glamour shot. Barb lounged in a brief crimson negligee against an oversized, white satin pillow in a provocative pose, but her eyes looked uncertain, hopeful, and vulnerable.

When Annie was trying to be an actress, she'd known dozens of girls like Barb with pretty faces and some talent. They all wanted more than they could afford, bewitched by styles and fragrances and a vision of elegance created by high-dollar advertising and films.

Annie wondered if Geoff Grant treasured his adoptive children for glimpses of their dead mothers or if he was often bewildered by personalities foreign to his. How did his new wife view them?

Rhoda Wickham Grant, 44. Born in Marietta, Georgia. Attended a business college in Atlanta. Married briefly to a Delta pilot, John Sanders. No children. She resumed her maiden name and was a real estate agent in Atlanta. She arrived on Broward's Rock six years ago. Worked for Sandpiper Realty. A longtime pilot. Credit history mixed. A tendency to run up credit card debt with exotic vacations.

There were two photographs from the *Gazette,* a wedding picture of Rhoda and Geoff, she in a mauve cocktail dress, he in a dark business suit, and Rhoda standing beside a Cessna Skyhawk at the Broward's Rock airport, the wind stirring her dark curls. She was smiling.

Annie picked up the final dossier.

Denise Howard Cramer, 37, born in Columbia. Older sister Helen married Geoff Grant. Various jobs as sales clerk, secretary, real estate agent. Marriage to Thomas Cramer ended in divorce in 1998. No children. She came to the island when her sister was diagnosed with terminal cancer. The former servants' cottage had long been used as a retreat for Geoff Grant. He turned it over to his sister-in-law. Denise remained on the island after Helen's death. She now rents the cottage. She is a successful island real estate agent. She introduced Rhoda to Geoff.

In one photograph, Denise stood near the Sandpiper Realty sign in front of a Mediterranean-style mansion. In the other, she presided at a Rotary luncheon. She looked bubbly with curly brown hair, a plump face, and a big smile.

Annie swept the sheets into a pile. The occupants of the house who deserved red flags seemed obvious, determinedly free-spirited Ben and financially irresponsible Barb. If Rhoda often spent more money than she had, she also might have been tempted by gold coins.

"However . . ." Annie murmured aloud. Sometimes it was the most conventional who had the most to lose. The decision to kill Gwen Jamison might have been made as much to protect a reputation as to profit from the theft.

The phone rang. Annie automatically checked caller ID. She saw the name and took a sudden quick breath.

Max sniffed. Ever a man to appreciate home baking, he sorted out appetizing smells of rising rolls, stew, and apple pie. He stopped in the wide doorway that opened into a spotless kitchen. Butter-topped rolls rose on several trays. Steam wreathed above large pots. Six apple pies cooled on a rack. Three black women with gingham aprons moved about purposefully.

Max knocked on the door frame. "Excuse me."

A tall woman with iron-gray hair looked up from a cutting board. "Yes?"

"I'm looking for Serena Shelby. Can you direct me to the preschool?"

Unsmiling, she walked toward him, her gaze questioning. "Who might you be?"

She obviously didn't intend to lead an unknown man to a young woman working at her church.

Max understood and knew he would have wanted the same protection for any of his sisters. He quickly discarded the idea of spinning a fake story. "I'm Max Darling. I'm working for the lawyer who's defending Robert Jamison."

Quick awareness flickered in the woman's dark eyes.

"I know Serena's a very nice girl." His smile was disarming. "Terry Phillips thinks the world of her. He gave me Serena's name, suggested I talk to her. I want to ask Serena for some information that may help prove Robert's innocence."

The woman's broad face folded into a thoughtful frown. Finally, she nodded. She pointed to the hall. "You can sit in the back of the sanctuary. Wait there."

"Death on Demand." Annie always answered with a lilt as she announced the finest mystery bookstore north of Miami. But this was no ordinary call to order a book. Who was phoning her from the Geoffrey Grant household and why?

"Annie Darling?" The woman's voice was soft and hurried.

"Yes. How may I help you?"

"The reporter called Geoff and said you talked to the police, told them about that woman on the pier." The caller struggled for breath. "Who was that woman talking about? Geoff's beside himself. He's gone to the police station to try and find out."

"Who is this?" Annie held tight to the receiver. When she'd tipped off Marian Kenyon, shared what she'd learned during that meeting on the dark pier, she'd hoped to stir up the Grants. Now she felt a qualm at the fear so apparent in her caller's voice.

"Rhoda Grant." The words came fast. "We met at Charlie Jamison's house. That doesn't matter. You have to help me." There was a note of anger as well as determination. "If that woman claims Gwen saw one of the family hiding the coins, she has to be found. Maybe she lied. That's possible, isn't it? You have to tell me what happened."

Rhoda Grant had every right to demand to know the circumstances. "The facts will be in the newspaper story, but here's what happened." It didn't take long to describe that short encounter in the darkness.

"What did she look like?"

"It was dark." Dark with night and heavy with the fleeing woman's fear.

"There was moonlight." Rhoda's voice was sharp. "You saw the boat. Was she a big woman? Slender? Heavy? Tall? Short? You've seen people row a boat. How big was she?"

Annie's memory was distinct. The woman had rowed jerkily, as fast as she could, angular arms pumping. She wasn't a big woman. She was likely no taller than five feet five or six. There had been nothing youthful in her movements so she was an older woman. How easy would it be for the thief to run through a list of Gwen Jamison's friends and find the one who knew too much?

Annie knew better than to create a false picture. Gwen no doubt had friends who were bulky and heavyset. Any description could be dangerous to someone. "It took me a moment to climb up the ladder. By the time I got up on the pier, I barely glimpsed the boat going around the headland."

"You don't have any idea who it could have been?" Rhoda sounded discouraged.

A sudden peal marked the opening of Death on Demand's front door. "I'm sorry. That's all I know. I have to go now. I have a customer." Annie clicked off the phone and stepped into the center aisle.

Geoff Grant walked toward her, his face grim.

Max sat in the last pew. The long, narrow, dim sanctuary reflected age, the natural cypress walls glowing with a rich softness.

Straight-backed pews were close together. The hymnals looked worn and well used.

A door opened near the choir loft.

Max rose and stepped into the aisle.

A big man in a dark blue suit walked toward him. He was impressive, a domed forehead, blunt chin, massive shoulders. Although his hair was white, his face was youthful with bright, dark eyes. Perhaps he was in his late forties. He was a good four inches taller than Max. He didn't offer to shake hands and his gaze was measuring. "Pastor Harold Shelby. I've been told you want to talk to Serena."

"Yes, sir." Max met his piercing gaze openly. "I understand she was with Robert Jamison yesterday morning." This was the critical piece of information Terry Phillips reluctantly revealed.

The preacher folded his arms. A muscle twitched in his cheek. "She was forbidden to see him." His face folded in an angry frown. "No-account, that's what Robert is. He grieved his mama. He couldn't hold a job and he hung around a nice girl, a good girl, even when he was told to keep his distance."

Abruptly Max understood. "Is Serena your daughter?"

Shelby glared. "Didn't Robert tell you? I warned him to stay away from my girl."

"Robert has told us nothing." Max spoke quietly. "He refused to say where he was yesterday morning. That's one reason he was arrested. He claimed he was driving around the north end of the island. His mother was shot between ten-twenty and ten-forty. If we can prove where he was during that period, the police will have to release him."

Shelby's eyes widened. "Robert didn't send you here?"

"No, sir. Terry Phillips, a friend of Robert's, thought he'd talked to Serena during that time. That's why I've come."

Shelby's voice was sharp. "Ten-twenty to ten-forty? You're sure of the time?"

"Absolutely."

Shelby stared at the floor. Finally, he lifted his eyes, his face grim, and jerked his head toward the door. "Come with me."

Geoff Grant's broad, capable-looking hands bunched into fists. His usually pinkish face was pale. He would have looked at home in a yacht's saloon in his yellow cashmere turtleneck, olive wool slacks, and burgundy loafers. Instead he was a picture of disbelief and anger as he hunched in a wicker chair in the reader's nook, listening intently.

When Annie finished, he said, "Do you know what you've done?"

She met his gaze steadily. "I reported information important to a murder investigation to the police."

"You did more than that. Reporting to the police is understandable even if someone told you lies. But you weren't satisfied with that." Anger toughened the words. "You called the newspaper. Now everyone on the island will know. You've accused someone in my family of theft and murder."

"I didn't make the accusation." She leaned forward. "I'm sorry if innocent persons are affected, but the police arrested Robert and they aren't looking any further. Do you believe Robert would shoot his mother? Do you think Robert is smart enough, sophisticated enough, to steal only the most valuable coins from your collection?" She watched him carefully.

Grant looked away, made no answer.

Annie felt sadness for a man confronting family anguish. His silent acquiescence meant the thief had carefully chosen from among valuable and less valuable coins.

She continued quietly, "Do you believe Gwen Jamison would cover up for her son if she suspected he was involved in theft?"

He met her gaze. "I don't know what to think. I'll be honest with you. Robert's a sweet kid. He always was. He got off the rails after his dad died. Gwen did her best, but he started running around with a wild bunch, stayed out too late, drank too much. Grief's hard on everyone, especially hard on kids." His eyes held memories of pain, the understanding of loss. "Anyway, last week Gwen told me he'd found a job and he was in love with a nice girl. She was really glad I'd helped with bail. Robert swore he didn't know about the marijuana, that somebody else had stuffed it behind the seat. She said, 'I know my boy. He's done things he shouldn't have, but I know when he's lying. He's telling the truth about this.' Still, maybe he fooled her. If he was strung out on drugs anything could happen."

"No." Annie was definite. Max had seen Robert as he learned of his mother's death. His pain had been deep and raw with no buffering by alcohol or drugs. Drug use was never hard to recognize. "Not yesterday morning."

The flat statement hung between them.

"If not . . ." His eyes reflected despair. "My kids are here for my birthday. I watched them grow up. I loved their mothers. I love them. I'll never believe one of them would kill."

Annie lifted a hand in appeal. "Tell me about them."

He looked shocked. "Betray them?"

"If they are innocent, nothing you say will cause harm."

Grant's face lightened. "I have nothing to hide. They have nothing to hide. Oh, they've made some mistakes in the past, but they're good kids." His shoulders lifted and fell in an impatient shrug. "They're young. Lots of kids make false starts and need time to figure out what matters in life." He spoke in a professorial tone.

Annie kept her face friendly and nonjudgmental, but her inner imp gave a sniff. The Grant progeny were in their mid-twenties, close in age to Annie. How hard was it to add and subtract and know what you could afford or couldn't? Her imp chanted, "Calvinist, that's what you are." Annie shrugged the thought away. The imp had taken his cue from Max who insisted she was a Calvinist with the saving grace of a sense of humor. She always protested that she wasn't grim about work. After all, work was simply the most splendid exercise of one's talents. Max always murmured something about lilies of the field and slid his arm around her shoulders and suggested that an afternoon—or morning or midday or midnight—frolic was just the ticket to increase joy in the workplace. She felt an inner glow, forced herself to focus on the Grant family.

"Justin sounds like a hard worker." Her tone was approving.

Grant beamed. "I'm proud of him. He's had a financial struggle. I helped as much as I could but I'm evenhanded with the children so my contribution had to be limited. I can only manage so much. Justin had to go into debt. Without student loans, he'd never have been able to finish. That wouldn't be so bad if he could pay them off, but now that he's planning to get married, it won't be easy."

Annie was puzzled. How expensive was it to get married? If you didn't have any money, you planned a modest ceremony.

She'd been on her own when she and Max married. She'd kept within a budget although she'd agreed to let Max and his mother plan the reception. It would have been ungracious to refuse. The wedding wasn't magnificent, but it was lovely and heartfelt on a sunny summer day. Happiness didn't cost a penny.

"Does he want a big ceremony?"

Grant was rueful. "Justin would be happy with a picnic on the beach, but Margaret, well, Margaret wants everything to be grand. She's talking about an evening wedding and a sit-down dinner at the Sea Side Inn with an orchestra. He wants his band, of course. She's a little put out about that. When she isn't happy, she won't say a word, and that gets to Justin. He wants her to be all bubbly. That's what he told me once, that Margaret was like a glass of champagne. I have to say she reminds me of champagne. She has white-gold hair, just like champagne. Margaret is incredibly beautiful and very charming, certainly one of the most attractive young women I've ever met." He didn't sound enthusiastic.

Annie looked at him inquiringly. "Does she care for Justin?"

"I'd say she does. But"—he looked worried—"she has expensive tastes. Sometimes a parent tries to make up for things by spending too much money. I don't want to be critical, but her mother has spoiled her. You see"—he hitched his chair closer—"Margaret's mother Jan is divorced. Her husband was a doctor so she was used to having whatever she wanted. After the divorce, she had to get a job. She's a paralegal and doesn't make a great deal of money. Nevertheless, Jan was determined that Margaret would have everything she would have had if her father hadn't left them. He paid child support but not a huge amount. When he remarried and had several more children, Jan spent even more money on Margaret, so she's grown up expecting to have anything and everything she wants. Justin is going to do fine as a vet, but he has to go into even more debt to buy into the practice here and they are planning on a new building. He's worried about how he's going to swing everything. He already has quite a bit of credit card debt. I'll tell you, it isn't easy for young people today. Everything is so expensive. I had no idea how much weddings cost, and her father isn't helping."

Annie had been poor before she married a rich man. She remembered living on a tight budget, but no one had ever pressed her to spend money she didn't have. She felt a quick sympathy for Justin.

"Still"—Grant brightened—"Justin will do well. He never gave Nancy and me a minute's trouble. He'll figure out a way." His smile was confident.

Annie smiled in return and wondered if Geoff Grant had any inkling he'd supplied Justin with a solid motive for taking the coins. Justin certainly would understand gradations in value among the coins. Moreover, she wasn't sure about requirements for a vet's license, but she doubted one could be granted or held by a man accused of grand larceny. Exposure would rob him of the career he'd sought so long and likely derail his marriage. If Justin were guilty, he couldn't take the chance that Gwen Jamison might speak out. She had promised the thief silence, but the thief either decided the risk was too great or was determined to reap the profits.

Grant continued to smile. "Nancy and I were always proud of Justin and"—his eyes were soft—"humbled by Kerry. She's been the same ever since she was little, always trying to help everyone. The only time she is ever angry is when she sees injustice." His smile slipped away. "I'm afraid she's often angry now. She's trying to raise money for a homeless mission and, of course, there are always more in need than can ever be helped."

Annie was thoughtful. "I suppose she'd like for people to give more for the poor and spend less on luxuries."

"Absolutely." Geoff was emphatic.

Annie pictured Double Eagles against black velvet. How did Kerry balance the value of Geoff Grant's collection against hunger, disease, and misery? How many people would eat if she stole the coins and sold them? But it would take an unbalanced mind to commit murder in the name of charity. Kerry's pictures showed a sweet face and kind eyes with no hint of zealotry.

"I understand Ben's an adventurous sort." Annie sounded approving.

Grant settled back in his chair. "It's all very well and good to enjoy travel, even to seek out the exotic." His frown made it clear he found Ben's attitude incomprehensible. "But a man has to settle down eventually and it's time for Ben to make something of himself." Geoff was indignant. "He had one of the highest SAT scores in the state his year. He could do anything. A lawyer or a doctor or an accountant."

Annie wondered if Geoff had ever read Ben's blog. *"I won't be trapped . . ."* "In any event, he's a free spirit."

Grant's lips pursed. "Free? Maybe too free. I give the children a substantial sum every year at this time. He uses the money for travel. The next thing I know he's broke again. But he's always the life of the party. He makes us laugh." Geoff's smile was reluctant, but admiring. "He does impromptu skits and somehow he can make you see anything. Last night he was imitating a giraffe talking to a beetle about global warming." He laughed aloud. "The giraffe was pompous and the beetle was sly and pretty soon he had us doubled up laughing. You can't be downhearted around Ben. He's even worked as a stand-up comic at some comedy clubs. I wish he'd take that energy and put it to good use."

Annie shrugged. "Since he's still single, his lifestyle doesn't affect anyone but him." She waited for Grant to ask how she knew so much about his family.

Instead, he looked grim. "Until he can be responsible, he certainly won't have my approval for marriage."

Annie looked at him sharply. In the twenty-first century, anyone of legal age was free to marry at will. Grant's suddenly pinched mouth was at odds with his usually genial expression.

"Ben's always in debt." Geoff shook his head in disgust. "As for Barb, it's the same old story. She wants to be a famous actress and the truth is"—he looked suddenly sad—"she doesn't have half of Ben's talent. She believes wearing the latest, most expensive styles will make her stand out. She goes to trendy places because she thinks she will see people who matter." A half smile was rueful. "But she's a sweet girl, one of the family. Family." He looked forlorn. "Now you're telling me that someone in the family is a thief and a murderer. I don't believe it. I saw them grow up. I know them." He stood up. "It would be decent of you to retract that story. Publicly."

Annie stood, too. "I can't. It happened."

His look was dogged. "That woman at the pier was confused. Or lying. Or perhaps Gwen was mistaken." He looked glum. "All of us will be suspected after that story is printed. I told the reporter that the informant was absolutely incorrect and that no one in the family could possibly be involved. She said she'd quote me very carefully."

Annie felt ashamed. Marian Kenyon couldn't report what the unseen informant told Annie because the material wasn't privileged and was possibly libelous on its face. However, now all Marian had to do was quote Annie saying the woman beneath the pier had been told by Gwen Jamison that she recognized the thief, explain that the lack of privilege prevented the *Gazette* from describing possible suspects, then follow with the quote from Geoff Grant insisting that the woman at the pier was absolutely mistaken and no one in the Grant family was involved. Readers would follow the bouncing ball without any difficulty.

Annie stared at the floor. She'd intended to rile the Grant family. She'd succeeded. Unfortunately, all of the Grants would now be suspects even though only one person was guilty.

"All right." He was terse. He stood. "What's done is done. Now we have to deal with the aftermath." He moved away, head down. Halfway to the door, he turned and looked back. "I told the police they have to find that woman at the pier. Officer Harrison said she would talk to the Jamison family, get a list of Gwen's close friends. How clearly did you see her?"

Annie had her story down now. "I scarcely caught a glimpse before she rowed around the headland." Thin and small and bony. Not a young woman.

He didn't move. "I sail in the bay. It's at least forty yards before the boat would be out of sight."

Annie said nothing.

His face hardened. He strode toward the front. The door closed.

Annie's heart pounded. Geoff Grant wanted to talk to the informant. So did his wife, Rhoda. As soon as the *Gazette* came out this afternoon, the residents of the Grant house on that fateful night would know that Gwen Jamison had seen and recognized the thief. The murderer could not take a chance that Gwen had told her friend the name of the thief. Annie was sure the woman possessed that deadly information.

Annie whirled and hurried to the storeroom for her purse and car keys. She'd unleashed a tiger and she had to rescue its prey.

Chapter 10

In the marble hallway, Max gestured toward a frosted door with a legend in gold letters:

BRICE WILLARD POSEY
CIRCUIT SOLICITOR

"You'd better take the Reverend Shelby in." Max looked at Handler Jones, his expression rueful. "If Posey sees me, he'll turn into a pit bull."

Tall and imposing in his dark suit, the Reverend Shelby stood with his arms folded, a man clearly unhappy to be there.

The lawyer shook his head. "I'll have to tell Brice how I found the reverend. You'd better come in. Brice will have some questions." Handler's easy smile was reassuring. "Brice and I were at the Citadel together. It will be all right."

As a plump, blond secretary announced them, Handler led the way. Max followed behind the Reverend Shelby.

Posey was on his feet, hand outstretched, mouth spread in a good-old-boy grin. "Hey, Handler." He sounded positively genial. "Are you hard up for clients? How come you've taken on a kid too dumb to ditch the murder weapon? Not even your golden tongue will sway a jury this time."

Despite the warm welcome for Handler Jones, Max saw the same old Posey, black brilliantined hair, watery blue eyes in a meaty face, a beer-and-barbecue potbelly.

Handler was relaxed. "I don't think we need to worry about a jury, Brice. I won't even need the twenty-four hours you were kind enough to promise." The lawyer pumped the solicitor's plump hand with every evidence of camaraderie. "You had a good prima facie case. No one can ever fault your preparation." There was great emphasis on the possessive adjective.

Posey stood a little straighter, lifted his plump chin.

Handler clapped him on the shoulder. "First-rate, always. As it happens, no fault of yours, the police work fell short this time, but clearly that was understandable since my client was less than forthcoming. But I've brought an unimpeachable witness for him."

Posey looked past Handler at the tall black man. Then he spotted Max.

Max tried to keep his face calm and unrevealing. He didn't like Brice Willard Posey. Brice Willard Posey didn't like him. Their enmity went back a long, long way. Posey's delight in charging Max with murder last summer set a seal on their mutual loathing.

Handler wasn't fazed. "Brice, this is the Reverend Harold

Shelby, pastor of Shady Grove Baptist Church on Broward's Rock. He has important information concerning the Jamison case. Max Darling is assisting me."

Posey looked sly. "When did you get your PI license, Darling?"

Max had no PI license. The sovereign state of South Carolina had particular and specific requirements for the granting of licenses to private investigators, including experience as a law enforcement official. Max insisted that Confidential Commissions was in no way a private investigative agency. He offered counsel and encouragement to clients seeking advice. He grinned at Posey, suddenly enjoying the moment. "In this instance, I'm working as a consultant with Handler. I was able to assist him by speaking with the Reverend Shelby."

Posey's porcine blue eyes glittered. "You're going to push me too far one of these days, Darling. All right." Posey was abruptly surly. "Sit down, gentlemen."

Handler looked appropriately grave as they took the chairs opposite the desk. "We won't take much of your time, Brice. Your schedule is always demanding. However, you will be pleased to avoid a false arrest. It was splendid of you to delay filing formal charges against my client and"—Handler's smile was brilliant—"that will save your office from embarrassment in the press. You know how the press can be." He paused to let Posey imagine headlines. "Not a good thing in an election year." The lawyer's gaze was supportive, his tone genial.

Posey picked up a pen, rolled it in his pudgy fingers. "What've you got?"

Handler gestured toward Max.

Max kept his recital brisk and nonconfrontational. He

described his visit to the Shady Grove Baptist Church. "Robert has a good friend in Pastor Shelby's daughter. I hoped to visit with her as I thought it was possible Robert had dropped by the church Wednesday morning. He was vague about his whereabouts—"

Posey was brusque. "Driving around the north end of the island. What kind of story is that?"

"—but the Reverend Shelby had made it clear he didn't welcome visits by Robert. Handler had an instinct that Robert's silence was not so much to protect himself as someone else. Handler directed me to inquire about Robert's friends. One of them told me Robert had the highest regard for Serena Shelby. I went to the church and was unable to speak with Serena, but I met with her father. Reverend Shelby, will you please tell the solicitor about Wednesday morning?"

Shelby's massive face might have been twisted out of steel. He looked directly at the solicitor. "At a quarter past ten, I needed to speak to the main teacher in the three-year-old class. We have a preschool and day care, infants to kindergarten." Some of the hardness seeped out of his face. "My daughter's very good with the little ones. She works in the three-year-old class on Wednesday mornings until she, herself, goes to class. She's a freshman at the Technical College of the Low Country. Certainly I expected her to be in the classroom. After I talked to Mrs. Greeley, who directs our program, I asked for Serena. Mrs. Greeley said she'd gone outside to see a friend. I was afraid it might be Robert." Once again his face was unyielding. "Serena was forbidden to see him. He isn't the kind of young man I want coming around my daughter. Serena is too kind and gentle. She doesn't see badness in anyone."

Posey was pleased. He leaned forward. "So Jamison's a known hoodlum?"

Shelby's frown was intense. Reluctantly, he shook his head. "That isn't correct. He's not mean or violent or dangerous. He's lazy and profligate and no-account. He's run around with a wild group for the last four or five years but the worst they've done is drink too much beer and be shiftless."

"Out to make an easy buck?" The solicitor looked eager.

"Hardly out to earn a penny, honest or otherwise." Shelby was disdainful. "However, Robert's character is not why I am here. I found Serena and Robert sitting in his car. The time was approximately ten twenty-five. They were talking." His tone implied Robert was fortunate indeed that the tryst was innocent of intimacy. "I yanked open the passenger door and directed Serena to go to my office at once. I then spoke with Robert. Our discussion lasted at least ten minutes. I made it clear to him that he was not to see or contact Serena in any manner."

Handler bent his head toward Shelby. "What time did you find Serena and Robert in his car?"

"The church bells tolled the half hour shortly after."

Posey flipped open a folder, ran a pudgy finger down the sheet.

Max knew the moment Posey reached the incontrovertible fact that Gwen Jamison's body had been discovered at eight minutes past the half hour. Max knew the times. Gwen Jamison called Confidential Commissions at ten-twenty. Barb tried to contact Max. When he didn't answer his cell, she called Annie, who set out to see Gwen Jamison. Barb again called the Jamison house. The phone was picked up but nothing said and the line remained open. Annie found Gwen dying at ten thirty-eight.

It was reasonable to assume that Gwen was shot after ten-twenty but before Barb called the Jamison house.

If Robert was speaking with the Reverend Shelby at ten-thirty, he couldn't have been at his mother's house when she was shot.

Posey looked up with a glower. "That's convenient for Robert."

The Reverend Shelby's frown was equally intense. "I have no interest whatsoever in making anything convenient for Robert Jamison. Ever."

Posey slammed the folder shut. "Do you people realize how much money and time the accused—" He broke off, drew a deep breath. "This uncooperative witness has cost the state of South Carolina? The man hours involved in this investigation? The damage that may result from the subsequent delay in focusing our investigative energies in the right direction?"

He shoved back his chair, rose, paced toward the fireplace. He swung about, an outraged prosecutor practicing for a news conference, and leveled a forefinger at Handler Jones. "I've half a mind to charge your client with obstruction of justice."

The Reverend Shelby stood. "This is typical of Robert. I don't blame you for being outraged."

Posey crossed the room, shook a surprised Shelby's hand. "Reverend, if we had more public-spirited citizens like you, our job would be much easier. Thank you for representing the best in citizenship."

Max knew that Posey, as always, was playing to the crowd, in this instance an admired and respected member of the black community. However, it had seemed an almost spontaneous gesture. Max came nearer to liking Posey than he would have thought possible.

Posey was glaring again when he swung toward the lawyer. "It will require the taking of statements to confirm this information." His nod toward the Reverend Shelby was respectful. "A matter of form, sir, a matter of form. I'm sure Miss Shelby and Mrs. Greeley will be happy to cooperate. Of course, the police must redirect the investigation. That takes precedence. However, as soon as the formalities are completed, possibly by tomorrow, Robert will be released."

His chief suspect was history, but Posey was demonstrating he was not a man to be stampeded and there were procedures to be followed.

Jones nodded agreeably. "Certainly, Brice. I'll make it clear to Robert that his actions have impeded the investigation. He will be available to assist you in any way he can."

Max was torn between irritation and amusement. Continuing to hold Robert might be petty of Posey—what else was new?—but another day of detention was a small price to pay for freedom.

Annie drove past the live-oak-bordered road that led to the Lucy Kinkaid Memorial Library. The island's library was housed in an old tabby home bequeathed to the city for library use. Annie drove until she reached an entrance to an adjoining nature preserve. Confident no one was behind her, she turned down a dusty narrow lane and eased the Volvo behind a tall stand of bamboo. She stepped out of the car and followed a faint path through the woods.

Vines spread across the trail and tree limbs interlocked overhead, making the way dim as twilight. She took off her sunglasses and stepped carefully, skirting fallen logs that might serve as a den for rattlers or copperheads. Of course, a snake could curl up for a winter snooze in a hole beneath a mound of leaves. If she stepped in the wrong place . . .

Annie picked her way as delicately as a long-legged heron. It was warm and sunny today and snakes might ease out of their retreats to enjoy a sunbath. The only danger would be if she disturbed them. Definitely she had no desire to disturb any snake.

By the time she reached the pine grove behind the library, she was perspiring and close to hyperventilating. She'd always had a horror of a close-up moment with either a copperhead or a red rat snake. Sure, they should be easy to differentiate—if she had half an hour and they were ensconced behind plate glass, not poised to spring at her. All right, she had a thing about snakes. She and Indiana Jones knew danger when they saw it.

When she reached the blacktopped parking lot, she shoved the sunglasses in place, turned up the collar of the trench coat she'd fished out of the lost-and-found at Death on Demand, and pulled low on her forehead the red tam found ditto. After a careful survey to be certain no one was near, she scuttled past a half-dozen cars to the back entrance. Inside, she opened a little-used door to a cramped back stairway. She climbed at the edge of the ancient treads to avoid telltale squeaks.

On the second floor, she stood in the corridor outside the administrative offices, an area off limits to the public. However, she was a member of the Friends of the Library so she would be fine if discovered. Her stealth had nothing to do with her location and everything to do with contacting Inez Willis unobserved by anyone.

She walked to the third office. A faint glow through the

frosted glass indicated a light shone within. Annie tapped, opened the door.

"Come in." Inez was seated, her back to the door. She half turned from a computer screen filled with text. Yesterday, at Charlie Jamison's house, she'd worn a mauve sweater and skirt and big-heeled black leather boots. Today she was a bright protest against dreary February in an orange turtleneck and mint-green slacks. She smiled politely. "These offices are restricted to staff. If you are seeking assistance, the research librarian on duty downstairs will be glad to help you."

Annie pulled off the tam and her hair sprang free. She dropped the sunglasses in her purse.

Inez looked bewildered. "Annie?"

Annie held a finger to her lips, closed the door behind her. "I don't want anyone to know I've talked to you."

"What's wrong?" Inez gestured at the chair next to her desk.

Annie slipped off the trench coat and sank into the chair. With the coat bunched in her arms, she blurted out, "I've made a mess of things. I'm terribly frightened about what may happen." As she described the story that would appear in the afternoon *Gazette,* she watched Inez's face.

The librarian's eyes widened. Once she gave a little gasp and placed her hand at her throat. "That's amazing."

Annie remembered the voice beneath the pier. It hadn't been as light and quick and brisk as Inez's voice. However, she had to be sure. "Were you the woman at the pier?"

"No." The disclaimer was quick and genuine. "I admired Sister Gwen, but we were never close friends. Her father and mine . . . No need to go into that, but we had a bar between us. I came to the house because I help with funeral arrangements at the church." Her face was grave. "What do you want of me?"

Annie reached over the bunched coat, caught Inez's right hand in her own. "I don't want to make things worse. I don't want anyone else to be in danger. As soon as the story comes out, everyone will be looking for the woman who met me. They'll want to know what she looked like, the sound of her voice, whatever I glimpsed of her. Don't you see? The police will ask me. I can't tell them. I can't say she was tall and heavy or little and thin or medium-sized. I can't say she had a high voice or a low one. Someone might recognize the description and word would get out. It always does. I can't tell anyone anything because the murderer will be looking, too."

Inez's dark eyes gazed at Annie. "What does this have to do with me?" There was a definite reserve in her tone. She pulled away from Annie, folded her arms.

"I need help." Annie wished for eloquence. She didn't know the women who had been present at Charlie Jamison's house. "I want you to find out the name of Gwen's closest friends. Everyone has friends who are there for them when they're sick or in trouble or sad. Who did Gwen count on?"

Inez's stare was challenging. "Call Charlie and ask him."

Annie had to be honest. "I'm afraid to do that. What if I got names and approached these women? What if I found the right person? People would talk and if the talk reached the murderer, the woman would be in danger. She knows too much. The murderer can't afford to let her speak."

Inez looked toward a leather folder on her desk. A teenage girl in a cheerleader's uniform reached high to catch a tumbling baton.

Annie followed her gaze. The picture captured an image of energy and enthusiasm. And life.

"I'm a single mother."

Annie heard reluctance edged with fear.

Inez whirled toward Annie, her face imploring. "I have to think of Daniela. She comes first. She needs me."

"You can find out the names of Gwen's closest friends without anyone realizing what you are doing. If I tried, everyone would talk and then the danger would be huge. You can be casual, offhand. You help with funerals. Tell Charlie you think it would be gracious to reach out to Gwen's closest friends, ask them to have a role at the reception. Then all you have to do is call them. There's no way anyone in the Grant family would ever know. You can use a public phone, whisper." Just as Gwen's friend had done when she called Annie. "No one will ever know. No one saw me come here. There's nothing to link you to me. There will be nothing to link you to the woman at the pier. You'll be perfectly safe."

Inez's narrow, intelligent face was thoughtful. "It could be done. I know a phone I could use. The number wouldn't be any more closely associated with me than with many others."

As if Inez had announced her intention, Annie pictured an extension at the Shady Grove Baptist Church. That would be good. That would reassure those receiving her call.

Inez spoke slowly. "I'm not promising, but I'll try. What should I say?"

Annie felt an overwhelming rush of relief. She picked her words carefully. "Tell them, 'If you met Annie Darling at the pier, you may be in danger because of the story in the *Gazette*. It is urgent that you call her.'" Annie gave her cell phone number, watched as Inez wrote it down. "'Or contact the police, tell them who Gwen saw that night, then you'll be safe.'"

Inez leaned back in her chair, her eyes wide. "If the message reaches the right person, you're asking her to take a risk. Why should the police believe her?" There was a bitter undertone to her voice. "They didn't believe Robert."

Annie understood her distrust. "Once she tells the police what she knows, she'll be safe. That's what matters. Who cares what the police think? What matters is that everyone must know she's given the information to the police and it won't do any good to come after her."

"Murderers don't think straight." Inez lifted a hand to forestall Annie's protest. "I said I'd call. I will." She gave Annie a puzzled stare. "You're going to a lot of trouble for a woman you don't know."

Annie turned her hands palms up. "It's my mess. I have to clean it up."

A sudden smile transformed Inez's face. She leaned forward, gave Annie a quick, hard hug.

It didn't melt the cold spot of fear in Annie's heart.

Max walked into Confidential Commissions, buoyant as if treading on clouds. Robert would soon be free. That lifted a ton of misery from Max's shoulders. A kid with a good-for-nothing rep found with a murder weapon in his trunk could easily have been convicted of a crime he didn't commit. Max broke off to sniff. The rich scent of dark chocolate hung in the air.

Barb poked her head out from the back room, which doubled as her office kitchen. She smiled at his wrinkled nose. "Decadent brownies. Chunks of Ghirardelli." She brushed flour from the cerise apron protecting her cream-colored dress. "You sound cheerful. Maybe you can cheer up Geoff Grant. He keeps calling, wanting to know where you are and how he can get in touch with Annie. He's either furious or scared. I didn't give him her cell."

Max wasn't worried about Geoff Grant. Maybe the police were already at the Grant house, pushing to find out more about Monday night. That suited Max fine. He strolled into his office, debated calling Geoff, decided to let him stew. Max settled behind his desk and picked up the morning mail. Ah, there was the small blue pamphlet he received occasionally from a rare book dealer in a quiet village in the Cotswolds. Max eagerly opened it. Would there be any rare Buchans or Chestertons? He was still looking for Buchan's *A Lost Lady of Old Years* published in 1899 and Chesterton's *Tremendous Trifles* published in 1909. Not even to Annie would he admit that these works attracted him because of their titles. How had the lady been lost? Which trifles seemed tremendous to the philosophical Chesterton?

Max ran his finger down the index.

The phone rang.

Max looked at caller ID, shrugged, picked up the receiver. He felt equal to any encounter today. He hadn't responded in time to help Gwen Jamison, but he'd saved her son. "Confidential Commissions." He spoke briskly as if he hadn't a care in the world.

"Max, Geoff Grant here." The words were rushed. "The police have fallen for that story your wife spun. I want some answers."

"Annie went to the pier." Max's voice was hard. "She reported what she was told."

"And announced it to the world." Grant's anger was obvious. "All right, all right." He made an effort to be conciliatory. "That's water over the dam now. But we've got to get to the bottom of that woman's tale. Who was she? Was she telling the truth or lying? We've got to find her. Your wife saw her run away. I want a description of that woman. She has to be found."

Annie reached her car without seeing anything but a startled deer who'd bounded away, crashing through undergrowth. Annie slipped behind the wheel, relaxed against the cushion, and breathed deeply. She'd done all she could do for the moment. Now she had to hope that Inez Willis felt safe enough, secure enough, to make those phone calls. Annie wrestled with uncertainty. Should she have given Inez a good description, narrowed down the possibilities to a very few, perhaps pinpointed Gwen's friend with certainty? *Thin and bony. Not young. Perhaps five feet four inches tall, five five at the most. A soft singsong voice.*

No. Not to Inez. Not to the police. Not to anyone.

She pulled out her cell phone, turned it on.

One message—11:22 a.m. "Hi, honey." Max's voice burbled with good humor. "Robert's got a solid alibi thanks to yours truly. Posey's on the warpath. That's thrown the cop shop into a tizzy. Ditto Geoff Grant. Geoff's determined to get a description of your informant at Fish Haul pier. I promised Geoff we'd drop by around three. We might glean some information and you can continue to stonewall about the woman. Meet me at Parotti's for lunch. Love you."

Annie was glad Robert was exonerated, but Max's good news did nothing to lessen the fear that weighed on her. If only she hadn't called Marian. If only she could bridle her impulsive nature, jerk the reins, stop and think before she acted. As poets and lovers well knew, words once spoken could not be recalled no matter the tears, no matter the anguish. *How many on the island knew the identity of Gwen's best friend? There were those who would know and please God don't let hasty gossip point the way for the murderer.* Annie clicked save and dialed to pick up messages at Death on Demand. Sergeant Harrison asked her to call the station as soon as possible. Annie felt in no hurry. She'd told the officer everything she knew.

There were two calls from Geoff and one from Rhoda, but that was settled now. She and Max would go to their house at three. She listened again to Rhoda's message:

> 11:15 a.m.—*"Annie, this is Rhoda Grant. Geoff asked me to call. Truly, we will be most appreciative if you and your husband will join us this afternoon at three for tea and sherry. We're sure you understand our need to contact the woman who is spreading such a damaging tale about us."*

Annie dropped the phone in her purse, turned on the motor, backed carefully from behind the bamboo. Afternoon tea. How civilized. Gwen Jamison lay lifeless in a morgue, but amber tea would curl into cups. *Oh, that dark figure in the corner? The one with a bloodstained hand? Oh, my dear, haven't you met our murderer?*

Ben Parotti plumped the steaming plate in front of Annie. "We heard the news on the morning radio show. The kitchen's got a pool going on the mysterious woman on the back side of Fish Haul pier. Geoff Grant told the radio the family isn't involved."

So much, Annie thought, for the *Gazette*'s exclusive. But it was good that word was out all over the island.

Ben stepped around the table, placed in front of Max a bowl of steaming chili topped with grated cheese and onions. "I put in a twenty on Gwen's cousin Lucinda. She could have played fullback for the Tigers if she'd been a boy. If she rowed a boat, it would fly." His tone was light, but his eyes were sharp.

Annie jabbed at a crisp fried clam and avoided Max's gaze. She didn't want to go to the Grant house. It was a relief to joust with Ben. "You tell the kitchen to keep their money and keep on frying the best clams in the Low Country. As far as I know it could have been an old lady or a teenage girl. As I told the police"—she lifted her voice to be heard and was certain that the dozen or so diners in Parotti's Bar and Grill were listening intently—"I didn't see the rower. I was on the ladder and I didn't climb up and reach the end of the pier until the rowboat was almost around the headland." She'd repeated this spiel so often now, it almost seemed real, but her mind held an indelible image of a small, bony woman hunched over the oars. "I don't think we'll ever know. Anyway, what difference does it make? She told me all she knew. She said Gwen was careful not to identify the person she saw." With that lie Annie poked a forkful of clams into the cocktail sauce.

"Pretty gutsy of you to meet somebody at night on the pier by yourself." Ben's tone was admiring. He turned toward Max.

"Everybody's proud of you for helping Robert. I hear he'll be home tomorrow."

Max grinned. He didn't doubt that Ben had up-to-date information. "Everybody helped, especially the Reverend Shelby."

"'All's well that ends well.'" Ben gave them a genial smile and turned back toward the kitchen.

Annie's fork sank to her plate. Ben quoting Shakespeare didn't surprise her, but his blithe pronouncement only made her more desperate. There could be no end until the murderer of Gwen Jamison was caught.

"Annie." Max's voice was low and urgent though his smile didn't waver. "People are watching us. Every word you've said will be repeated and they'll describe how you looked and how you sounded."

Annie forced a smile, but her eyes were stricken. "If the murderer finds Gwen's friend, it will be my fault."

Max reached across the table and caught her hand. "She came to you. She could have contacted the police. She can still contact the police. Now, eat with your usual gusto and grin, grin, grin. Everything's fine in Annie Land. You don't have a care in the world." His smile was huge, as if they were enjoying the moment with no clouds on the horizon. Yet his gaze was serious and stern. "We have a gilt-edged invitation, Annie. We have to go to the Grant house this afternoon."

Annie continued to smile brightly though she felt cold inside. "They want to know about the woman at the pier."

"Sure they do. You can regale them with the misgivings you felt as you walked out on the pier by yourself into the darkness with only the empty water on both sides and your shock when addressed by an unseen figure. You hope this woman will respond to the urging of police and come forward. You'd be glad to help find the speaker, but, of course, you scarcely had a glimpse of her." Max lifted his iced-tea glass as if making a toast. "To Robert coming home tomorrow. To the innocent members of the Grant family."

Annie's lips felt stiff. She clinked her glass against his. "To Gwen. To her friend."

Chapter 11

Annie picked up Agatha, nuzzled her face against warm, sweet-smelling fur. "I'm sorry lunch is late."

Agatha wriggled free and loped toward the coffee bar and her cat bowls nestled against the wall.

Annie shook dry pellets with a yeasty scent into the blue plastic bowl, refreshed the water in the red bowl.

Agatha ate and growled, growled and ate.

"You'll get indigestion." Sometimes she worried about Agatha's longevity. Wasn't a sunny temperament supposed to increase life span? That was what one study suggested in humans. Laugh, be merry, and tiptoe into the twilight as an octogenarian.

Completing her meal, Agatha proved her mercurial disposition by jumping to the coffee bar and leaning against Annie. A satisfied purr rumbled.

Annie glanced at the telephone. The blinking light signaled

more messages. Undoubtedly Officer Harrison was among them. Annie stroked Agatha. "I wish I could stay here and spend the afternoon with you and the books." She wanted to unpack the new Deborah Crombie books. Instead, the flashing red light beckoned.

Annie sighed. She was only putting off a difficult moment. Annie dialed. The exchange was short and swift. "I'll be there shortly, Mrs. Darling." Officer Harrison hung up without a farewell.

Annie wrinkled her nose at the phone, accessed the messages. She deleted messages that didn't matter (two from Officer Harrison) and listened to three.

> 12:05 p.m.—*"Hal Porter. [His voice sounded strong and untroubled.] I wanted to let you know I'm fine. I left a message for Max, too. Everything's okay at your house. The carpenter's there and he said nobody's been around. I'm working on the birdhouse at the Grant place. I've been checking your place every little while and I'll be there to stay around six. If those kids show up tonight, I'll be ready for them. Let me know if I can do anything else."*

Hal's encounter with the black teenagers last night was still a puzzle. Since Robert had been cleared, Hal's attackers were not Robert's confederates. However, they could have been friends trying to divert suspicion or possibly adventurous teenagers looking for treasure. Most islanders now knew about Gwen Jamison hiding the packet in the Franklin house, so it was possible the young men were otherwise unconnected to the case. Or was the truth darker and more dangerous, the men somehow involved in the theft? That didn't jibe with the claim that Gwen recognized the thief as a member of the Grant family.

Annie felt a sudden uncertainty. Could the woman at the pier have been lying? In her mind, she heard the grave, serious voice. "'It's gospel, girl . . . One of the family.'"

Annie knew truth when she heard it. The woman was repeating what she'd been told. *One of the family.*

If the young black men who'd struck down Hal Porter were involved in the theft, they had to be working at the direction of a family member. Justin and Ben had graduated from the island high school. It was hard to picture Eagle Scout Justin with friends willing to break and enter, but Ben likely was on good terms with the swashbucklers in his class. Last night's duo might have been young men in their twenties, not teenagers as they'd assumed.

The next message was the one she'd hoped for.

12:25 p.m.—*"The calls have been made."*

Annie heard the crisp voice with a surge of excitement. If only the mysterious figure responded.

The last message brought a smile.

1:03 p.m.—*"Are you boycotting your computer? [Static blurred some words.] . . . check your e-mail." [Emma sounded disgusted.]*

Annie wondered if the intrepid trio hungered for a crime update or if they had something to contribute. Smiling, she clicked off the phone, turned to go to the storeroom. The bell tinkled at the front door. Annie looked over her shoulder. Her smile slipped away.

Officer Harrison marched determinedly down the central aisle.

Max unloaded a cot, sleeping bag, and provisions. He carried the gear into the kitchen of the Franklin house. Fortunately the appliances had been installed and were in service. He heard the distant whirr of a buzz saw, smelled the sweet scent of fresh lumber. He set up the cot in the drawing room then strolled down the main hall to check the fresh panes in the back window. Sun spilled through the window and the wide hallway was light and airy as he'd known it would be even when the Franklin house had been an abandoned derelict. He made a circuit of the rooms, admiring fresh paint and wallpaper.

This was going to be a happy house for him and for Annie. He grinned, imagining the shrill cry of children's voices. He stopped at the foot of the steps, looked up. The slick handrail would be irresistible to small adventurers though the figure of the griffin carved in the newel post might preclude flights on the banister. He reached out, tapped the eagle head, felt ridged wooden feathers.

He walked upstairs, his expression thoughtful. The house was almost ready. Everywhere there was freshness—and emptiness. There didn't seem to be a nook or cranny that would provide a hiding place. Max checked out the master bedroom, the small den that would be a special retreat for him and Annie, the other bedrooms and baths.

He frowned as he headed downstairs. Somewhere the coins were hidden. Would their hiding place ever be found?

Officer Harrison sat stiffly at the round wooden table nearest the coffee bar, a pad, pencil, and green folder in front of her. Her pale blue eyes seemed to dissect Death on Demand as she scanned the bookshelves. She glanced up at the watercolors.

Annie offered a smile. "I run a contest every month. The first person who identifies the book and author pictured in each watercolor wins a prize."

Harrison gave her a level look. "I saw a display on one of the front tables. A bunch of books—"

Annie pictured the titles with their stylish covers: *Dear Miss Demeanor* by Joan Hess, *Murder Makes Waves* by Anne George, *I Gave You My Heart but You Sold It Online* by Dixie Cash, *Night of the Living Deb* by Susan McBride, and *Hurricane Homicide* by Nora Charles.

"—with a sign: LAUGH OUT LOUD. MURDEROUSLY FUNNY." The policewoman's angular face folded in a disapproving frown. "Murder's not funny."

Annie's eyes glinted, but she kept her voice pleasant. "Murder is never funny. People are funny."

Harrison was cold. "If they had my job, they'd find something else to read."

Annie knew the somber policewoman didn't read mysteries, so she didn't understand them. This wasn't the moment to explain that murder was never the point of a mystery, that mysteries have to do with goodness and justice and the triumph of right over wrong, that decent and moral people read mysteries because they want for a fleeting moment to inhabit a world that celebrates goodness.

Annie remembered the officer's anguish when she spoke of her partner's death. Murder was real and personal to Officer Harrison. Annie turned a hand out in appeal. "People who read mysteries admire the police. They want crimes to be solved."

Officer Harrison's eyes widened in surprise.

She hoped that Harrison saw respect in hers. Maybe the policewoman lived in a black-and-white world, but she worked every day to make that world a safer place. She did her job, knowing she faced danger every time she stopped a car, approached a door, walked out into the night.

"Would you like a cup of coffee?" Annie gestured toward the coffee bar. "I have Colombian freshly made."

Harrison started to shake her head, stopped, slowly nodded. "Thank you."

Annie filled the mugs, brought them to the table, slipped into the opposite chair.

Harrison lifted a spoonful of sugar crystals, dropped them into the hot black coffee, stirred. "The investigation into the murder of Gwen Jamison continues. Last night you met an informant on Fish Haul pier. Please describe what happened, beginning with the phone call setting up the meeting."

Annie spoke carefully and clearly. Harrison interrupted a half-dozen times, pressing for information:

"The sound of the voice?" *A whisper.*

"Length of the conversation?" *Ten minutes, fifteen.*

"Did she speak with an accent?" *She was an islander.*

"Was her voice high or low?" *She whispered, how could I know?*

"Ability to see?" *Hidden beneath the pier.*

"Informant's sex?" *Female.*

"A description?"

Annie held her mug tightly, feeling beleaguered. Every scrap of information gave a clearer picture. How secure would this information be? If she told Harrison that the woman was middling height, bony, thin, middle-aged from her voice, it might sign a death warrant. If the informant called the police as Annie had urged, there would be no need for Annie to describe her. Annie's lips parted. When she spoke, she listened to her words with a sense of finality. "I can't describe her. I scarcely caught a glimpse. By the time I reached the end of the pier, the boat was rounding the point."

Harrison looked at Annie hopefully. Without her customary expression of reserve and wariness, her angular face had a shy appeal. "Robert Jamison set the investigation back more than twenty-four hours when he didn't reveal his whereabouts Wednesday morning. I talked to the chief this morning, but they're all sick with a stomach flu and can't travel for at least a couple of days. The baby's been real sick. He said you're a good friend, that you'll help me."

Annie felt anguished, torn between instinct and duty. *It's my mess. I have to clean it up.* She tried to sound normal. "I'll do everything I can." She was willing to do everything she could to be helpful, short of putting Gwen's friend into even more danger. "Max and I both want to help."

Harrison looked relieved. "Even if you didn't get a good look, maybe you'll see a resemblance in these pictures." For an instant, her eyes flashed. "We aren't getting any help from the black community. None. Nobody will talk. To hear them, you wouldn't think the woman had a best friend. Instead, she had lots and lots of friends. Nobody special. I don't believe that. A woman always has a best friend. Sometimes it isn't another woman, but she's got a best friend. Nobody we've talked to knows from nothing about who tried to break into the Franklin house last night. So we got some pictures of people who've been in and out of Charlie Jamison's house. I figure his mother's best friend showed up." She opened the folder, pushed it across the table.

Annie leafed through the color photos. They were sharp and clear, likely taken with a telephoto lens, the subjects unaware.

Annie stared down, her shoulders stiff. Three women were plump, one decidedly obese. Five women were of middle height, thin, bony, almost indistinguishable in physical appearance.

Relief almost made her giddy. Her description of that dimly seen figure would provide no help. She was spared making a terrible choice. "I have no idea." Truth has a genuine sound. "I know she isn't one of the bigger women, but it could be any one of these." She tapped the pictures of the slender women. "I'm sorry."

The policewoman slid the pictures into the folder, closed it. "Thank you for your time. If you hear anything further from her, call us." She stood.

Annie rose. She took comfort in the fact that she had indeed been helpful. If she hadn't gone to Fish Haul pier, there likely would be no suspicion of the Grant family. "Please tell Chief Cameron I hope they are well soon."

A quick grin touched Harrison's face. "The sooner the better." Abruptly, she was formal again. "We appreciate your assistance, Mrs. Darling."

Annie almost asked her, for heaven's sake, to call her Annie but Harrison, after a short nod, moved quickly up the center aisle. Annie watched her go with a sense of relief. The investigation was now on course. Harrison might lack charm, but she was honest and thorough. Perhaps she would quickly solve the crime and Gwen's friend would be safe.

Max felt transported into wilderness as he followed the faint, overgrown path through the woods. He pushed aside palmetto fronds and ferns, heard the rustle of twigs and acorns underfoot. The rat-a-tat of an unseen woodpecker and the chit of squirrels were joined by the crack of a hammer as he reached the end of the unchecked growth. He came out on a broad, well-kept path. He walked faster, passing a narrower path that branched to his left. With a clear mental picture of the terrain, he identified the offshoot as the route to Gwen Jamison's house.

The rattle of the hammer grew louder. Max stopped at the foot of the elaborate Grant garden with its banks of azaleas and replicas of classic statuary: Diana with a bow aimed skyward, Bacchus beaming and garlanded with laurel, the somber dying Gaul. Hal Porter stood on a ladder, intent as he hammered on a birdhouse.

Max walked swiftly toward him, circling a bricked fountain with a centerpiece of Neptune hoisting his trident. Freshly set cement held a shiny new metal pole topped by a redwood house for purple martins. The birdhouse was equidistant between the fountain and a partially constructed wooden bench. Hal paused and swiped a bandanna across his face.

Max's steps crunched on the oyster-shell walk.

Hal turned to look. He stuffed the bandanna in a pocket

and came down the ladder, tucking the hammer in a belt loop. He looked fit and robust, the only evidence of his encounter in the woods a small gauze bandage on his left temple. He walked toward Max, hand outstretched.

"How're you feeling?"

They shook hands.

"A little sore." Hal lightly touched the bandage. "Not nearly as sore as those kids are going to be when I catch up with them. I've got people asking around. So far nobody's come up with names. I'm going to check out Robert's friends."

"Why not let it go for right now? I'll give Robert a ring tomorrow when he gets home, ask him if he has any ideas."

"Home?" Hal looked surprised.

Max felt buoyant. "Robert's in the clear for yesterday. Rock-solid alibi." He pointed toward the Grant house. Quickly he recounted Annie's encounter on Fish Haul pier. "The story starts there and ends there."

"One of the family?" Hal stared at the house, his gaze appraising.

"Gwen identified the thief as one of the Grants."

Hal shrugged. "She could have been mistaken. It's hard to see in the middle of the night. Maybe the lady she told misunderstood. You know what I mean. One person tells another and they tell somebody else and pretty soon the story's twisted as a licorice stick. I can't see Mr. or Mrs. Grant faking a robbery, then blowing away somebody. They're nice people. Not the type."

"Type?" Max looked at him with interest.

Hal stepped closer, dropped his voice. "Grant's a nice old boy, but not a tough dude. The other day he was looking over the purple martin house and all of a sudden he started quoting some poem. Something about 'These are the days when the birds come back . . .'" Hal's tone was bemused. "Mrs. Grant's the kind that won't step on a palmetto bug. I don't see either of them as criminals. Now, I don't know their kids and they've got a bunch visiting right now. I'd say if there's something funny going on it's got to be one of the young ones."

"That's what we have to find out. You may know the answer."

Hal frowned. "Me?"

"Wednesday morning someone may have walked through the garden to go to Gwen Jamison's house." Since Annie had heard no car nor had Max later heard a car, Max thought it likely that the murderer was on foot. Max pointed at the new birdhouse. "You were working here. You have a clear view of the path."

Hal looked thoughtful. "You're saying that if one of the Grants walked to the Jamison house, they had to go by here. What time?"

"Around a quarter past ten." Max shrugged. "It could have been a few minutes earlier or later. Gwen was shot between ten-twenty and ten-forty."

Hal shook his head. "I wasn't paying any attention to time. I had a good view though I couldn't see all the way to the woods because of the fog. I was moving around, back and forth between here and the far side of the house." He touched the metal pole. "I mixed the concrete there, brought it over here in a wheelbarrow." He gestured at the fresh patch. "I didn't want to make a mess here. I wasn't paying any attention to people. Come to think of it, I saw Gwen Jamison go by. I don't know what time it was."

Max thought quickly. Gwen had gone to the Franklin house to retrieve the packet of coins. When she found new locks on the doors, she'd hurried home and called Confidential Commissions. "She probably came by around nine-thirty. Did you see anyone after that?"

Hal slowly shook his head. "Not on the path. A little later Mrs. Grant came out to see how I was getting on. But somebody could easily have gone past when I was on the far side of the house mixing the concrete. I was setting the pole into the cement when I heard the shots from your place."

Max was disappointed though not surprised.

"You can ask Mrs. Grant. Maybe she saw somebody." Hal reached for the hammer. "I got to finish the birdhouse. It's for purple martins. They'll start arriving pretty soon. They're great to keep mosquitoes down."

As he turned away, Max called out. "One more thing. Robert Jamison came here looking for his mother. He probably arrived between eleven and twelve. Did you see him?"

"I guess so." The handyman was casual. "When I came back from your place, I was loading up my stuff and a black kid came out of the kitchen door and got into a beat-up old car parked next to my truck."

That was another confirmation of Robert's movements, not that it mattered now. "Did you see anybody in the family when you were at your truck?"

Hal hesitated. "I didn't *see* anybody. About that time, I looked up and I think somebody was watching out the second-floor window. I saw a curtain move. I don't know that it matters."

Max pictured a hidden watcher. How easy and how damnably clever it had been for the murderer to slip through the house and place the gun in the trunk of Robert's old rattletrap while Robert was in the kitchen.

Annie beamed as the front door of Death on Demand closed on the departure of a plump and voluble widow enjoying a winter holiday at the Sea Side Inn. It wasn't up to Chamber of Commerce standards to admit to astonishment on making a substantial sale in February, but it certainly was true.

Agatha leaped to the cash desk, eyes gleaming.

"One hundred and forty dollars! Cash!" Annie picked up Agatha and swooped into a cautious waltz, cautious because sudden movements were likely to turn Agatha into a razor-clawed vortex. But this sale had to be celebrated. "What fun! And I introduced her to authors she's going to love, Mary Saums and T. Lynn Ocean and Jimmie Ruth Evans and Charles Benoit."

The shrill peal of the telephone ended the impromptu dance. Annie grabbed the phone. "Death on Demand, the finest—"

"Apparently you are ambulatory." Emma Clyde's raspy voice quivered with ill-suppressed fury. "We had assumed incapacitation accounted for your lack of response."

Response? Oh, dear. Emma's crusty message had directed Annie to check e-mails. Obviously, it had been a royal command. Annie stiffened her shoulders. "Emma, I haven't had a minute. I've been dealing with Officer Harrison." It wasn't necessary to reveal the policewoman had departed a good half hour ago. "Anyway, I'm glad you called because I have a lot to tell you." She felt as if she were talking into a cavern, which suggested Emma's ship-to-shore telephone had speaker-phone capabilities.

"Dearest Annie"—Laurel's husky voice exuded pleasure—"we can't wait to be with you."

"We're in port." Henny was brisk. "Now we can do an online video conference. Hurry, dear. We're delaying our departure until we have our talk."

Annie found herself at her computer and, with Webcams at work, she was looking at the traveling trio and they at her. Of course, her small cramped storeroom scarcely had the élan of the teak-appointed saloon on *Marigold's Pleasure*. Emma's caftan this afternoon was burnt orange with splashes of silver. Annie was irresistibly reminded of sherbet and slivered almonds. Henny looked professorial with reading glasses low on her nose and silver-streaked dark hair in a bun. As always Laurel was gorgeous, silver-blond hair in a flattering feathered cut, Nordic blue eyes clear and bright, her white shirt and slacks and blue canvas thongs perfect for a rum and Coke at a jungle plantation house.

Annie brought them up to date with the great news of Robert's imminent release. "Thanks to Max."

Emma cleared her throat, which sounded like iron scraping on concrete. "Had you checked your e-mails, you would have realized we have important contributions to make to the progress of the investigation. I'll go first."

"Of course you will go first." Laurel's husky voice sounded like a cross between a psychotherapist and a kindergarten teacher. Her smile was benign.

Henny lifted a hand to her face to hide a quick smile.

Emma's piercing blue eyes narrowed.

Annie rushed to smooth things over. "Emma, you are wonderful to take your precious time and spend it helping us. I know you had hoped to make progress on a new plot on the cruise and here you are, sharing your insight and experience."

"Yes?" Emma's square face looked expectant.

Annie wrinkled her nose. How much obeisance did the old monster need? Obviously more was required. "No one but you has the brilliance and panache"—Annie wondered if she was overdoing it— "to discern what truly matters!"

"Good of you to say so." Emma was grudgingly mollified. "Certainly I wouldn't presume to take precedence except for the undeniable fact that Marigold and I are experts in understanding motivation. Motivation is the key here. The moment I read the story about your interlude on Fish Haul pier, I understood everything. I must say I rather liked that bit of business."

Annie recalled the chill of the night and her sense of isolation and the sadness in the voice of Gwen's friend.

"Marigold may well enjoy such an adventure her next time out." Clearly Emma was intrigued. "Moreover, I had an epiphany."

Annie's eyes slitted. Much as the mystery writer often annoyed her, it wasn't usual for Emma to be trite. Annie loathed the casual use of "epiphany" as a synonym for a thought, revelation, or, as in this case, a hunch.

"As Marigold often reminds Inspector Houlihan, 'Beware the Trojan Horse.'" Emma came to a full stop and beamed.

"Horse?" Annie felt confused.

Emma was patronizing. "My dear Annie, think about it. Why did this woman contact you instead of the police?"

"She was afraid." Afraid of what she knew, afraid no one would believe her.

"Marigold sees right through that. The woman contacted you to avoid incisive questioning by the authorities that might reveal her to have an ulterior motive. Obviously, she wanted to fasten suspicion on the family. I suspect collusion. The informant knows who committed the crime. Discover her identity and that will lead you to the person she is trying to protect. Or she may simply be someone who holds a grudge against the Grants. Marigold is always suspicious when an apparently peripheral witness purports to offer clinching evidence."

Annie restrained herself from caroling, "Good for Marigold." No matter how maddening Emma might be, she was trying to be helpful. "That's an excellent suggestion, Emma. I'll do my best to find out more about the woman at the pier."

"Dear Emma." Laurel gazed admiringly at her hostess. "If only we all were as perceptive as you, as intelligent, commanding, and intuitive. I am humble in your presence."

Annie grinned. Laurel was about to overdo the accolades.

"Years of experience, my dear, years of experience." Emma's becomingly modest tone indicated full acceptance of Laurel's panegyric.

Laurel turned her brilliant gaze toward her daughter-in-law. "That is a perfect color choice, Annie. The cornflower blue of your blouse is so becoming to you." She nodded approval. "Annie dearest, we'll be home by Saturday evening at the latest. I feel guilty to confess"—a trill of laughter—"that we've become a trifle tired of Parcheesi and even canasta has lost its charm. Although we've played a number of games, our every thought is focused on Gwen's murder. I can't claim an epiphany, but I was jolted by the story linking a member of the Grant family to the theft and subsequent murder. That changed everything."

Suddenly her voice was crisp and incisive. "I never like to fuel gossip—"

Annie murmured, "Of course not."

Did Laurel's gaze sharpen a little? Annie maintained a sweet smile.

"—but you should know there was a rumor a year or so after Helen died that Geoff and Denise might be headed for marriage. Instead, he married Rhoda. Passion, my dear, is so often the background to crime."

Annie frowned. A previous romantic link between Geoff and his former sister-in-law hardly seemed relevant to a current theft and murder. "Are you suggesting Denise stole the Double Eagles to get back at Geoff and Rhoda?"

Henny patted Laurel's knee. "I heard that rumor, but I never gave it credence. I don't think Denise was interested in Geoff. Denise loves everybody, her ex–brother-in-law, the postman, the clerk at the hardware store, her doctor. Everybody's always her Instant New Best Friend, including me. Besides, Denise doesn't hold grudges. She's a dear. She threw herself into all the island charities after Helen died. I got to know her fairly well when we were working on the campaign to get fast foods out of the high school. Denise loves everybody, including Rhoda. In fact, Denise introduced Rhoda to Geoff. Rhoda works for Island Realty and Denise and Rhoda are great friends. Denise gave the sweetest toast at the wedding, something like, 'To our dearest Rhoda and Geoff, now and forever, living, laughing, loving,' and she was obviously delighted for them."

Laurel brushed back a feathery curl. "I'm afraid something isn't right in Geoff and Rhoda's marriage. My Esperanza's sister Gloria assisted Gwen Jamison in cleaning the Grant house."

Laurel's voice dropped. "Gloria told Esperanza that the Grants no longer share a bedroom. Last fall Rhoda moved into a room of her own. My dears. That is the first step to divorce." Her voice vibrated with distress.

Annie wasn't surprised at Laurel's conclusion. Laurel foresaw disaster when a couple no longer shared the conjugal bed. Laurel had difficulty envisioning occupying a bed alone whether married or single . . . Annie sternly corralled her thoughts.

Henny threw up graceful hands and laughed with delight. "A separate room doesn't prohibit marital bliss. Maybe he snores. Maybe she snores. Nothing prevents an assignation in the night. Or morning. Or afternoon."

Laurel didn't smile in return. Her face was grave. "I haven't shared some knowledge I possess. I'm very much afraid that Rhoda has a lover. I may be wrong—"

Annie felt certain that Laurel had an extra special awareness of love affairs. Those who indulge . . . Annie again firmly corralled her thoughts.

"—but I was in Chastain one evening recently. I saw Rhoda with another man. They were leaving the Caballero Club."

Annie raised an eyebrow. What was Max's mother doing at a high-class gambling joint?

"I caught a glimpse of him from the back. He was much bigger than Geoff, sandy hair not dark. The way he held her arm told me they were lovers."

Henny shook her head. "That's sad, but it doesn't have anything to do with theft and murder. I doubt that sex matters here. What matters is character." Suddenly her thoughtful face was grave. "I suggested earlier that the authorities might want to take a close look at Ben Travis-Grant. But it isn't fair to single him out. I was still teaching when the Grant children were in high school. There were two incidents I should mention. There was an ugly hazing scandal. A freshman was left tied to a stake in the woods overnight. The boy was found the next morning by a couple out for an early bird watch. He was hysterical. Apparently there was a den of snakes nearby and several crawled near him. Fortunately they were not poisonous, but the boy had no way of knowing that. Justin Foster-Grant was part of the group responsible. Criminal action was threatened, but the family was persuaded not to bring charges. Also, Barb Travis-Grant was caught shoplifting and narrowly escaped being charged." Henny sighed. "People make mistakes. Especially kids. But I felt I should make it clear that Ben isn't the only member of the family with some question marks about character."

Annie felt chilled. What kind of self-absorption or lack of empathy did it require on Justin's part to leave a younger boy captive in woods known to harbor wild boars, cougars, foxes, rattlers, and copperheads? As for Barb, shoplifting as a teenager could have resulted from peer pressure, but stealing could also indicate a hunger for possessions untroubled by any sense of right or wrong.

Henny's face softened. "The only one universally admired is Kerry Foster-Grant. Every nice thing said about her is deserved. A fine girl."

In the background, the yacht's whistle sounded. The traveling trio stood and waved.

A blown kiss from Laurel. "We're on our way, darling. Take care."

Henny looked impatient. "Wish we were there. We're coming as fast as we can."

"Beware the Trojan Horse." Emma's voice was deep and confident.

Annie leaned closer to the Webcam. If only she could make Emma understand that the woman beneath the pier was terrified. Before she could speak, the picture was gone.

Chapter 12

Max walked through the garden to the parking area east of the Grant house. A wheelbarrow sat next to a huge black pickup with an alligator emblazoned on the driver's door. That would be Hal's truck. Max noted a half-dozen cars.

He looked up at the second floor. The curtains hung still and straight in the windows that overlooked the parking area. There were many vantage points where Robert's arrival in a noisy rattletrap might have been noted. And acted upon. The gun in Robert's trunk had almost succeeded in a charge of murder against the hapless teenager.

The decision to place the murder weapon in Robert's trunk reflected an opportunistic quickness, but it revealed much more. Gwen Jamison's murder could have been an act of desperation, a frantic effort to prevent exposure or save a reputation. Or perhaps the motive was greed. However, Robert posed no threat to the murderer. Implicating Robert indicated a self-serving ruthlessness. Whoever they sought was calculating, callous, and dangerous by nature.

Max turned and walked swiftly back to the garden. It would soon be time to meet Annie at the Franklin house and return here to speak with the Grant family. There was one more stop he wanted to make.

The garden sloped gracefully. Dark green mounds of azaleas curved in banks all the way to the woods. Hal Porter stood on his ladder at the birdhouse, a screwdriver in one hand.

Max stopped at the fountain and surveyed the back porch and its inviting wicker rockers. In the fog and chill Wednesday morning, it was unlikely any of the chairs were occupied. There was the possibility that someone might have glanced from a back window as the murderer walked toward Gwen's house. That could be checked out.

His gaze stopped at the attractive cottage that sat among weeping willows. The cottage front porch overlooked the garden and the paths. That's where the former sister-in-law lived. She was a real estate agent. Perhaps she'd been home Wednesday morning.

As Max walked toward the front steps, the front door opened and a plump, curly-haired woman bustled outside. She clutched two manila folders, a pot of geraniums, and a massive purse. Spotting Max, she skidded to a stop next to a redwood bench with an intricately carved back.

Max smiled and came up the steps. "Denise Cramer? I'm Max Darling, and I'd appreciate a moment of your time."

She gave him a bright smile. Her gaze was frankly admiring.

"I know. My friends sent you to celebrate my birthday. Tall, blond, and handsome, just what the birthday girl ordered. But you're six months late. Or have I won the lottery? I'll take the cash now. Or maybe you want to buy a house and you couldn't wait for me to get to the office." She calculated the expense of his blue cashmere sweater, worsted wool slacks, and Italian loafers. "Am I about to smart-mouth my way out of contention to be your real estate agent? I can be serious"—she sucked in her cheeks and looked grave—"and I've got some listings to die for."

Max laughed. "None of the above, but may you have many happy returns whenever you celebrate." He gestured to the south. "My wife and I—"

"That's what I figured. The choice ones are always spoken for. Oh well, better luck next time."

"—are your new neighbors. We're going to move into the Franklin house."

"That's swell. Maybe we can play badminton sometime. Right now I've got to run. Glad to meet you and all that sort of thing." She clattered down the steps. "If you're making neighborly calls, I'm a tenant. Geoff Grant's the man you're looking for."

She swept past without a backward glance. In a moment, a shiny red Cadillac wheeled from behind the cottage and roared out the front drive.

Max jingled coins in his pocket and wondered at Denise Cramer's hurry. Was she always this ebullient? Or was she clever at avoiding questions she might not want to answer? Or—his mouth turned down in wry self-doubt—was he seeing every action by a member of the Grant household through a lens of guilt? After all, Denise Cramer could not have had any idea why he wanted to see her.

Annie nosed the Volvo into a spot of sunshine next to Max's Corvette. The shadows were lengthening even though it wasn't quite three o'clock. She didn't bother to click the car lock. That was one of the joys of living on an island. Since cars don't have water wings, theft wasn't likely.

On the back porch, she checked the windows. Everything was in order. She heard the distant whir of a buzz saw.

"Yo, Annie." Max's voice rose clear and strong.

She turned and looked down into the garden. Max strode toward her, smiling.

Her lips curved. She moved toward the steps. Suddenly the muffled peal of her cell phone sounded. Annie's eyes widened. Cell phone. It might not be anything important, but it might be very important. She opened her purse and grabbed the phone.

"Hello."

"You shouldn't ought to've put it all in the paper, girl." The whispery voice was familiar and especially the cadence and the appellation. *Girl.* There was something poignant about that title.

Annie's hand tightened on the cell. "I was afraid the police wouldn't pay any attention."

There might have been a faint laugh. "You got their attention, girl. You got mine. I be gone now for a spell. But I got friends. Five of us together, we're taking a trip so nobody will know which one of us talked to Gwen. You're no fool, girl. You knew Gwen told me who she saw. Might you should read tea leaves, girl. I didn't want to tell you. I can't prove anything. But I thought about what you said and how I couldn't have blood on my hands if there was more trouble so I did what you asked. I called that police number even though I don't expect them to pay no never mind. I told them who it was Gwen saw, so now they know. You keep out of it, girl. Don't go meeting nobody else in the dark. Leave it to the police."

Annie felt a rush of relief so intense she felt giddy. "Thank you. Oh, thank you."

The line was empty, the caller gone.

Max ran up the steps. "What's happened?" His arm curved around her shoulders, held her tight.

She leaned against him. "Good news. Finally, we have good news. Gwen's friend called the police, told them who Gwen said she saw that night. I was terrified the murderer would find her. Now I don't have to be afraid any longer."

Max looked startled. "Who did she say Gwen saw?"

Annie shook her head. "She didn't tell me. She said she'd called the police. That's all she said. She hung up before I could ask."

Max nodded swift approval. "Smart woman. She's told the people who need to know. It's up to them now. She didn't want to put you in danger, too."

Annie moved out of his clasp, walked to the porch railing, and looked toward the pond and the woods that lay between the Franklin house and the Grant home. "Do you suppose we still need to go there?"

Max joined her at the railing, his face thoughtful. "Definitely. Don't mention this second call. If the police want to announce anything, let them do it. As far as you are concerned, you met this unknown woman at the pier and you're glad to share what you were told with the Grants. Leave it at that."

The wide front piazza of the Grant house was inviting on this bright, sunny, capriciously warm afternoon. Red cushions decorated green wicker furniture. A white wooden swing hung at one end.

As they climbed the steps, a distraught Geoff Grant opened the front door and came outside. "The police just left. That's the second time today. They're hounding us. I don't like the tenor of their questions."

Max was unruffled. "They're trying to solve the crime."

Annie was elated, though she was careful to give no hint of her pleasure. She felt sure the second round of questioning was in response to the Crime Stoppers tip.

"I hope"—Geoff stared at Annie—"that you can help us prove these suspicions are baseless."

Max's gaze was direct. "Robert Jamison has been cleared."

Geoff's face was suddenly older. "I see." His tone was heavy. "We'll go to the library."

They walked down a spacious central hallway. When they stepped into the library, the murmur of conversation ended. All of the family had gathered, but there were no looks of welcome. The stiff silence was in marked contrast to the serenity of the decor. Soft green woodwork provided a lovely backdrop for a Chinese painting of five robed figures. Silk wall panels depicted peach blossoms and a winding shallow stream. On the Georgian mantel above a flickering fire, glazed green and orange replicas of Tang dynasty tomb figures evoked a world far distant in time and space. A hand-painted royal peacock posed majestically beneath a stylized tree on a black lacquer screen. A suit of armor, dark and tarnished, stood by the fireplace.

Annie and Max followed their host past a figurine of a green celadon horse on a rosewood stand and a glass display case and lustrous gold Double Eagles. She noted several empty spots, the velvet darker than the surrounding field.

Geoff tried to be a good host. "Tea? Sherry?"

"No, thank you." Max shook his head.

Annie accepted a cup of tea.

Rhoda poured, her hand shaking a little. There was a flurry of movement to the tea table or to the sideboard for sherry.

Geoff stood in front of the fireplace. He looked around the room at the assembled family. "Max and Annie Darling have agreed to help us try to make some sense of what's been happening." He came to a full stop. Finally, he said, "I understand Robert Jamison is no longer a suspect in Gwen's murder." There was an instant of shock at his words. "Max has been in touch with the circuit solicitor." Geoff's expression was bleak as he sat down. "He will tell us what he knows."

Annie waited by the fireplace. The room seemed hot and crowded. Perhaps standing near the fire contributed to her discomfort, that and the knowledge that the faces turned toward her were hostile.

She tallied those present: Geoff and Rhoda Grant, Kerry Foster-Grant, Justin Foster-Grant and his fiancée, Margaret Brown, Barb Travis-Grant and Ben Travis-Grant, Denise Cramer. Annie felt a sharp disappointment. They were all here. No arrest had been made despite the call received by Crime Stoppers. Knowing and proving were separate and distinct. The police had to have more than a name. They had to be able to prove that the suspect could have been in Gwen Jamison's house. They had to find evidence. Everyone present appeared uncomfortable, some angry, some fearful, but not one more than the others. Apparently the police hadn't revealed interest in a particular suspect in the second round of questioning.

Max stepped forward. "This morning in a meeting with the circuit solicitor . . ." Max spoke easily and well. Annie took strength from his strength. He was forceful, confident. "It is fortunate that Reverend Shelby is an honorable man and . . ."

His audience was unmoved. Robert's release signaled danger for them.

Geoff Grant's dark head bent forward as if he were intent on capturing every word. His rounded face was somber. Once he glanced toward Ben Travis-Grant who stood near the door. Geoff as quickly looked away.

Annie tried to define the quicksilver impression she'd received from Geoff's hurried glance. Suspicion? Fear?

Ben tossed off his glass of sherry. His muscles bunched as if he were ready to engage in a fistfight or possibly bolt into the hall. His curly chestnut hair was scarcely combed. His reddish face folded in a frown. His yellow and black flannel shirt was open at the throat, sleeves rolled up to the elbows. The leg pockets of his travel khakis bulged. He could carry a great deal in those pockets. A flashlight. Maps. Food. A gun?

Perhaps he felt Geoff's scrutiny. Ben glanced at Geoff, a quick, cool, defiant look.

A small hand reached up to touch Ben's arm. Kerry Foster-Grant, lovely and slender, perched on the edge of the petit-point chair near Ben. Her narrow face was troubled. When Ben looked down, she gave him a quick, sweet smile.

Ben's face softened. He reached down, brushed back a lock of her raven hair.

Kerry held his hand against her cheek for a moment.

Annie knew she'd glimpsed a private moment, a display of deep affection.

Geoff Grant watched, too, his face drawn in a frown.

Barb Travis-Grant huddled in a Queen Anne wing chair. Barb's pinched face made her look ill. The cup of tea on a nearby table remained untasted.

Rhoda sat stiffly behind the tea table, her hands tightly folded. Her dark hair gleamed in the light of the chandelier. She was stylish in a pale blue sweater and gray slacks, but her face was strained. The vermilion, jade, and gold beads in her necklace emphasized her worried expression. Every so often she darted a covert glance at her husband.

Denise Cramer stood near a curio cabinet a little behind and to the left of Geoff Grant's wing chair. Her glass of sherry was almost empty. Her bright, curious eyes moved quickly around the room. Her plump face looked interested and excited. She had the air of an onlooker at an unexpectedly interesting meeting.

Justin Foster-Grant's teacup clicked against a tabletop. He abruptly stood, pushing back his chair with a clatter, and moved with a quick, hurried energy to the center of the library to stand next to the case that held the Double Eagles. His bright red hair and luxuriant mustache gleamed in the light from the chandelier. He challenged Max. "I don't believe in foolproof alibis."

Margaret Brown, slim and elegant in a red sweater and cream slacks, nodded approvingly at her fiancé. She appeared relaxed on a small sofa, stirring her tea. She had an aura of privilege, a young woman accustomed to deference and admiration.

Max was unruffled. "My wife found Gwen Jamison dying at approximately ten thirty-eight. At that precise moment, Robert Jamison was speaking with Reverend Shelby. Moreover, Robert had arrived at the church at ten-fifteen. My secretary spoke with Mrs. Jamison at twenty minutes past ten."

Justin waved away Max's claims. "The clock could be wrong at the church. They could all be lying. Robert went to see his girlfriend, right? Maybe he told her he needed an alibi. Have you thought of that? Or your wife could be wrong. Or maybe she's lying."

Justin jerked toward Annie. "You've had a lot to say about all of this. One thing sticks out. You claim the woman at the pier told you Gwen hid the Double Eagles and a note about who took them in your house. How come your house? Sure, Gwen used to work there but"—he spaced the words—"it seems odd to me that all the accusations are coming from you and the coins were taken to your place and Gwen was on the phone to you people and you hotfoot it to her house and say you found her shot. Maybe you and your husband set it up to have the coins stolen. Then it makes sense to fling around accusations at other people." He looked around the room for support.

His fiancée's thin high voice was patronizing. "It may be much simpler." A faint flush lighted the pale face framed by sleek silver hair. "Obviously, Gwen Jamison was the thief and working with someone else. She wanted to keep police suspicion away from her so she told a friend that she saw a member of the family, but her partner decided to kill her and keep all the loot. Then her friend contacted you." The red-tipped finger leveled at Annie was accusatory. "You repeated a lie."

Annie was solemn. "I repeated what I was told. I felt I heard the truth."

Emotion surged in the room. Worry, anger, and distress were justified if the accusation was false, but Annie detected a current of fear. Annie glanced quickly at each in turn. Surely that fear must be imprinted on one face, clear to see.

Geoff Grant looked much older. He stared into the fire, his face drooping with weariness. Rhoda folded her arms, her posture rigid with disavowal. Denise moved uneasily, her round face puckered with dismay. Ben glowered. Dark-haired Kerry glanced up at him, her violet eyes wide with concern. Barb clutched the chair arm. Justin's chin jutted in disagreement. Margaret's frown made her face disagreeable.

Justin strode toward Annie, stood a foot away. "Accusations by a person or persons unknown have no standing. Not here. Not in a court of law. It's your responsibility to help discover this accuser's identity. We have a right to confront her. You are the one who talked to her, or at least that is what you claim. What did she look like? Describe her."

"I've already spoken to the police about that." Once again Annie sensed a flood of panic. "Unfortunately, I scarcely caught a glimpse of her as she disappeared around the headland. I saw only a shape against the horizon. But the police are certainly seeking her."

Max stepped nearer. "I'm offering a reward for any information that leads to the arrest or conviction of the murderer."

Annie felt a cheer inside. A reward would be wonderful.

Max looked around the room. "Someone may possess information that will prove the woman wrong. Moreover"—Max's tone was easy—"I suggest we let the police deal with this woman. We don't have any way to find her. Annie didn't see her well enough to describe her. But the police can reach out into the community. Instead of focusing on her, let's pool the information we have. Let's work together. We may learn facts that will lead to the right person."

It was utterly quiet.

Max pointed at the glass display case. "I understand the original case was smashed open. Did anyone hear an unexpected noise Monday night?"

No one spoke.

Max persisted. "Was there any kind of noise either inside the house or outside the house?"

Again, he was met by silence.

"Did anyone come downstairs at any time that night?"

No response.

Annie looked around the room. The faces were shuttered against Max.

Geoff was impatient. "No one saw anything because it wasn't one of us. The best thing we can do is find that woman, get her to admit she made a mistake or at least insist she own up publicly if she's going to accuse us. We have to prove that she's wrong."

Max was emphatic. "Every fact we learn helps protect the innocent."

Ben Travis-Grant's gaze was pugnacious. "Why do you care? Why should we tell you anything?"

Max met his stare directly. "I run a business that helps people with problems. I find out answers. Gwen Jamison called me for help. I didn't help her. I can't change what happened. I can't change what I didn't do. I know what I can do. I can look and hunt and see what I can discover. There's no law against asking questions. Maybe a fact or idea we come up with will help the police find her murderer."

Kerry Foster-Grant shivered. "The police keep coming. They talked to each one of us alone. I didn't like it. None of us would steal Geoff's coins or hurt Gwen. The thief had to be a stranger. What can we do to find someone like that?"

Rhoda nodded energetically. "Kerry's right. We don't know anything."

Geoff was on his feet. "That's why there's no reason for us to avoid talking with Max and Annie." His voice was resolute. "Gwen was a good woman." He took a breath. "Everyone in this room is good, too." There was a tremor in his voice. He looked at Max. "We'll do everything we can to help."

"Murder doesn't have anything to do with us." Barb Travis-Grant's voice was shrill. "I don't know anything. I wish we could have a good time this week like we always do when we come home. Everything's ruined."

Ben moved to his sister, patted her shoulder. "It's okay, Barbie. I'll take care of you." His voice was soft and soothing.

Barb's lips trembled. She pressed her head against his hand.

Justin Foster-Grant flung himself into an easy chair next to Margaret. He stared at Max with no effort to mask his disdain. "Okay, miracle man. What's your plan?"

Max's expression was pleasant. "While we are together, let's clear up a few points." He turned toward Geoff. "How many bedrooms are on the second floor?"

Geoff looked bewildered. "Eight."

"Four on the east side, four on the west?"

"Yes."

"Who is staying in each of the east rooms?"

Geoff frowned. "What difference does it make?"

"It may be helpful." Max didn't explain.

Annie hadn't realized how strained the atmosphere had been until she felt a sudden easing of tension. No one saw a threat in Max's queries about the inhabitants of the bedrooms. She wondered why he cared.

Geoff shrugged. "On the east side, Ben has the first bedroom to the north. Barb is next to him. Across the hall is Kerry. Justin has the south corner room."

"The bedrooms on the west side?" Max was casual.

"The northwest room is mine. Rhoda has the adjoining room. The room across the hall is empty and our guest"—Geoff smiled at Margaret—"is in the southwest corner room."

"That's clear." Max smiled his approval. "Now let's place everyone yesterday morning about a quarter past ten."

Denise bent forward, her brown eyes curious. "What's important about a quarter past ten?"

"Gwen Jamison was alive at twenty minutes after ten. Annie found her dying about ten-forty. Obviously if some of you were together here in the house or can prove you were somewhere else at ten-fifteen, that will go far to eliminate you as suspects." Max sounded reassuring.

Ben gave a sour smile. "You think we're all pretty dumb, asking about who sleeps where when that obviously doesn't matter. Why beat around the bush? Why not ask which one of us hustled through the garden to Gwen's house at a quarter past ten?"

Rhoda lifted a hand to her throat. "That's terrible. It isn't fair to suspect us because we were here. We live here. I was outside yesterday morning. I don't know what time. I went to check on the birdhouse. I came right back inside. I didn't see a soul." She stopped, looked startled. "Oh, wait. I talked to Hal Porter. He's doing some repair work for us."

"When you came inside, where did you go?"

Rhoda looked flustered. "I went to the pantry. I wanted to get some preserves. That may have been later. I looked around for Gwen. I wanted to talk to her about dinner, but I couldn't find her. Then I went upstairs."

"Did you see anyone?"

Rhoda brightened. "Barb was coming downstairs. I remember that."

Barb brushed back a lock of golden-brown hair. "You're mixed up, Rhoda. I didn't come down until almost eleven." Her look at Max was emphatic. "I'd just gotten up."

Ben moved impatiently. "I don't think you're going to find anybody in the garden at the right time. We're on holiday. We sleep in. Everybody but Justin. He's always bright-eyed. How about it, Justin. Were you out in the garden eating worms?"

Ben's tone was disagreeable. There was no brotherly affection.

Annie felt startled for an instant then realized there was no reason why they should have been close. They weren't brothers. Ben Travis, now Ben Travis-Grant, and Barb Travis, now Barb Travis-Grant, had been pushed into a melded family by their mother's marriage to Geoff. That held true for Justin Foster, now Justin Foster-Grant, and Kerry Foster, now Kerry Foster-Grant. All these adoptive siblings had in common was the fact their mothers had married Geoff. There were no family ties among the four. Obviously, Ben and Justin disliked each other. That was unfortunate since Ben and Kerry clearly were in love.

Justin gave Ben a look of active dislike. "I had an early appointment at the bank. Then I went by the lot where the clinic will be built."

Max nodded. "You drove?"

Justin's gaze at Max was equally cold. "I drove."

Kerry hurried to speak as if to make up for her brother's rudeness. "I didn't sleep late." She smiled at Ben. "You've always loved sleeping in. I was up early and the only one down for breakfast." Suddenly her face was sad. "Gwen was there. I fixed an English muffin with orange marmalade and asked her about Charlie. She was so excited about the baby coming. But there was something wrong. I asked her if she felt all right. She said everything was fine, but I knew something was bothering her. Oh, if only I'd insisted she tell me. But I didn't want to press. I knew she'd had trouble with Robert and Geoff had helped them. On my way upstairs, I gave her a hug. I'd intended to take a walk, but when I looked out the window I saw it was foggy. So I settled at my desk and worked on some files I'd brought with me."

Annie enjoyed hearing Kerry speak. Her soft voice was kind and cheerful.

Max smiled at Kerry. "Did you look out of the window again?"

"I got up to stretch around ten." She smiled at her brother. "I saw Justin's car leave."

"Which," Justin snapped, "proves nothing."

"Justin called me from the bank and told me about his meeting." Margaret sounded smug. "The clinic's going to be beautiful."

"Did he call you on your cell phone?" Max was courteous, but Annie knew full well he didn't like Margaret.

Margaret smoothed back a strand of ice-blond hair. "Of course. I was relaxing in my room. And no, I didn't look out of the window. Who looks at fog?"

Max turned toward Geoff.

"I was in my study." He gestured to his right. "It adjoins the library. I was working on notes for my class."

Max glanced toward the closed door. "Does your study have a window onto the terrace like the library?"

"French doors. I open them in the summer. I can smell the honeysuckle when I'm working. I like that. It was too cold yesterday morning."

"Did you look out into the garden?"

Geoff shook his head. "I sit with my back to the doors. I was absorbed in my writing."

"Monkeys no see, monkeys no hear, monkeys no speak." Denise pushed back her chair, jumped up. "This has been . . ." She giggled. "Well, a little peculiar but definitely not boring like some of my appointments. Speaking of appointments, ladies and gentlemen, I have one. To show a beach house. For that kind of money, I'd better be on time." She moved toward the door.

Max stepped into her path. "You haven't said where you were at a quarter past ten."

She stopped. "Me? On the phone, handsome. Drumming up business."

"Could you see into the garden?"

Just for an instant, there was a flicker of uncertainty in her eyes. She parted red lips, looked past him, abruptly shook her head. "Not to speak of. Sorry." She adroitly sidestepped Max and was out the library door.

As it closed behind her, Max once again faced the family. "Annie and I are looking forward to a few private minutes with each of you."

Chapter 13

The sunroom was a haven of warmth from its southern exposure. A quartet of wicker chairs with gay chintz cushions overlooked the garden. Yellow-orange abutilon blossomed in four hanging baskets, the tapered bell-shaped flowers glowing bright as Seville oranges. Annie admired the healthy plants. Someone had a green thumb. Every time she tried to grow abutilon, spider mites attacked. A glossy-leaved rubber tree dwarfed one corner. Ivy climbed on posts between the chairs. Pots of ferns nudged the windowsills, flanked the doorway. Annie felt as if she'd been dropped into a tiny pocket of jungle. At any moment Tarzan might burst from behind a robust Royal fern.

Geoff sat in an opposite chair. The blaze of sunlight emphasized every line in his face. He looked worried and tired. "I wish I'd been here yesterday morning instead of my study." He pointed out the windows at the sweep of the garden, gleaming statuary, banks of azaleas, the broad well-kept path. "If I had, I'd be able to tell you no one took the path to Gwen's."

"Let's not worry about that for the moment." Max's tone was soothing. "I know you've been under stress ever since the robbery." Max leaned back in the wicker chair. "Though I suppose the coins were covered by insurance."

Geoff massaged one temple, squinted as if the sunlight hurt his eyes. "The collection is insured but that won't bring the coins back. Double Eagles. They're the most beautiful coins ever made. I loved holding them, trying to imagine who might have owned them. Some are from the San Francisco mint and I thought about the gold rush. Can't you see a miner striding into an assayer's office, his hat filled with gold nuggets? Maybe the miner had been a riverboat gambler or a druggist or a horse thief, and there he was, part of the most exciting gold hunt the world has ever known. That's the kind of thing I used to think about when I held the coins. I had some really rare ones." His animation fled. "Those are the ones that were taken, the special ones." He looked up suddenly, his eyes sunken in his face. "The ones"—his voice was almost a whisper—"I used to tell the family about. I like talking about the coins. I'd pick different ones and give their history. Last summer the family was here for the Fourth of July and I asked each one to make up a story about a 1927 Double Eagle. Rhoda's was cleverest. She pretended the coin had been in Lindbergh's pocket when he made the flight in *The Spirit of St. Louis*. Did you know sometimes the plane skimmed only ten feet above the water?" He let the question fall into silence. Last summer's fun had no life now. "I always brought the coins out when they visited. We sat around the fire and turned out the lights and I held my beauties up to let everyone see them glow in the firelight. I wanted them to see the beauty, but I don't believe in keeping treasures private. I gave the collection to Chastain College to receive upon my death. The collection is insured and they'll receive the money, but they won't be able to replace some of my coins."

Rhoda moved uneasily in the chair. "I didn't see a soul in the garden. I'm sure there's been a mistake."

"Except Hal, of course."

Rhoda's fingers wrapped around the strands of her necklace. "Oh, Hal." She took a quick breath. "He was working in the garden. I told you that. Maybe he saw someone."

"Only you. Apparently he must have been in the side yard when someone passed."

"If someone passed." Her voice was sharp. "It looks to me as though there's nothing to these accusations. With all the people here in the house, surely someone would have noticed." She looked relieved.

Annie pushed away a tendril of ivy. "Did you talk to Gwen yesterday morning?"

Rhoda's eyes flared like a horse ready to shy. "It was just a regular morning. I asked her to be sure and water the plants. I try to keep to a schedule. Water once a week. If you water too often, the dirt gets mushy and the roots rot and sometimes with houseguests it's hard to remember . . ." She trailed away.

Max leaned forward. "Were you aware that Gwen was troubled?"

"Troubled? Oh, that's just Kerry being sympathetic. Maybe Gwen looked tired. I don't know. Kerry's always worrying about people. I hardly spoke with Gwen. I was in a hurry." Rhoda moved impatiently in the chair. "I needed to get some washes on and I wasn't sure whether Geoff was going to grill for dinner. He was in such a good humor. And now—" Suddenly her look was imploring. "He's terribly upset. He never wants to admit—" She broke off, her gaze dropping.

Annie felt that Rhoda had almost revealed something important. "What won't he admit?"

Rhoda lifted a shaky hand to her lips. "I don't know what to do. He believes the kids are wonderful. Well"—her voice grew stronger—"I don't think they're wonderful. Justin's calculating and two-faced. He always acts like Mr. Perfect when he's around Geoff, but he's furious with Geoff. I heard him talking to that icy little rich girl he's going to marry. He'd better make money. He'd better beat a path to the bank because it's going to take a boatload of money to make her happy. They were in the swing and I was checking on my tomato plants. I heard him tell her Geoff wouldn't cosign for the note on the lot for the clinic." She lifted her face, her eyes burning. "It isn't right. Geoff's hard up for money. He's lost a lot in the stock market the last few years. And then he sold low and everything went back up. They don't realize how little money there is now. He doesn't want them to know. They're always after him for money. Kerry wants it for people who don't have jobs. Well, why don't they get jobs? I've worked—"

Annie thought about the sick and the old, the mentally ill and the incompetent, those devoured by drugs and alcohol, bad luck, poor judgment. *Well, why don't they get jobs?*

"—all my life. But Kerry's always got a sob story. Ben's already tried to get some money from Geoff. I heard them arguing

Sunday night. Barb's broke, of course, and she's heard about this modeling school in Hollywood and all you need is a five-thousand-dollar down payment for training. She's such a silly little fool. It can't be legitimate. It's a scam and if she went out there, who knows what would happen to her? Geoff told her no." Tears brimmed and rushed down pale cheeks. Rhoda came to her feet, rushed to the door. With one hand clutching the handle, she turned. "If you tell Geoff what I've said, he'll be furious. But it isn't right to pretend like they're all so wonderful." The door slammed behind her.

Justin Foster-Grant sat bolt upright, arms folded, feet planted, eyes narrowed in a glare. In the sunshine, his unpleasant expression and luxuriant red mustache gave him a piratical look.

Max was low-key. "I'm convinced that vets come equipped with plenty of empathy. Your patients can't describe their symptoms so you have to have a sense of what they'd tell you if they could."

Humorless eyes watched Max coldly. "I'm a good vet and I've got plenty of empathy to get it when somebody's soft-soaping me. For the record, I don't cheat old ladies or orphans, rob banks, rip off my stepfather, or kill the cook. I was at the bank like I said."

Max persisted. "You said you were on your way at a quarter past ten."

"I didn't detour by Gwen's house. I don't know where anybody was Wednesday morning. But I'll say this, sometimes I don't sleep well." His hand tugged at his mustache. "I've got a lot on my mind." His voice was no longer combative. "Interest rates are high. I've got student loans to pay off. Margaret's looking at a house on the south end of the island. Anyway, I couldn't sleep Monday night. There's a board that squeaks near the stairway in the hall. It's loud enough that I hear it with my door closed. It was late. I thought it was odd so I got up to take a look."

"Someone going to a bathroom?"

Justin shook his head. "The bathrooms are between the rooms. There's no need to cross the hall." His eyes glittered with malice. "Ben was walking into his room. I don't know where he'd been, but he sure stepped on that board."

Margaret Brown was composed and confident. "I hope this is settled as quickly as possible. Justin is going to be a force in the community, and it's most unfortunate to have his name associated with this unpleasantness."

... *unpleasantness.* "Murder is unpleasant." Annie's voice trembled. "I watched Gwen Jamison die." The stark words were cold in the overwarm Carolina room.

Margaret suddenly looked young and scared, her eyes uncertain. "Murder doesn't have anything to do with Justin or his family."

Max spoke without emphasis. "Justin has serious money problems. You could say he's desperate for money. More than a million dollars could make a big difference for him."

Margaret's elegant features sharpened in distress, giving her a witchlike appearance, a preview of how time might deal with her beauty. "Not Justin. Never Justin." She lifted a shaking hand to her throat. "If you go around saying things like that, you'll ruin his life. And mine. Everything's going to be wonderful. He'll have his practice and the new building, and we're going to buy a house. Some crook broke in. That's what happened." She jumped to her feet and hurried out.

Kerry Foster-Grant was forceful. "There are almost seven thousand homeless people in Atlanta right this moment. People who have no place to go, no kitchen, no car, no job. The only food they can hope for is at a shelter. More than a third of them have been homeless for more than a year. Eighty-seven percent are African American. Most are men between the ages of thirty-five and fifty-four. They can't find jobs. They have no way to get to a job. They don't have clean clothes to wear. A huge number are battling drug or alcohol dependency." Kerry's eyes blazed. "They are people without hope. We want to give them hope."

Max smiled. "You make a difference in many lives."

"I hope I can help." She looked discouraged. "It's hard to make people listen. They say, 'Oh, the poor are always with us.' That's true, but it doesn't change what we should do. God wants us to care."

Annie looked at her searchingly. "How did you feel when you looked at your stepfather's collection of Double Eagles?"

Kerry met her gaze directly. She spoke with defiance. "The same way I feel when I see a Lexus or handbags that sell for a thousand dollars or pictures of an elegant resort in Tahiti. I have a wish." She leaned forward, her violet eyes stern. "The people who own everything, who can go and do and be whatever they wish, make them homeless for a night. Just one night. Take away their cars and clothes and luxuries. Let them hear voices in their heads or try to stay warm on a winter night or stand in line at a homeless shelter for a meal or struggle against the demon of addiction. Just for one night."

Ben Travis-Grant lounged at his ease in the wicker chair, made it look small. "Sorry I can't be helpful. I was online for a long time Monday night. I was checking out a sweet travel deal to Bolivia. I've got to see the Concordia Tin Mine before I die. Butch and Sundance tried to go straight. Too bad it didn't work out. Last stop San Vicente Cemetery. Maybe. Or maybe not."

Max grinned. "Sometime we'll trade Butch and Sundance tales, but right now I'm more interested in outlaws here than in Bolivia. I'm hoping you can clear some things up." Max's smile slid away. "Especially since you were out of your room late Monday night."

Ben's amused expression didn't alter. "I don't recall saying that I left my room."

"You were seen."

Ben's half smile remained in place.

Annie had a sense that Ben, despite his casual attitude, was thinking fast and hard.

"By whom?" Ben's voice was soft.

"Does it matter?" Max's tone was equally soft.

Ben flicked away a strand of ivy. He glanced down, turned over a leaf. "Mealy worms. Now there's a real problem. I'd better alert Rhoda. She'll want to know." And he was on his feet and across the room and out the door.

Barb Travis-Grant looked like a waif with huge frightened eyes in a washed-out face despite her bead-spangled orange blouse, supertight crimson cropped pants, and glistening orange high heels. The garish colors emphasized her pallor. She hunched in the chair, knees to her chin, and stared at Annie and Max.

Max's voice was gentle. "It may be a good thing you were late coming down Wednesday morning."

Wide brown eyes watched him warily.

Annie would have liked to tell Barb to suck up her guts and act like somebody. Or, Annie's eyes narrowed, was Barb already acting a part, the terrified heroine trapped in a cellar and the villain coming down the steps, one creaking step at a time?

Max smiled at Barb. "That means you were in your room at an important time."

Barb forgot to act. She blinked in thought. "My room doesn't overlook the garden."

"I know." He was matter-of-fact. "Your windows overlook the side of the house where everyone parks. Did you look outside?"

Barb's feet slid to the floor. She sat up straight, curiosity overcoming histrionics. "What's the big deal about the side yard?"

Max was casual. "It would be helpful to know what cars you saw and when."

Barb looked interested. "I was in my chair by the window about ten. I like natural light to put on my makeup." She lifted a finger to touch her cheek. "It makes all kinds of difference. You look splotchy if you put on too much."

Annie bit her lip to keep from smiling. She had an inkling

of Barb's appeal, a girlish hopefulness, a transparent desire to be beautiful and admired and loved. No wonder Ben hurried to reassure his little sister when she was frightened.

Barb scooted forward in the chair. "I was doing my makeup and I looked out the window a couple of times. The crows were cawing like mad. I've always liked crows. They make me think of Shakespeare. You know, striding out on a stage, bumptious and loud. I tried out for Juliet in a summer outdoor theater, but I didn't get a good part. If I had the right training, I'd have a chance." She puffed her cheeks in a pout. "Geoff's mean not to help."

"Maybe you'll be the one to get the reward. I'm offering five thousand dollars."

Barb's eyes glistened. "I'll try to help."

Annie looked sharply at Max. Was everything fair in the hunt for a murderer? Perhaps. But she hated to see the avid hunger for money on Barb's face, hated to know Max was dangling bait. Had he settled on offering five thousand because that was the sum Barb needed for the modeling school?

"You looked out the window around ten?" Max prompted.

She lifted her shoulders, let them fall. "Not much to see. Crows. A raccoon trying to open the garbage pails. Justin came out all dressed up in a suit. He has a new station wagon. I don't see why he can have everything he wants." Her eyes were dark with envy. "I didn't see anyone else. 'Course, I wasn't looking every minute. I had to do my makeup."

Max was patient. "What cars did you see?"

She held up a finger as she thought, gave a swift nod. "Rhoda's Lexus. Geoff gave it to her for a wedding present. Maybe he'd have money for us if he didn't spend so much on her. Geoff's old

Chrysler. He's the one who needs a new car. Kerry's car is boring, a little old Toyota. She keeps it polished. You'd think it was a fancy car. Ben's MGB is cool even if it's old. My car's a junky little Ford. I don't know if it can make it to L.A. or not. And" —she suddenly looked eager—"maybe this is what you've been trying to find out. There was a big black pickup parked there. It doesn't belong to any of us. I don't know who it belongs to."

"Did you see anyone near it?"

"Nope. Just before I went downstairs, I happened to look out again and I saw Robert Jamison's old jalopy."

Max's gaze was intent. "Did you see Robert?"

She shook her head regretfully. "I didn't see him, but I'm sure it was his car."

Max looked puzzled. "How do you know Robert's car?"

She looked at him earnestly. "That was our first car."

Max looked blank.

Barb laughed. "It was a piece of junk, but we loved it. It looked like a mangled can, but it ran, got us everywhere we needed to go. Geoff bought it from a guy who worked on one of the shrimp boats. It was passed down from Justin to Ben and me and then to Kerry. When we'd all left and got our own cars, Geoff sold it to Robert, let him pay for it by doing yard work."

Geoff came out of the library as Annie and Max left the sunroom. Annie felt sure he'd been listening to the sunroom door open and shut. Barb was the last family member to be interviewed and here was Geoff, walking toward them, eager but anxious.

Max smiled. "Everyone was helpful."

"Is there anything new?" Geoff sounded apprehensive.

Annie wondered how he would feel if he knew one important fact had been established with certainty: Every member of the Grant family was familiar with Robert Jamison's car. Its presence at the house Wednesday morning must have seemed providential to a calculating murderer.

Max's expression was bland. "I have a much better picture of the household now. There's one more thing I'd like to check out. Do you mind if Annie and I run upstairs for a minute? I'd like to have a better idea of the view from the hall windows."

"Why, yes. Of course. I'll—"

"That's all right. You don't have to come with us. It will only take a minute. Come on, Annie." Max turned on his heel and headed for the stairs. Annie hurried to catch up.

On the second floor, he gave one swift glance behind to be sure Geoff hadn't followed. He scarcely glanced toward the east window. "Ben and Barb's rooms to the left, Kerry and Justin to the right." He stepped on the landing. A board creaked. "If Justin's telling the truth, Ben had just crossed this spot."

Annie understood the implication. Anyone coming up the stairs and going to Ben's room would step on that board.

Max was grave. "What was Ben doing downstairs?"

No wind stirred the dangling fronds of the weeping willows. The shadows across Denise Cramer's front porch faded as the sun slipped behind the tall pines, turning the sky a rich orange, throwing deep patches of darkness across the lawn.

As Max knocked on the front door, Annie took a sidestep and glanced past a red pottery rooster on a chrome-and-glass table framed by the uncurtained front window. Though the living room was dim, it was light enough to see that the colors were gay, a turquoise pottery lamp, a handwoven sweet grass Gullah basket with bright balls of coral and green and blue yarn, a purple pottery sandpiper.

Max turned. "We'll try again in the morning. Why didn't she want to talk about her view of the garden?"

Annie fell into step beside him. "Do you think that's why she shot out of the library so fast?"

"Maybe. Maybe she really has a million-dollar deal. We'll catch her. Right now I want to talk to our favorite lady cop, bring her up to date." His tone evidenced no joy at the prospect.

Annie grabbed his hand. "I haven't had a chance to tell you. Harrison's okay, Max. She came to the store this morning. I liked her. She's trying hard."

Max waved at Hal Porter who was concentrating as he screwed an owl guard over the purple martin entry holes. Hal didn't look their way.

Annie gestured toward Hal. "He left me a message this afternoon. He plans to camp out at the Franklin house again tonight. I think he hopes those kids come back. This time he'll be ready for them." She frowned. "I hope he doesn't have another shotgun."

Max grinned. "That kind of guy always has another gun."

Annie looked worried. "I hope he's careful."

"He called me, too." Max grabbed her hand, walked faster. "Come on, Mrs. Darling. After the cop shop, we'll swing by and feed your razor-fanged cat—"

"She loves me," Annie protested.

"—then head for home and a Max Darling gourmet dinner and conversation with a civilized feline."

Max touched Annie's arm, looked pointedly at a series of tiny scars, mementos of Agatha's affection.

"She isn't perfect." Annie tried not to sound defensive. "Who'd want a perfect cat?"

"Like mine?" Max boasted that plump, white-furred Dorothy L. had the charm and good humor Agatha lacked.

"Agatha's smarter than Dorothy L."

"Depends," Max said airily, "upon which reader you ask."

Officer Harrison invited them into the break room. "My office is kind of small. I've got some coffee ready." She looked shyly at Annie.

When they settled at the Formica-topped table, there was also a plate of Lorna Doone cookies with a batch of homemade fudge in the center. Harrison nodded at the candy. "Lana Edwards is filling in for Mavis. Lana's taken some hot soup to Lou. She says the hospital food tastes like soap and he needs to get his strength back. She knows I like fudge. She makes it with Karo syrup and evaporated milk."

Annie took a cup of coffee in the thick white pottery cup. Harrison retrieved a carton of half-and-half from the refrigerator. Annie took a splash and a piece of fudge. "How's Lou?" She felt a pang that she hadn't called to ask how he was progressing after his appendectomy.

Harrison's face furrowed. "He's doing better. He gets to go home tomorrow. I don't think he'll be back until next week. But"—and she sounded delighted—"Billy called a little while ago. If Lily keeps some food down tomorrow, they'll start home Saturday. Of course, he's aware of everything we've learned and has given me instructions."

It seemed odd to be in the police break room without Billy.

Max was forthright. "After you left the Grant house, we met with the family. As you may know, the Grants were disturbed by the article in today's *Gazette*. They wanted to talk to Annie."

"When the reporter called, I felt our investigation was being criticized." She looked at Annie. "I had done as I promised you and informed the solicitor. He dismissed the episode on the pier as an effort to divert suspicion from Robert. I agreed. However, since Robert Jamison is no longer a suspect, we reviewed the case. We can't rely on an unsubstantiated identification, but obviously the family must now be included as possible suspects. When Mr. Grant called about the article, I realized the family was on the defensive. That"—and she gave a sudden bright smile—"is good. Now, what brings you to see me?" She flipped open a notebook.

Max cradled his steaming cup. "We picked up some information you might want." Harrison made notes as Max talked. When he concluded, she was judicious. "Let me confirm what you've reported:

1. *No one admitted hearing anything out of the ordinary Monday night.*
2. *Rhoda Grant and Hal Porter were in the garden Wednesday morning near the time a resident of the house could have walked to the Jamison house. Neither observed anyone else in the garden.*

3. *The garden is visible from Geoff Grant's study, from the library, and from the corner guest rooms occupied by Justin Foster-Grant and Justin's fiancée, Margaret Brown.*
4. *Denise Cramer was home Wednesday morning, but she claimed not to have looked out her front windows.*
5. *Justin Foster-Grant departed in his car at a little after ten en route to the bank.*
6. *Geoff Grant often described the coin collection to his family. The family was well aware of which coins were most valuable.*
7. *According to Rhoda Grant, all the Grant children desperately want money. Also, Geoff Grant is pressed for cash.*
8. *Justin claims he saw Ben Travis-Grant returning to his room late Monday night.*
9. *Robert Jamison's jalopy was familiar to every member of the Grant family."*

Harrison tapped her pen on the notebook. "The last is a big help. The murder weapon in Robert's car and his refusal to state his whereabouts resulted in his arrest. There didn't seem to be any reason other than guilt that the gun could be in his trunk. Now its presence appears to be a direct link to the Grant household."

"Dinner was divine." Annie slid the last plate into the dishwasher.

Dorothy L. observed from the windowsill and looked for all the world as if she were smiling benignly.

Max wrung out the dishcloth, hung it on a rack above the sink. "The okra makes all the difference."

Annie came up behind him, slid her arms around him. "The chef makes all the difference. I've tasted plenty of gumbos"—she pressed against him—"but yours is special."

Max swung around and held her. "Not nearly as special as you."

Annie lifted her lips and felt the warmth of his. After a long moment, she sighed happily. She stepped back, caught his hand in hers. She was ready to turn and walk up the stairs until Max gave her fingers a squeeze and loosened his grasp. She looked at him in surprise. "You have a better idea?"

He looked rueful as he pointed at the clock. "I told Hal I'd be over no later than eight. He wanted to go by his place for a little while."

"So you'll be gone an hour or so?"

Max was abruptly hearty. "You can relax and enjoy that new Donna Leon book. I'll fix you some cocoa before I leave. With marshmallows and cinnamon."

Annie folded her arms. "And you?" she inquired sweetly.

"I'll give Hal some backup. I dropped my stuff over there earlier today, a cot and sleeping bag and food. I even laid in some firewood. But it's pretty spartan. There's no need for you to be uncomfortable." He avoided her gaze. "I'd better be on my way."

He turned and reached for his leather jacket.

Annie was right behind him. "Great. A sleepover. Count me in."

Chapter 14

The unfurnished drawing room glowed with fresh paint and repaired woodwork. Two cots in front of the fireplace looked small in the great expanse. Flames flickered red and orange as logs crackled. Annie walked near, held out her hands for warmth.

She grinned at Max. "This isn't exactly what I had in mind for our first night in the Franklin house." They'd already planned the menu for that wonderful beginning. She had yet to choose the wine. Perhaps they'd enjoy champagne at evening's end. She watched the dancing flames. The grand moment of their first official night would be the presentation of the Franklin house history to Max. Would she give Max his surprise before dinner? Or when they had coffee here in front of the fire? Or should she save it for their first morning together as he awoke? She could put the slender volume with its long-ago tales of the lives and loves of the Franklin house on his breakfast tray.

"Hey, Annie. You're a million miles away."

"Actually," her tone was light, "I'm totally here in the Franklin house."

Max put another log on the flames. He strode to the kitchen, returned in a moment with two green plastic garden chairs. He placed them near the fire. "Madame, make yourself comfortable. And hey, I'm glad you're here."

Annie slipped into a chair, welcoming the warmth of the fire.

Max poked his chair. "No brocade but it will do for now." He sat down. "All the comforts of home. Almost."

She gazed up at the pale lilac coved ceiling with its elaborate cornice. The graceful and fluid garlands of vines looped from the center were as lively as rippling forest ferns in a spring breeze. "Max, it's lovely. I wish our beautiful house wasn't part of a crime."

Max's reply was swift and firm. "When we find out what happened, you won't feel that way. There will be too many happy things to dwell on this. Every old house has had good days and bad days. We're going to have good days. But we can't ignore trouble when we're right in the middle of it." He came to his feet, gestured to her. "Come on, we should be able to figure out where Gwen hid the coins. She needed a space"—he spread his hands perhaps six inches apart—"at least this big. Now"—his eyes scanned the big room—"the floors have been refinished, so we can knock out any idea of lifting a board."

Annie came to her feet. Surely they could work out the secret of the Franklin house. "The hiding place had to be within reach and she was no taller than I am." Annie stepped to a wall, placed her hand high above her head.

Max stepped to the mantel, ran his hand along the loops of

carved ivy. He pushed, tugged, pulled to no avail. Annie moved to the doorway and studied the lintels. They poked, pressed, and yanked, including wainscoting and baseboards. Everything they touched remained secure.

Max led the way to the dark dining room. He flipped switches and the chandelier burst into brightness, the freshly cleaned crystal prisms and hurricane lamps brilliant as the day they were made almost two centuries before. The cascade of light emphasized the blackness of the night beyond the dark panes of the uncurtained windows. Max concentrated on the mantel. Annie studied the lintels, pulled at marble windowsills. She moved in a crablike crouch to check the baseboards.

Annie shook her head in discouragement. She pushed up and moved to the center of the room where their Sheraton dining table would sit, looked skeptically around. "This is a wild-goose chase."

Max frowned. "She put the coins somewhere in this house."

They continued from room to room, turning on lights as they went. Annie rapped on a cypress panel in the library. "Oh wait, this is what the carpenter just replaced." But she was talking to herself. Max's voice floated from the hall. "Think I'll pop down to the basement. That's where people hide things."

Annie recalled the basement's pristine walls with a bright coat of new white paint, the newly installed heating unit on a solid concrete base, the almost endless rows of new shelving. Empty new shelving.

If it were the old basement, Max might be right, but the walls had been torn out and replaced. A hiding place would have been exposed. Exasperated, she put her hands on her hips and turned in a slow circle, seeking inspiration.

Had Max been in the library with her, she might have dismissed the sound as the click of his shoe on the wooden floor. Max wasn't in the library. Her sneakers made no sound.

There had been a sound. A sharp click.

If a figure moved behind the shrubbery at the window, pressed near the windows, a button or zipper on a jacket might snap against a pane. That was the kind of sound she'd heard.

Annie tried to continue to look perplexed and thoughtful though her heart thudded. The sound came again.

Someone watched her from the darkness. Casually, she strolled toward the mantel, gave it a sharp rap. Shaking her head, she walked to the hall. Once out of sight of the window, she flung herself toward the kitchen. In a flash, she was at the top of the basement stairs. "Max!" Her whisper was piercing.

He looked up, startled.

Annie put a finger to her lips, then gestured for him to come.

Max ran lightly up the steps.

She gripped his arm, whispered, the words tumbling in a rush. "Someone's outside. Watching us. Outside the library."

"Stay here." His voice was low. He moved to go past her.

Annie held on tight. "Let's get Hal. He has a gun."

Max's expression was grave. "If it's too dangerous for us, it's too dangerous for Hal. You go back to the library, wander around, keep it casual. I'll slip upstairs and go out on the side porch and see if I can spot anyone. No confrontations with a killer. All we need is a look."

Annie nodded and walked swiftly up the basement stairs, Max close behind. In the central hallway, Max hurried up the main stairs. Annie strolled into the library and called over her shoulder as if Max were just outside the door. "The rosewood cabinet will fit perfectly between the windows." She half turned as if listening, then smiled and walked to the fireplace. She lifted her hand, knocked on a side panel. "Sounds solid as a rock to me."

In a moment, Max wandered into the library. "We've almost finished downstairs. Let's check the hallway and stairs."

Once out of sight of the library window, Max spoke softly. "I looked from the upstairs porch, but the shadows are too dark. I think someone's there. Get my flashlight from the kitchen. Go upstairs and out on the porch. I'll turn off the hall light and ease out the front door and down into the yard. Once I'm in the shadows, I'll move where I can throw this." He waggled a can of soda from the refrigerator he'd stocked earlier. "I'll toss it about thirty yards away from the house. It should make a racket. If somebody bolts from the bush, turn on the flashlight, and see if you can get a look."

Annie found the flashlight in the kitchen. Back in the main hall, Max waited in the dark foyer, ready to step onto the porch. She ran lightly up the stairs. It was also dark on the second floor. She moved with a hand outstretched. At the porch door, she opened it carefully. On the upper porch, the cool night air smelled of dampness and wood and foliage. There was an aromatic scent from the cedar near the front walk. She took one noiseless step at a time to the end of the porch. She stood behind a massive column and strained to see.

Max threw the can and brush crackled west of the house, the sound explosive in the night silence. The shrubbery near the library windows rustled. Annie pressed the button. Light speared over the side of the porch down toward the shrubbery.

A shot rang out.

"Annie," Max shouted. "Get down."

She ran for the door, struggling to breathe. Max had called out and he was in the yard, alone, unarmed.

Another shot exploded.

Annie ran through the upper hall to the stairs, calling out, "Max, get inside." *Be safe. Be safe. Be safe.*

Muffled but terrifying came the crack of three shots in quick succession.

When she reached the kitchen, the back door burst open. Max plunged inside. They came together in the center of the kitchen.

She clung to him.

In an instant, he pushed her toward the hallway. "Get out of sight. If the door opens, I'll go for him. You get out the front door."

Steps pounded on the back porch. "Max? Annie?" Hal yelled. "Are you there? Are you all right?"

Max flung open the door.

Hal rushed inside, a revolver in his right hand. "I was in my tent and I heard shots. They came from the west. I grabbed my gun and hustled outside. Someone ran toward the woods. I got off a couple of shots, but I was shooting blind." He swiftly looked them over. "You all right? What's going on?" He clicked the safety on his gun, stuffed it in the side pocket of his jacket.

Max described their effort to catch a glimpse of the observer. "We tried to be clever. We're lucky the shots went wild."

Hal looked disappointed. "I didn't think anybody'd try to get in with the lights on, so I was taking a break. I was watching the Lady Tigers play North Carolina State. Man, I like lady athletes." At Annie's look of surprise, he smiled. "I was married to a basketball player once. I don't miss many games. I got a battery-powered TV. All the comforts of home." His smile was brief. "I feel bad I messed up. But"—he looked puzzled—"why would somebody watch you guys? And why shoot at you?"

Max gestured toward the library. "We were hunting for the coins. That was obvious. When Annie realized someone was out there, I thought we had a chance to see who it was. We came too close. The watcher couldn't afford to be seen. That has to mean it was the murderer."

Hal looked glum. "If I'd been on my toes, we might have it all wrapped up right this minute." He was gruff. "I would've gone after him, but first I had to check on you two."

Max flicked a glance toward the porch. "Think there's any chance we can find him now?"

"Not likely." Hal gestured to the woods. "He didn't hang around."

Annie looked quizzically at Max and Hal. "Why do you both keep saying 'he'?"

Hal gave an odd sideways smile. "You got a point. My ex-wife was a whiz at trapshooting." He gave a humorless chuckle. "If she'd been out there, one of you would be dead. Are any of the Grant ladies trapshooters?"

"We'll find out." Max looked determined. "We're too late to catch anyone and there's no point calling Harrison now. But we can take a look by the library windows."

Annie remembered the distinctive clink that had betrayed the silent watcher. There might be a trace of that presence.

Camellia sasanqua ran the length of the west side of the house. In the glare of the flashlights, fragrant white blossoms were vivid against the shiny dark green leaves. The shrubbery was cut back to permit a good foot of clearance between the house and the planting.

Max knelt and aimed the light beam down the narrow space. "The leaves look like they've been kicked underfoot." His voice lifted in excitement. "About six feet from here, the leaves are mashed down. Looks like someone skidded. There's a muddy place near a water faucet. I can see the edge of a footprint."

Annie bent near. "A man's shoe or a woman's?"

"The print isn't large enough for me to tell. I can see treads, maybe a portion of a running shoe. Every shoe wears differently." Max backed out of the opening, came to his feet, reached down to brush twigs and leaves from his knees. In the upward glow from the flashlight, he looked like a man with a winning Derby ticket. "Tomorrow Harrison can get a cast. Finally, we have something concrete, a link to the murderer."

Curious, Hal knelt to get a look. "I see it. Maybe I should get a board to cover it up."

Max shook his head. "Better not. In daylight, Harrison can go slow. There may be other prints we'd mess up if we got in there."

Officer Harrison was crisp in a fresh uniform, the French blue shirt and pants immaculate. Her dusky red hair shone in the soft morning sun. The cloudless blue sky promised a seductive February day with a gentle breeze. A cardinal's trill sounded amid the glossy leaves of the magnolia near the sundial.

Annie felt the kind of happiness that good days bring. No matter the dark reason for this morning's early outing, it was a gorgeous day to be alive. She felt like wrapping her arms around her world, the tall pines, the live oaks with their dangling Spanish moss, the saw palmettos. Annie's rush of affection extended even to the several hundred chattering, milling jackdaws that dotted the trees and strutted atop the roof.

Max led the way as he described the night to Harrison.

Harrison's face looked stiff. "You should have called the authorities immediately, Mr. Darling."

Annie noted that Harrison's high-polish black leather shoes left a clear print on sandy portions of the ground.

Max gestured toward the woods. "When Hal Porter got here from his tent, the murderer was well into the woods. By the time you could have arrived, he'd have been long gone. But there's a footprint behind the hedge. There may be other prints as well. That's why we waited until morning. It would be easy in the darkness to miss a print."

The narrow tunnel between the house and the camellias was dusky. Harrison pointed the brilliant beam of her Maglite into the opening.

Annie shivered a little and fastened the belt of her cardigan. It would be in the sixties by midafternoon, but now the air was cool. She leaned close to Max, whispered, "We're always in trouble with Harrison."

Harrison backed away from the hedge. She turned pale blue inscrutable eyes on Max. "You left the site undisturbed?"

Max looked puzzled. "When we saw the partial print, we left it exactly as it was."

Harrison held out the Maglite, jerked her head toward the hedge.

Max took the light and moved to the opening.

Annie saw the sudden tension in his shoulders. When he faced Harrison, he looked grim. "Not a trace."

Annie heard Harrison speak, but the sound was lost in a rush of feeling. She stared at the nearby woods. Last night they'd been watched when they thought the trespasser was long gone. A dangerous, cool-headed gunman had calmly observed them and waited until it was safe to smooth away any trace behind the hedge.

The police cruiser pulled away.

Max stood with his hands on his hips, frowning. "I don't blame Harrison for being irritated. We busted it."

Annie's objection was swift. "How could we know the murderer was still out there?"

"It should have occurred to us." He was dour. "Now we've lost our best chance to get some kind of lead, something specific. It's like fighting smoke. We reach out to grab and nothing's there."

Annie's eyes were drawn to the trees. Despite the cheerful sunlight, the woods now looked sinister.

Max was abrupt. "Anyway, you're out of here. You stay at the house tonight. Our old house."

Annie glared. "While you and macho man hold the fort? If you're here, I'm here."

Max suddenly grinned. "You have that edge to your voice. I know when I'm licked. But"—he was firm—"we won't provide a target tonight. It's pretty obvious we're safe as long as we don't spot our trespasser. We need to stay because as long as we're here, nobody can get in to hunt for the coins. I'm afraid they may stay hidden until the next century. I'm going to go at it another way." He reached for his cell phone, rang. "The number for Denise Cramer, please." In a moment, he punched the buttons, then gave Annie a thumbs-up. "Mrs. Cramer, this is Max Darling." He grinned. "Sure, I'd love to come up and see you sometime. In fact, how about right now?" Abruptly, he was serious. "Someone shot at my wife and me last night here at the Franklin house. It's important to know who you saw Wednesday. . . . Nobody? . . . You're sure? . . . All right, but I want to talk to you. . . . You can't make it sooner? . . . All right. I'll be over at ten."

He hung up and frowned at the phone. "Why do women always procrastinate?"

Annie cleared her throat.

He smiled. "Okay, I know. Not all women do. In fact, you are the least procrastinating woman I've ever known. You act first and think later."

Annie didn't smile. "Excuse me?"

He laughed aloud. "I'm not excelling in tact this morning. Anyway, Denise is taking a bubble bath, and she'll smell lovely for my arrival. She sounded much too cheerful to be harboring any dark secrets. In fact, she made it clear, 'I didn't see anyone. It's crazy to think one of us would hurt anyone. Ever. But if you want to ask me questions, I'm your gal. My dance card's full this morning. The lady policewoman's coming at eleven. Maybe you and I can talk about something more interesting than Geoff's garden.' She gave this giddy laugh and hung up."

Agatha's meow was sharp. Her green eyes glittered. She advanced toward Annie with a hunter's stealth.

"I know. You've contacted the Cat CLU." Annie was conciliatory and she walked fast, grateful for her ankle-high brown boots. "I wouldn't have been late"—Annie sidestepped and broke into a trot—"but I had to go by the house and feed Dorothy L." Possibly this wasn't tactful.

She yanked open the cupboard behind the coffee bar, lifted out a can of gourmet cat food, flipped the lid, and spooned it into Agatha's bowl. Before she could place it on the mat, Agatha poked her head into the bowl and ate in gulps while firmly planted on the coffee bar counter.

"The health department would not be pleased." Annie tried to pull the bowl away.

Agatha gave a deep-throated growl.

Annie yielded and left the bowl on the counter. She hadn't bothered to flip the sign on the door to OPEN. She didn't intend to stay long. She definitely intended to accompany Max to see Denise Cramer. Denise might just be having fun. She obviously liked to have fun. But fun with Max included fun with Annie. Period.

Annie put the mail on the counter. A slim cardboard envelope, marked URGENT, didn't carry Uncle Sam's postage. Annie opened it. The label held a note in Henny's handwriting:

> *A dear friend was flying to the States and promised to drop in on the island and leave this for you. Most of the footage reflects our glorious trip, but we inserted personal messages at the beginning. We're on our way. See you soon.*

Annie slid out a DVD. In a moment, she'd inserted it in the player:

Emma's deep orchid caftan glittered with silver spangles. Her spiky hair was silver with purple streaks. Holding a laptop, she sat in her usual regal posture in a mahogany chair with silver cushions.

Annie blinked at the arresting colors.

Emma's square face looked satisfied. "I wish Marigold and I had time to help you." Her tone indicated her conviction that Annie would certainly be in need of help. "However, the Muse calls." She cleared her throat. "I'm on page nine."

Annie folded her arms. "You are the most self-centered creature I have ever met." Talking back to a DVD might be strange, but it was very satisfying. "When I tell you we almost got shot last night, I hope it doesn't disturb the Muse." If "Muse" sounded like a snarl, it was no accident.

The scene moved to Henny standing on deck. A breeze ruffled her dark hair. In the background was the lush vegetation of a Caribbean island. "I hope you will take time to talk to Denise. She can be silly, but she is loving and generous. If you gain her confidence, she may have better insights than almost anyone in the family. The others are much more self-absorbed. Perhaps that's what makes it so difficult to know who might be guilty."

Annie glanced at her watch. She and Max would talk with Denise in less than an hour.

Laurel relaxed on a chintz sofa. She was lovely but her face had a haunted quality. "Dearest Ones, I have a terrible premonition. You know that I am sensitive to impending events. There is great danger. Do not under any circumstances attempt action on your own. Stay together. Beware the false face."

Annie shook away a momentary shiver. Maybe there was such a thing as ESP and Laurel had become aware of their peril last night. As the DVD moved into a scene of their departure from Broward's Rock several weeks ago, Annie hit stop.

She gave no more thought to the DVD as she hurried toward her car. What could they learn from Denise? Max was convinced she'd evaded talking to him because she had seen someone in the garden Wednesday morning. Annie didn't think Denise would keep quiet if she believed she'd seen the murderer. But Annie wanted Denise's help. Maybe she would agree to talk to Ben and find out where he'd been Monday night when Justin saw him.

Chapter 15

Sunlight speared through the overhead canopy. Cardinals trilled. Crows cawed. A white tailed deer bounded across the overgrown path, followed by a spindly legged fawn. Annie felt ebullient. Sunlight did that for her. She hurried to keep up with Max. "We should be up front with Denise, tell her that Justin claims Ben was out of his room late Monday night, and Ben won't explain. That ought to get her attention."

Max looked skeptical. "I don't think a doting aunt is going to assume he was burying coins in Gwen Jamison's family cemetery."

"I don't see why not. If there's an innocent explanation, why doesn't he give it?"

Max laughed. "Because he's Ben, and he won't be bullied."

Annie accepted Max's judgment. "Okay. No bullying. Maybe Denise can cajole."

They left the woods behind and reached the well-kept path

to the Grant house. The Grant garden was lovely in the sunshine though no one was taking advantage of the weather for a stroll or to sit on the back piazza. The wail of a buzz saw shattered the morning peace. The shrill sound came from the other side of the house and was enough to keep everyone inside.

Max knocked on the cottage door. Annie looked through the open curtains. She smiled. Yesterday she'd noted that Denise was a casual housekeeper, books stacked on end tables, magazines in a lopsided pile on the coffee table, a sweater tossed carelessly over a chair, a tray with a mound of mail. Today there was even more clutter, car keys tossed carelessly on the coffee table next to a green leather purse.

Max banged again, louder. After another try, he was irritated. "I guess she's pretty irresponsible. But she's going to have to answer some questions sooner or later."

They walked back toward the main house. Annie stopped, frowning. She pointed at the bright red recently polished Cadillac parked near the cottage back door. "I guess that's Denise's car. Her purse and car keys are on the coffee table in the living room."

They both looked toward the white screen door. The door into the kitchen was open.

Max moved fast, his expression determined. "If she's home, she's going to talk to us."

But once he reached the steps, he stopped and turned toward Annie. "Wait here."

She looked past him, saw a brownish-red smear on the lintel.

He pushed open the kitchen door.

She waited by a cheerful yellow bench, her eyes fixed on the screen door. It seemed a long time though it was only a moment before he returned. He stepped outside, his face grim.

"She's dead. I need your cell." He took the phone, punched 911. "Max Darling calling from Denise Cramer's cottage. She's been murdered. I found her body in the passageway between the kitchen and living room. Somebody beat her to death. There's a baseball bat covered with blood." He looked sickened. "And a bloodstained coat on the floor."

Red light swirling, siren blasting, the police cruiser jolted to a stop behind the shiny red Cadillac. Harrison banged out of the car. Thorpe scanned the surroundings, alert and wary. As they strode toward Annie and Max, Harrison spoke briefly to Thorpe. Thorpe nodded and veered toward the Grant house.

The front door of the Grant house opened. Geoff Grant came out on the porch, a newspaper in one hand. He stared at the whirling police light and the police officers. He hurried down the broad front steps. "What's going on? What are you doing here?"

Thorpe held up a hand and Geoff stopped. He looked toward the cottage. "What's happened?"

Thorpe's low voice didn't carry.

Geoff looked as if he'd been struck. Once again he started for the cottage. Thorpe barred the way, spoke briefly. Reluctantly, Geoff turned and walked back to the house, Thorpe beside him. They disappeared inside.

At the cottage, Harrison gave Annie and Max a quick, cool glance. "Stay here." She pulled on plastic gloves, eased open the screen door, stepped inside.

A rattle and wheeze announced the arrival of Dr. Burford's old sedan. He didn't hurry. He knew there was no need for hurry. He nodded at Annie and Max as he passed. His seamed face looked angry. He loved bringing babies into the world. He hated death, especially death come too soon.

The crime van pulled up alongside Burford's car. Frank Saulter swung down. He carried a video camera and satchel. As he passed, he looked at Annie. Warmth touched his light brown eyes for an instant. Then his face re-formed, taut, impersonal, controlled, a police professional at a murder scene.

Annie turned her back on the cottage, though turning away did nothing to erase an image in her mind of a plump, cheerful, affectionate woman lying in a pool of blood.

Max gripped her arm. "Sit down." He led her to the brightly painted bench.

Annie sank onto the hard wooden seat. "Was she killed because we were coming?" It hurt to speak.

Max grabbed her hand. "Not because of us. Harrison was scheduled to see her at eleven. The murderer's running true to form. Gwen Jamison promised to keep quiet, and it didn't save her. I don't think Denise intended to reveal what she knew."

"Why not? Why protect a killer?"

Max looked toward the Grant house. "Because"—and his voice was sad—"she loved someone and didn't believe that person could be guilty."

Annie stared at the house. Denise's generous foolish heart had cost her dearly.

Chief Saulter stood in front of the fireplace in the Grant library. Ashes were clumped in the grate from yesterday's blaze. A sherry glass with sticky residue was tucked behind the celadon vase. Everyday household tasks hadn't received their usual attention. The chief's hair was grayer, his face more lined, but his air of authority was undiminished. Annie always thought of him as chief even though he'd long been retired.

The hall door opened again. Officer Thorpe held it wide for Margaret Brown.

She entered, looking haughty, her champagne-bright hair perfectly coiffed. "I resent being treated like a criminal." A rose silk blouse emphasized the deeper rose of tweed slacks. She walked regally across the room to sit on a leather sofa next to Justin.

Thorpe ignored her, spoke to Saulter. "This is the last one. She took her time getting ready."

Family members had been ushered to the library singly or in pairs by Thorpe to join Geoff, Max and Annie, and, later, Hal Porter. Geoff, Justin, Margaret, Kerry, Ben, and Barb were present. Everyone in the family was there except Rhoda.

Annie and Max sat a little apart from the family with Hal Porter. He looked out of place among the Chippendale and Sheraton chairs in his plaid work shirt, stained Levi's, and worn brown cowboy boots. He sat on a wooden bench, massive hands on his thighs, expression remote and wary. Occasionally, he gazed at one or another of the Grants, his eyes narrowing in scrutiny.

Yesterday the gathering in the library had been contentious with an undercurrent of defiance. Now the mood was fearful and grief-laden.

Geoff's face was the color of old snow. He slumped in a wing chair, head sunk on his chest, eyes staring at nothing.

Barb scrubbed at tearstained cheeks. Her golden-brown hair was straggly. Her red cotton blouse was only half tucked into faded jeans. She huddled on a love seat next to her brother. Ben was unshaven. His white T-shirt hung loose over khaki slacks. He patted his sister's back, occasionally spoke softly to her. He had lost his swagger.

Kerry had pulled an ottoman close to Barb and Ben. Every so often she murmured to one or the other. Occasionally she bent forward, rested her head against Ben's shoulder, her soft black hair screening her face.

Justin bent close to Margaret, listening as she murmured to him. He frowned and turned his hands over in helpless resignation. She glared at him. Finally, reluctantly, he turned toward Saulter. "Look, we know this is horrible and we want everything possible done to find out who hurt Denise, but what's the sense of penning us up?"

Saulter glanced from Justin to Margaret and back again.

A bright flush touched Justin's face.

"Sorry to inconvenience you." Saulter's voice was measured. "A basic investigative technique is to gather possible witnesses in one place and prevent private conversations. When Officer Harrison completes her investigation of the crime scene, she will conduct an interrogation. The process has been slowed because the department is shorthanded. I am former Chief of Police Frank Saulter. I am assisting Officer Harrison. In this instance, everyone in the vicinity of Mrs. Cramer's cottage this morning has to be considered a suspect in her death."

Margaret came to her feet, outraged. "That is absurd. I scarcely knew the woman."

Saulter's expression didn't change though his eyes had a sardonic gleam. "Then I suppose you will have to consider your proximity to murder an unfortunate introduction to the reality of police work, Miss Brown."

Hal Porter smothered a bark of laughter.

Geoff cleared his throat. "Margaret, please sit down. We have to cooperate with the authorities."

Justin tugged at Margaret's sleeve.

She tossed her head. "Rhoda isn't here. What makes her special?"

Geoff looked miserable. "Rhoda went to the mainland this morning on the first ferry, so she doesn't know what's happened. It's going to be awful for her." He looked at the china clock on the mantel. "She'll be back in a few minutes. She'll drive up to the house and see the police cars and ambulance and that crime-scene tape." He reached out a pleading hand. "Let me call and warn her, at least tell her there's been an accident."

Saulter was firm. "Witnesses awaiting interrogation may not make telephone calls."

The room sank into a watchful brooding silence. Occasionally Barb muffled a fresh sob. Kerry held one of Ben's hands in both of hers. Margaret stared stone-faced at Saulter. Justin tugged at his shirt collar as if it choked him. Geoff moved restlessly in his chair. When the clock chimed the quarter hour, he stood and walked to the French windows and peered to look out.

Annie wondered if he was watching for Rhoda's car or if he was surveying the cottage.

There was a distant sound of a car motor.

Geoff turned back to the room, started for the door.

A door slammed. Running steps crossed the hall. Rhoda burst into the library. She was trembling, her eyes wild, her mouth working. "What's happened? There's crime-scene tape around the cottage and the ambulance has its door open and they're bringing out a stretcher that's all covered over."

Barb gave a keening cry. "Somebody killed Denise. She's dead, Rhoda. Mama's dead and now Denise is dead."

Ben wrapped his arm around her shoulders. "Don't cry, baby." Several voices rose at once.

Saulter strode to the center of the room. "Quiet, please. Mrs. Grant, Denise Cramer was killed this morning between nine and ten a.m. Officer Harrison will be here soon to inquire into the whereabouts of everyone concerned. Please take a seat and refrain from discussing the circumstances."

Rhoda wavered on her feet. She looked from face to face as if hoping that someone would say none of this was true. "Denise?" She lifted her hands, pressed them to her cheeks. "She can't be dead." Abruptly, Rhoda began to cry, great gulping sobs.

Geoff hurried to her, took her in his arms. He glared at Frank. "She's too upset to make her stay. Let me take her upstairs."

Hal Porter moved restively on the bench. He shot a sharp look at Rhoda, his tough face folded in a frown. Annie thought he wouldn't have much patience with women who couldn't cope.

Saulter frowned at Geoff. "I need for you to remain here." Saulter looked around the room. His eyes fastened on Annie. "Annie, will you go upstairs with Mrs. Grant? Officer Harrison can come up and speak with her."

Annie dipped a washcloth in cold water. Rhoda lay propped up on two pillows. Tears streamed unchecked down her face. She lay with her hands open and limp, her body sagging heavily, her makeup smeared, her facial muscles flaccid.

"The cool cloth will help." Annie handed it to Rhoda. In happier days, the bedroom was cheerful and light with flower-patterned lilac drapes and comfortably sized easy chairs in pale lemon. Annie looked toward the windows. Would it be better to draw the blinds, make the room dim and quiet? Or was the splash of sunshine across the hardwood floors cheering?

Rhoda held the cloth to her face. "I can't bear it." Her voice was muffled, her tone bereft. "I asked her to go with me this morning. She said she couldn't, she had to see some people. She was fine. Everything was fine. If she'd come . . . If I hadn't gone . . ." A fresh paroxysm of weeping shook her.

Annie felt helpless. Should she offer another cloth? Call Rhoda's doctor? A brisk knock sounded and the door opened. Officer Harrison stepped inside. "I'll have a word with Mrs. Grant. If you'd like to go downstairs, Mrs. Darling, you may do so. Please wait in the library."

Annie moved toward the door.

Rhoda called after her. "Don't go. It's all right if she stays, isn't it? She's been nice."

Annie heard a plea for support. She looked at the policewoman.

Harrison nodded. "Whatever you wish, Mrs. Grant. I have only a few questions."

Annie moved back to the bedside.

"About Denise?" Rhoda's voice shook.

Harrison came nearer. "I understand she was a special friend—"

Rhoda's face crumpled. She held the washcloth against her eyes.

"—so I'll be brief." Harrison's voice was gentle. "Am I correct that you left the island on the eight-thirty ferry?"

Rhoda took a deep breath, smoothed the cloth over her face. She pulled herself into a sitting position, held the cloth tight in her hands, and stared at Harrison with misery in her eyes. "I took the eight-thirty ferry."

Harrison was brisk. "When did you return to the island?"

"On the ten-thirty ferry." Her voice quivered. "I wanted to get away for a while. I went to Chastain and did the antique shops on Ephraim Street. I didn't even buy anything. I thought I'd feel better if I had a little while alone." She held tight to the damp cloth. "What happened to Denise?"

Harrison's look was bleak. "She suffered fatal head trauma when she was repeatedly struck by a baseball bat sometime this morning between nine a.m. when she spoke on the telephone—"

Annie remembered Max's lighthearted conversation with Denise.

"—and ten a.m. when her body was discovered. When did you last see her?"

Rhoda's splotched face made her look old and defeated. "This morning on my way to the ferry." Her voice was dull. "I had coffee with her. I asked her to come with me. She said she was busy."

"What was her demeanor?" Harrison looked hopeful.

Rhoda's eyes filled with tears. "She was her usual self."

Harrison frowned. "She didn't indicate fear or worry of any kind or suggest she had information that might connect a member of the family to the murder of Gwen Jamison?"

Rhoda hunched her shoulders. "The last thing she told me was that she was sure no one in the family had done anything wrong." She bowed her head. "She hugged me and I left."

Harrison looked disappointed. Obviously, she had hoped for more. She gave a quick nod. "Thank you, Mrs. Grant. Mrs. Darling's presence is now required downstairs. I will send your husband up to be with you as soon as possible."

"It's all right." Rhoda's voice was muffled as she turned against the pillow. "Nothing can make any difference."

When Annie and Officer Harrison entered the library, Annie hurried to join Max. He gave her hand a squeeze.

Geoff's blue eyes were anxious. "Is Rhoda all right?"

"She's resting." Annie knew it was inadequate.

Harrison stood beside Saulter, conferred for a moment in a low voice. He nodded and walked swiftly out of the room. He left open the door into the central hall.

Harrison folded her arms. "Denise Cramer was murdered between nine and ten a.m. this morning in her cottage which is on the grounds of this property. It is necessary to determine the whereabouts at that time of everyone in proximity of the crime." She flipped open a notebook. "Does anyone have information relating to the crime?"

No one moved or spoke.

Annie looked curiously at Ben. Yesterday he would have objected. Now he held Barb's hand, his face drawn in a tight frown. Annie's gaze swung to Justin. Yesterday he would have sneered and snarled. Now his vivid red hair and mustache emphasized the paleness of his face, the empty stare in his green eyes.

"Very well. Let's start with you, Mr. Grant." Harrison looked at Geoff. "Your whereabouts between nine and ten a.m.?"

Geoff sat forward in his chair, elbows on his knees, hands clasped. "I was working in my study. I was there until I heard the siren."

Harrison pointed. "Ben Travis-Grant."

Ben gave his sister a reassuring smile, released her hand. "I don't pay a lot of attention to time. I went out for a jog. I suppose I came back a little while before ten. I was heading upstairs for a shower when I heard the siren."

Harrison's gaze was intent. "Where did you jog?"

Ben made an indeterminate gesture. "I took the path, went over to Calliope Lane, came around by the road and down the front drive."

"Did you see Denise Cramer?"

Ben leaned back, folded his arms. He looked uncertain.

Harrison took a step forward. "Did you or did you not see her, Mr. Travis-Grant?"

Ben looked grim. "I did not see her."

Harrison stared at him for a moment, her gaze suspicious, then turned to Barb.

"Miss Travis-Grant?"

Barb licked her lips. She had a hunted look. "I was in my room the whole time. I didn't see Denise." She sagged back against her chair.

"I saw him." Margaret's voice was higher than usual, but steady and determined.

Harrison looked toward her. "Saw whom?"

Margaret stared at Ben with icy blue eyes. "Ben was at the back door of the cottage. I was standing at my window, brushing my hair, and thinking about Wednesday. I didn't look out that morning. It was foggy. But today was beautiful. I saw him."

Ben's face closed down, his expression became smooth and impenetrable as marble.

Harrison took another step toward him. "Were you at the cottage door?"

Ben hunched his shoulders. "I knocked and there wasn't any answer. I waited a minute and knocked again. I did not go inside."

"You didn't mention this earlier." Harrison's voice was stern.

Ben moved uncomfortably. "What was the point? I don't know anything. All I can tell you is I knocked on the door and there wasn't any answer. I'd just got back from my jog, and I wanted to talk to Denise. When she didn't come to the door, I went in the house. That's all I know."

Harrison wrote swiftly in her notebook. "Miss Brown, what time did you see Mr. Travis-Grant at the door to the cottage?"

Margaret looked uncertain. "I didn't notice the time. I wasn't in any hurry to come downstairs. After I brushed my hair, I decided to do my fingernails. I had to let them dry. I hadn't dressed when the siren sounded. I looked out and decided to stay in my room." Her tone implied that her world held no place for police and whatever the excitement, it was of no interest to her.

Kerry jumped up from the ottoman. Her face was flushed. "I took a walk this morning, too, and I saw Ben go up to the cottage and knock on the door. He did just as he said. He knocked several times, then he turned and left."

Annie didn't think a single person in the room believed Kerry.

Harrison's eyes narrowed. "You didn't speak up when Mr. Ben Travis-Grant failed to mention his visit to the cottage."

Kerry lifted her chin. Her soft black hair swirled around her face. "I was waiting until my turn."

Harrison looked sardonic. "Yes, indeed. You claim that you went for a walk?"

"I went for a walk." Kerry's tone was sharp.

"Where?" Harrison held her pen above the notepad.

Kerry glanced across the room at Annie and Max. "Their house. I was curious to see it. It used to be an old dump when we were kids. They've made it beautiful again. Gwen had lots of stories about when she was the housekeeper there." Her stare was defiant. "I went up and tried the door. It was locked. I was going to see if I could figure out where Gwen hid the coins."

Max's expression was wry. "You're welcome to come and look. We've searched everywhere."

Harrison studied Kerry. "If you went to the Franklin house—"

"I did."

"—and returned here, how did you have occasion to see Mr. Ben Grant at the back door of the cottage?"

Kerry stiffened. "I saw him when I came back."

"You came straight back from the Franklin house and came inside here?"

Slowly Kerry nodded, her violet eyes wary.

Harrison had the air of a teacher writing an equation on the board. "The Franklin house is directly south of the Grant house. The cottage sits approximately forty yards to the northwest of this house. The back door of the cottage is not visible on the walk from the Franklin house to here."

Kerry's eyes were brilliant. "I was enjoying being outside. I came past the house and in the front door. I saw Ben when I came up on the porch."

Harrison turned toward Ben. "Can you confirm Miss Kerry Foster-Grant's claim."

"I didn't see her." His voice was toneless, but his eyes were soft.

Harrison glanced at her notes. "Mr. Justin Foster-Grant?"

Justin was brief. "I was in my room until I heard the siren. I did not see Denise today."

Harrison walked to Annie and Max. "Mr. and Mrs. Darling, you discovered Mrs. Cramer's body. Did you see anyone near the cottage?"

Max answered for them. "No one."

Justin cracked the knuckles of one hand. "Our ever-present neighbors again. What business did you have with Denise?"

Max was somber. "I wanted to ask who she saw Wednesday morning on the path to Gwen Jamison's. I was too late."

There was no sharp denial. Instead the silence was filled with foreboding.

Harrison looked toward Hal Porter.

Hal sat with his arms folded, booted feet solidly planted. He had the air of a man constrained to be present, but clearly he considered himself an unwilling onlooker. At Harrison's glance, he spoke up. "Look, I don't know these people. I'm a handyman in the winter. I'd never spoken with the lady who got killed. I don't know anything that will help. I was working on the east side of the main house, cutting wood for an arbor that Mrs. Grant ordered. I wasn't paying any attention to people coming and going." He stood. "So if it's the same to you, I'd like to get back to work."

Harrison held up a hand. "We are almost done, Mr. Porter. Please remain until we finish."

Hal looked irritated, but he sat down.

Harrison flipped her notebook shut. "I want to ask if anyone can identify two objects taken from the crime scene. Chief Saulter?"

Frank entered through the hall door. He moved to the center of the room.

There were quick indrawn breaths, a gasp, a shrill cry. Barb clutched at her throat.

Annie steeled herself against horror. Max reached out to take her hand.

A baseball bat dangled from Saulter's hand. He held an inch-wide band of rubber that was wrapped around the thinnest portion of the shaft. Blood smeared the white ash. Portions of hair clumped near the end.

Geoff came to his feet, his hands clenched. "No one should be asked to look at this."

Barb buried her face in her hands.

Justin came to his feet. His voice was hoarse. "That's my bat. I burned my initials on it when I was a kid. Mid-shaft."

A crooked letter *J* was clearly visible.

Justin looked frightened. "I haven't seen it in years."

Annie averted her eyes. The bat was dreadful, as Geoff had

said. She tried hard not to picture Denise's cheery face and hear her buoyant voice. How terrible to be hurt and, worse, to back away helpless from someone known and loved.

Geoff tried to keep his voice steady. "There's a lot of sports equipment in the garage. Anyone could have taken it. We don't lock the garage."

Harrison looked toward the hall. "Officer Thorpe?"

Every face turned toward the door. They waited, eyes staring, bodies rigid.

Thorpe gripped a four-foot square of cardboard. He held it as he would a plate. He carried the cardboard and its grisly burden to the middle of the room and carefully placed it on the floor. With a plastic-gloved hand, he reached down and lifted up a crumpled tan plastic poncho that looked as though handfuls of blood had been flung against it.

Geoff came slowly forward. He stared at the poncho. "That's Rhoda's. She keeps it hanging on a hook in the garage."

Chapter 16

Annie opened the microwave, lifted out a paper plate with steaming chicken tamales. Mixed veggies, nachos, and mango-pineapple salsa completed the menu. They stood by the food island since the tall stools had yet to be delivered.

Max used his plastic fork to spear a chunk of tamale. "How can you defend Ben?" He tapped his fork against his plate, ticking off his points. "He can't seem to hold a steady job." He grinned. "Not that a casual attitude toward work is bad."

Annie grinned in return. Max was capable of intense effort. On occasion. However, he insisted that work should never take precedence over living and loving. Especially the latter.

Max added a spoonful of salsa. "Ben sneers at convention. He was out of his room Monday night. He asked Geoff for money and was turned down. He was seen on the murdered woman's back porch."

Annie spooned more salsa over the nachos. She and Max had been wrangling all evening, Max insisting that Ben Travis-Grant was the prime suspect, Annie stubbornly disagreeing.

She munched a nacho, said indistinctly, "If he were the murderer, he'd never admit he went to Denise's cottage."

Max raised an eyebrow. "If you recall, he didn't admit it until Margaret Brown said she'd seen him. He had no choice."

Annie shrugged that away. "All he had to do was say she was mistaken, his word against hers."

Max lifted his Dr Pepper bottle. "What about Kerry?"

Annie did her best to balance mixed veggies on the plastic fork. "She didn't see Ben." Annie looked at Max with suddenly doleful eyes. "That's why I don't want it to be him."

Max looked bewildered. "Because Kerry didn't see him?"

"Kerry loves him." Annie's voice was sad. "She's such a good person."

"Not," Max said dryly, "apparently an always truthful person."

"Oh, it was true. True in her heart."

Max put down his fork. "You are beginning to sound a lot like my mother."

Annie looked at him in dismay, then saw the smile tugging at his lips.

"Laurel would understand." Annie pictured Laurel with her glorious golden hair and patrician features and empathetic blue eyes. "Laurel knows all about love. She understands how people care. Kerry wouldn't even think it was a lie because she believes in Ben. She knows if he said he was on the back porch and didn't go inside, every word was true, and so she decided to say she saw him and that would make him safe. It matters terribly to her that Ben be safe."

Max took a last bite of tamale. "Then I'm sorry for her. I think he was lying." He stood and moved to the counter. "Do you want a brownie or raspberry sorbet?"

"Both." The answer was quick and automatic.

Max topped the brownie with sorbet, placed the dish on the food island. "It's almost Ben by default. We know the murderer is a member of the family. Gwen made that clear. When you look at the family, what do you see? Geoff's got some money problems, but he doesn't seem greedy. Justin's a jerk, but he's not stupid. He'd never use his own bat as a weapon. That garage has to be full of stuff that could be used as a weapon, golf clubs, an ax, hockey sticks, probably a stack of old bricks. So much for Justin. As for his fiancée, she has all the charm of an anaconda, but I can't picture her draped in a poncho and wielding a bat. Ditto for Kerry and Barb. That leaves"—he gurgled the rest of his Dr Pepper—"Ben. Case closed."

As they cleared up, Annie was silent. Max had logic on his side. All she had was a feeling that a woman with Kerry's heart wouldn't be deceived, that if she saw worth, worth was there.

Annie dumped the last paper plate into a black plastic trash bag, determined to push away all thoughts of the Grant family. Let Officer Harrison handle the investigation. There was nothing more she and Max could do. She held the bag open for the cardboard dessert bowls. "Maybe we should go to paper plates after we move in. Look how quickly we cleared up."

Max swiped the food island with a damp dishcloth. "Not on my watch." He sounded firm. "Food needs proper presentation."

For an instant, Annie felt lighthearted. This was her familiar world. Oh, they were only camping out in their home-to-be, but Max was here and that was all she ever needed to be happy. She smiled at him. If she had to be trapped in an unfurnished house that attracted too much stealthy attention, it was lovely to be trapped with Max. Her moment of happiness lasted until she looked toward the uncurtained kitchen windows. Annie kept her smile bright, but she was acutely aware of the night.

Max saw her glance. His face was suddenly serious. "Go home, Annie. I know it's grim here."

"It would be grim there, too." She would be haunted by images of Denise Cramer crumpling beneath the blows of the bloodied white-ash bat. Annie resolutely tied the trash bag, plunked it next to the door.

Max reached for it.

She grabbed his arm. "In the morning. Too much happens around here to go out in the dark. Maybe everything will be over by morning." Ben in jail? Kerry's world shattered? "Harrison intended to get formal statements from all of them this afternoon."

Max didn't look hopeful. "More detail maybe. But nobody saw anything. Unless someone's lying."

"Someone's lying for sure." Annie looked toward the hallway. "And somebody still wants the coins. They're probably locked up somewhere in this house."

"Lightning doesn't strike twice." He sounded confident. "We'll have a calm evening. Hal said he'd settle in with a good book tonight. No TV. We won't be caught by surprise."

A frenzied knock rattled the back door.

As Max strode to the door, Annie followed close behind.

When the door opened, Barb Grant timidly looked inside. In the wash of light from the overhead fluorescent panels, she looked wan, eyes reddened from weeping, no makeup, her hair frowsy. She reached out a shaking hand. "Can I talk to you?"

Annie looked past her, saw Hal Porter near the hedge. She gave a tiny shake of her head. He nodded and slipped back into the shadows.

Max held the door wide. "Sure. Come on in." His voice was gentle.

Barb edged inside. "Everything's awful." Tears spilled down her cheeks. "They've taken Ben to Beaufort. Tomorrow they're going to charge him with murder."

Annie's heart ached, even though the news came as no surprise. Maybe Harrison had made the right choice. Still, Annie didn't believe Ben had twice committed murder. All right. Face it. She didn't want Ben to be guilty because of Kerry. But if not Ben, who? She saw faces in her mind: gentlemanly Geoff, arrogant Justin, supercilious Margaret, tender Kerry, forlorn Barb. None of them fit.

Barb stood in the bright fresh kitchen and looked as though her world had collapsed. Her hands twined together, twisting, twisting. She looked at Annie. "You were nice to Rhoda today. I took her a tray tonight, and she said you were kind. I know it may seem strange for me to come here. There's no reason you should help me, but your house seems to be part of everything, and I know you helped Robert. I don't have anyone else to ask."

Annie moved toward her, slipped her arm around thin shoulders. "Let's go in by the fire." She knew Barb was cold, the deep pervading cold of shock. "Would you like to have something to drink?" They weren't equipped for hospitality. At home they had brandy or cocoa, something to pump warmth into a body diminished by grief and anguish. Here there was hot coffee in a thermos, nothing more.

"I don't want anything. Thank you." Barb spoke almost primly, remembering her manners.

Max stood by the mantel as Annie and Barb sat on the folding chairs.

"I thought Ben would come home tonight. Everyone else came home." Barb's voice was thin and wavery. "We all had to go to the police station this afternoon. Everybody but Rhoda. I guess they don't care about her since she was in Chastain when Denise was killed. The rest of us were there, Geoff and Justin and Margaret and Kerry and me. They made us wait on benches in that front entrance place. They talked to us one by one. I came home with Kerry. Justin and Margaret were next. About six, Kerry and I decided to fix something to eat. We cooked bacon and scrambled eggs and made English muffins. I took a tray up to Rhoda, but she couldn't manage a bite. She just lies there and cries. Geoff didn't come in until seven. I should have known. He wouldn't look at me and he ate real fast and then he sent Kerry up to get Justin and Margaret and he had us come into the library." She massaged her temple. "Me and Kerry and Justin and Margaret." She stared at them with heartbreak in her eyes. "I can't blame Geoff. He said they asked him about the check that was forged. He didn't know how they found out. Maybe they talked to someone at the bank."

Max looked puzzled. "Check?"

She crossed her arms tight against her body, her head sank forward. "We were in college. It was spring." She came to a full stop.

Annie scooted her chair forward, patted Barb's shoulder.

Barb looked at her with hollow eyes. "It wasn't even that much money. Six hundred dollars isn't that much."

"Six hundred dollars?" Annie wished that Barb did not look so defeated.

"I had a chance to go on a cruise and somebody told me there was going to be a producer there. I thought if I could meet him . . ." Her voice trailed away.

Max was brisk. "You took a check out of Geoff's checkbook and forged his name."

Barb's eyes widened. "How did you know?"

Annie would have liked to take her by the shoulders and give her a good shake. "What does this have to do with Ben?"

Barb's gaze fell. "We'd been home for Geoff's party. I'd asked him for the extra money and he'd said no and so I went down in the middle of the night and got a check out of his checkbook. I didn't think he'd notice."

Max frowned. "What happened when he found out?"

"He didn't exactly find out. He wrote a letter to all of us, me and Ben and Justin and Kerry, saying there was an irregularity of six hundred dollars in his checks and he would be forced to contact the authorities if the matter weren't cleared up immediately. Ben called me." Again she came to a full stop.

Max's tone was thoughtful. "How did Ben know it was you?"

"I'd asked him for money, too. Six hundred dollars." Her voice wobbled. "He told me I was an idiot and why had I done it and I tried to make him understand and he was furious, but he told me he'd take care of everything."

Annie's eyes opened wide. "What happened then?"

Barb looked at her timidly. "Nothing."

"Nothing?" Annie stared in disbelief.

Max pushed away from the mantel. "You never asked Ben?"

"No." Her face mirrored guilt and heartbreak.

"Ben took the blame for you." Annie wondered at Barb's willingness to protect herself at her brother's expense and at the ostrich mentality that had avoided finding out what Ben had done. Perhaps in Barb's world not knowing the outcome of Ben's talk with Geoff almost made her feel as if nothing had ever happened. "Have the police come up with that old story?"

Barb's face was etched with misery. "Geoff told them Ben was a thief. Geoff thinks Ben took the coins and killed Gwen and Denise. Geoff said he had to tell the police what he knew because it all added up. Justin saw Ben out of his room the night the coins were taken and this morning Ben went to Denise's cottage and he needed money and he was a known thief." She shrank against the chair. "When Geoff said that, Kerry turned so white I thought she was going to faint. She got up and walked out without a word. And then"—Barb struggled for breath—"Geoff said he'd called a lawyer to see to Ben. Geoff walked out of the room. I went after him." Her eyes were desperate. "I called out to him as he started up the stairs and told him I had to talk to him and he said not tonight, he was sorry but he'd had all he could take and he had to go up and see to Rhoda. I wanted to tell him. I tried to call after him and say it was all wrong, I was the one who'd forged the check, but he was gone. Then I knew what I had to do. I had to tell Kerry. I went up to her room and knocked and she didn't answer. I tried the door and it was locked. I whispered that I had to tell her something important, that Ben was innocent. But she wouldn't come to the door."

Max's tone was gentle but firm. "You have to tell the police."

She clenched her hands. "I don't know where to go or who to talk to. They took Ben to the mainland. I'll tell them I forged the check and"—she took a deep breath, dragging in air—"I'll tell them that Monday night I'd gone downstairs"—she talked so fast the words were slurred—"because Geoff wouldn't let me have the money for the modeling school. I knew Ben needed money. He wouldn't tell me why, but he said it was life and death and I knew he couldn't help me. Kerry doesn't have any money, and Justin's a pig and would never help anyone else out. Geoff has this old drawing in his study and once Mother said it was amazing how much money it was worth, thousands of dollars, an original sketch by Klee or Klass or something like that, and I thought if I took it to Los Angeles somebody there would know how much it was worth and I'd have the money I needed. I'd got it and all of a sudden Ben was there. He took my wrist so hard it hurt and he said I couldn't do it, that Geoff would find out and if I didn't stop doing things like this, someday I'd end up in prison and it would be awful."

Annie looked forward. "You and Ben were downstairs Monday night?"

Barb nodded, her face weary.

"Did you see anyone? Did you hear anything?" Everything depended upon timing. Very likely Barb had waited until deep in the night when the house was quiet. Certainly the theft of coins would have taken place when the house was utterly still.

Barb frowned. "I don't know. Once I thought I heard a creak, but it might have been Ben." She shook her head. "No, that was when I first got to the study."

"Did you turn on a light?"

"I used a flashlight. I wore gloves." There was a hint of pride at her careful preparations.

Annie wondered if the thief, fresh from digging in Gwen's family cemetery, had started to cross the hallway to return upstairs and been frozen into immobility by the gleam of a flashlight in Geoff's study or by Ben's hurried descent from upstairs.

"Anyway"—Barb's tone was resentful—"Ben made me put the drawing back. He marched me upstairs and waited until I went in my room before he went to his. And now"—it was a wail—"they're going to put Ben in jail and it's all my fault."

Annie hurried to the kitchen. She grabbed a roll of paper towels, ripped off a piece, dampened it. She took it to the living room and handed it to Barb.

Max waited until Barb's tears subsided. "Nothing can be done tonight. You need to speak with the circuit solicitor in Beaufort. His office is closed now. I'll ask a lawyer I know to see if he can arrange for him to be in his office tomorrow even though it's Saturday. Let me see what I can do."

Max took his cell and walked near the windows. He dialed. "Handler?" Quickly he brought the lawyer up to date. "Barb's explanation might dissuade Posey from filing charges against Ben. Could you set it up for him to meet with Barb in the morning? Whether it changes his mind or not, he'd probably like to hear what she has to say." Max listened, nodded. "All right. Nine a.m. She'll come over on the early ferry."

He clicked off the phone, turned back to Annie and Barb. "Handler picked up the call at his son's basketball game. He said Posey's one of the referees and he'll talk to him after the game. If we don't hear back, everything will be set."

Barb lifted beseeching eyes. "Will you come with me?"

Max looked uncertain. "The solicitor and I aren't on good terms. However, I'll take you if you wish."

"Please." Her gaze dropped. "Will he tell Geoff?"

Max was gentle. "Posey may feel that it will be necessary for him to talk to Geoff again. Don't you think it would be best if you told Geoff yourself?"

"I guess I'll have to." Barb's voice was small.

"Everything will be better tomorrow. Now I'll walk you back to your house. Go straight to your room. Don't talk to anyone. Lock your door."

Barb stared at him, her hand at her throat.

Max looked at her steadily. "If Ben is innocent—"

"Oh yes, he is!"

"—and if you are innocent, there is still a murderer in that house."

The dying fire flickered. The wash of moonlight through the uncurtained windows made the living room seem huge. Oddly, Annie felt no menace now. Was that because Ben Travis-Grant was being held? She wasn't sure. She only knew that for the first time since Wednesday morning, she felt safe in their lovely old house with no sense that danger lurked outside. She wondered if Max was asleep. "Max?" Her whisper was light.

"Mmmm?"

"Barb could have been lying."

"With Barb"—his tone was dry—"that is always a possibility. But"—he rolled over on one elbow, propped up—"I can't see her volunteering as a noble sacrifice. In fact, I expect she fudged her story when she said she tried to tell Geoff. Still"—and now his tone was kind—"she's doing her best and probably that's a lot better than she usually does."

Annie propped up on her elbow, faced him. "What do you suppose Posey will do when we show up in the morning?"

Max's head shake was immediate. "Not us. Much as I love you and think you enhance any outing, if there is anyone Posey loathes more than me, it's you."

Annie knew Max was right. Posey had been quick to charge Max with murder last August. His office and the island's mayor had both looked hasty and foolish when Annie, with the assistance of Billy Cameron, proved Max a victim of a clever and calculated frame-up. Posey's antipathy to Annie went back a long time ago to their clash when Ingrid had disappeared and Posey concluded she'd committed murder.

She laughed. "Okay. I don't mind staying home." She had a vision of a cheerful morning at the bookstore, opening boxes and shelving new titles. "You can do your best to disappear into the wallpaper and let Barb win him over with her waiflike appeal."

Annie flew past Max, pulling on her windbreaker. Not a cloud marred the silky blue sky. It was going to be another gorgeous day in paradise with the temperature nudging seventy, although it was still chilly as the sun spilled over the pines. Annie took a deep breath of pine resin, marsh water, and cinnamon-scented japonica. "I've got to rush. Agatha was furious when I was late yesterday. She doesn't care if Dorothy L. ever eats."

"Better wear gauntlets. I'm sure there's a catalog with falconry equipment." Max strolled toward the Corvette.

Annie ignored the calumny. Agatha wasn't vicious. She simply had a strong personality. As she flung into her Volvo, she called out, "Good luck with Posey. You're the one who may need gauntlets."

"I'll imitate wallpaper and hope for the best."

She was still smiling as she drove too fast. First she'd drop by the house and feed Dorothy L. and then she'd go to Death on Demand. It was shaping up to be a perfect Low Country day, a glimpse of sea, a splash of sun, and the best mystery bookstore north of Miami.

The Corvette pulled up behind a decade-old beige Toyota sedan. They were the only cars on the ferry. The *Miss Jolene*'s deep whistle blared three times, and the ferry eased away from the dock.

Barb clutched Max's arm. "That's Kerry's car."

The driver's door of the Toyota opened. Kerry Foster-Grant stepped out and turned to look at the car behind her. As she walked toward the Corvette, the breeze rippled her feathery dark hair. She was slim and lovely in a charcoal-gray wool suit set off by a cherry-red silk blouse and black pumps. A pearl choker emphasized the grace of her throat. She looked businesslike and determined.

Barb took a deep breath. "I have to talk to her." On deck, she hesitated then moved slowly forward, a contrast in style and demeanor, her raglan sweater multihued and shapeless above black wool trousers and black leather flats, her posture defeated.

Max slid out of the car. The air off the water was cold. Gulls cawed. Frothy whitecaps lipped the water. The ferry chugged steadily westward across the sound, the mainland not yet in view.

Kerry's face was set and stern, her deep violet eyes filled with anguish. "I'm on my way to Beaufort. It's all a lie about Ben. Geoff said the police think he stole the coins because he needed money. He'd asked Geoff for help, offered to sign a note, but Geoff turned him down. Ben should have told him why he wanted the money. A good friend of his in Thailand needs an operation and can't pay for it. Ben didn't want to say. He was afraid Geoff wouldn't believe him. Now the police think he took the coins to sell them. He didn't. Ben wouldn't steal, not ever."

Barb looked insubstantial, as if the brisk wind that ruffled the water could topple her overboard.

Kerry stared at Barb. "You forged the check. I know that's what happened. You're the only person Ben would lie for. You shouldn't have done that to him. You shouldn't have made him lie."

Barb lifted a hand in appeal. Her face was drawn. "I tried to tell you last night. I tried to tell Geoff. I'm on my way there now. I'm going to see the circuit solicitor"—she stumbled a little over the title—"and tell him the truth."

The hardness eased out of Kerry's face. "I knew that's what happened. I knew that was the only answer. Ben didn't steal. He wouldn't steal. Oh Barb, Barb." Kerry's face crumpled, tears sliding down ashen cheeks. "Oh Barb, thank you."

They came together in a tight embrace.

"Gauntlets." Annie's tone was derisive. However, she still wore her jacket and she moved with alacrity, slipping the bowl onto

Agatha's mat and evading a quick slash of fangs. It wouldn't be necessary to tell Max that Agatha had at first evidenced displeasure. Now the sleek and elegant black cat was purring as she ate.

Annie shed her jacket, hanging it in the storeroom. She returned to the coffee bar, started a pot of Colombian coffee, and settled at a table with the previous afternoon's *Gazette*, which she'd retrieved from the house when she fed Dorothy L.

The headline was big and black:

MURDER CLAIMS ISLAND REALTOR

Annie scanned the story. It was amazing how much detail Marian Kenyon had included even though she'd had to work against a quick deadline. There was a portrait shot of Denise Cramer, photos of the Grant house, the Franklin house, and Gwen Jamison's home. A boldface sidebar read:

Is there a deadly triangle on Broward's Rock?
See artist's rendition page 3.

Annie flipped to page 3. A bright red isosceles triangle was turned on its side with the base perpendicular. A black skull marked each end of the base with a third at the tip.

The caption was worthy of a 1930s radio serial:

> Death stalks the island. Should residents beware the sinister happenings that have occurred at three residences which form a perfect triangle?
>
> Skull 1 marks the home of Gwen Jamison whose body was found Wednesday morning.

> Skull 2 marks the residence of Geoffrey Grant which was the site of a high-dollar theft of gold coins Monday night. Island Realtor Denise Cramer was found bludgeoned to death Friday morning in a cottage on the grounds.
>
> Skull 3 marks the unoccupied but refurbished antebellum Franklin house where the stolen Double Eagles reputedly are hidden, accounting for several attempts to break into the house. Gunfire has erupted though there have been no injuries. An armed guard is now on duty at all times.
>
> Police officials are discouraging any visits to these sites.

Annie reached for the phone. She wondered if it would faze Marian if Annie suggested that the next issue might as well dub the houses the Bermuda Triangle of the Low Country and be done with it. She doubted Marian would feel an iota of shame. In fact, she was likely floating on a cloud of self-approval. Her husky voice would proclaim, "It's the new journalism, baby, up close and personal. Get 'em in the gut."

The phone rang.

Annie glanced at caller ID. Miss Pinky's Pantry. Miss Pinky, aka Paula Paine Pratt, was the proud proprietor of a combination tea shop and secondhand store crammed with antiques, collectibles, and dusty old books. Miss Pinky, as might be expected, was always garbed in pink, fluffy, frothy, filmy masses of pink. Her white hair had a pinkish tinge, she chirped in a high sweet voice, and never, never, never had an unkind word to say. She also had a shrewd gleam in her eye, likely the inheritance from a Yankee trader forebear who'd landed on the island shortly after the Civil War, married a local girl, and never left. Woe betide any outlander who thought Miss Pinky could be gulled. Smiling sweetly, she was famed for coming out the better in any trade.

Annie smiled as she lifted the phone. "Hi, Miss Pinky." The old dear had a passion for Patricia Wentworth titles and was eagerly replacing some of her tattered copies with the new editions now coming out.

"Oh, my dear, it always gives me a moment's pause when I phone and before I can say a word I'm already known. It almost smacks of the occult though I know it's just more of that connectedness they are always telling us about. I swear the next thing you know we'll all have to wear implanted chips that tell more than we want anyone to know. Why, now they can identify you by taking a picture of your eye and they say it's even better than a fingerprint. I for one would like to go back to the days when they didn't have records on us that go six ways from Sunday. But of course it's such a help to historians, though everyone says digital cameras are a bane. How can you make a scrapbook or have a box of old pictures when everything's on a silly little disk? But it's history that worries me now."

Annie was smiling. Miss Pinky was in vintage form. "History is troubling you?" Annie wondered what aspect of history was causing Miss Pinky's distress.

"It's been my experience and quite often a source of profit to me," the high sweet voice was confiding, "that there is always something behind a flurry of interest in a particular subject. Mark my words. If I get several calls for an early silver coffeepot by Samuel Kirk of Baltimore, I know one must have sold on eBay for a huge sum. Or if that film actress who built that mansion on the south end of the island calls and asks for a Hepplewhite armchair made before 1790, you can take it to the bank that one of her neighbors just found one in Charleston. This morning I received an inquiry from Maggie Owens. She owns the Silver Horse in Chastain."

Annie sipped her coffee, remembering the collectible shop on Ephraim Street. Its proprietor was a lean woman who favored turtlenecks and jodhpurs and who indulged her passion for horses with the largest collection of horse memorabilia in the Low Country.

"Maggie wanted a copy of *A History of the Franklin House* by Miss Agnes Merton, the very one you bought a few weeks ago. She offered me a substantial sum for it. She said she had a customer come in Friday morning who was desperate for the book. That waved a red flag because I had an inquiry about the book this week. This morning I read yesterday's *Gazette*. When I saw that triangle, I knew I had to call you."

Annie no longer felt comfortable and mildly amused.

"I heard that Gwen Jamison hid those stolen coins in the Franklin house and you'd been having all kinds of trouble there, so folks wanting to know all about the Franklin house may be up to no good. Now I don't go around talking about my customers. Least said soonest mended. And a mote in my eye may not be a beam in yours. And maybe it's nothing more than somebody putting two and two together and thinking they might as well skim the cream as anybody else."

Annie looked toward the bookshelf where the slim gray volume was tucked. She held tight to the receiver. "Who's hunting for the book?" And for a fortune in coins. Was it going to be this simple? Would Miss Pinky in an instant tell Annie in a breathy, dithering voice the name of the figure who'd moved unseen leaving death behind?

"She looked like she'd traveled a long road when she came into the shop. That was Thursday afternoon. By that time there wasn't a man, woman, or child on the island who didn't know there was a fortune somewhere in the Franklin house. She asked me to try and find a copy, said she was collecting books about old island houses and she needed that one." Miss Pinky's sniff was delicate as a cat's sneeze. "I could have told her she didn't have me fooled. I taught first grade for thirty years and I can tell you that when a body's eyes skitter like a marionette's jerky foot, there's not a word of truth being said. I told her I didn't have a copy on hand but I'd see if I could round one up. Then I got that call from Maggie. I asked her if Rhoda Grant was the customer and she'd asked me to hunt for it and no sense in both of us . . ." —Miss Pinky's words danced in Annie's mind—". . . online . . . who else would know better that those coins . . . maybe trying to help out her husband . . ."

Somehow Annie thanked her and ended the conversation and all the while she fought bitter disappointment. For a moment, she'd thought the answer was at hand and hoped to take a name—the name—to Officer Harrison.

Rhoda Grant. It would do no good to call Officer Harrison. No matter what Rhoda's motive in seeking the history, she was not on the island Friday morning when Denise Cramer was murdered, that was certain and definite. Now Annie knew what Rhoda had done off island. She had canvassed the antique and secondhand and collectible stores in Chastain, seeking a copy of *The History of the Franklin House*. She hadn't taken the ferry Friday morning to leave behind the pressures of theft and murder, she had hurried to the mainland seeking information about the Franklin house. If she discovered the hidden cache, what was her intention? To restore the coins to her husband and deliver a murderer's name to the police? Or was she working for her own advantage, seeking the coins for their value?

Annie hurried to the bookcase. She lifted out the thin little book with its pebbled gray cover.

Chapter 17

Max pumped another quarter in the parking meter. He resumed his slow stroll up and down the street. The state flag, a palmetto and silver crescent against a blue field, and the Stars and Stripes hung above the broad double doorway of the courthouse.

He hoped he'd made the right decision to stay outside and have Kerry and Barb speak to Posey unaccompanied. Without Max there, Posey was more likely to listen. Max reached the corner, turned back. He picked up his pace when the doors opened and Kerry and Barb came out. He felt a shock of disappointment. Kerry moved as if she were old and sick. Barb clung to her arm for support.

Max met them at the bottom of the steps. "Did you see Posey?"

"He accused me of lying." Barb's voice shook. "He said I was trying to protect Ben. He said Geoff made it clear Ben was guilty."

Kerry's eyes looked empty and lost. "They found bloodstains in the well behind the seat of Ben's MGB. Posey said it was top-notch police work that they found the stain. Thorpe used a dog to smell around the property including the cars parked on the east side. The dog pawed on the door of Ben's car and whined. They got a search warrant. The dog sniffed in the seat then poked his head in the well. They used a special light and found a blood smear. Posey's convinced Ben had blood on his hands and he cleaned them up and hid the cloth there until he had a chance to get rid of it later, but the blood was so dark he didn't see the smears. If lab tests show the blood matches Denise's, they're going to charge him with murder. Posey said the poncho protected his clothes but his hands got bloody."

Annie opened the small volume, skimmed a history of the settling of the island—"Captain Josiah Broward, an experienced planter from the West Indies, built the first plantation in 1724 and made a fortune with early crops of long staple cotton"—until she found a description of the Franklin house:

> Built in 1805, the Franklin house is an excellent example of Low Country architecture with two-story verandahs that wrap around three sides, inset chimneys, and a hipped roof. The drawing room ceiling is in pure Adam style. Its first inhabitants were Walter Franklin, his wife Matilda, and their six children, Juliet, Andrew, Carson, Harold, James, and Nathaniel. Franklin was a sea captain who was often absent on long voyages. His ship went down off Cape Hatteras in 1820. Of the children, Carson, Harold, and James

> were lost to yellow fever in 1809. Thereafter, their mother Matilda was often seen in the still of the night, circling their graves. This may account for the legend of the grieving lady in white, a ghost still glimpsed in the cemetery on Locke Road. The house was passed to Andrew, the eldest son, upon his father's death. Andrew achieved great wealth as a plantation owner with rice and indigo . . .

Impatiently, Annie flipped through the pages: the house served as a hospital during the War Between the States . . . was later sold for taxes . . . owned by a Northern industrialist . . . a gift to his daughter Rosemary upon her marriage in 1907 . . . a portion lost to fire in 1927. . . . Annie continued to flip through the pages, then a passage gripped her:

> Miserly Horace Kingsley, at one time the wealthiest man on the island, distrusted banks after the failures during the great depression of the nineteen thirties. He was reputed to have built a "safe" place in the house where he kept a fortune in diamonds. There are many stories as to the disposition of the jewels. One tale has it that Horace bestowed them upon his mistress Theodora, who went to Paris and held a great salon for poets and writers. Another suggests that his wastrel son Frederick stole the diamonds and gambled away the proceeds in New Orleans. Whatever the truth and whether the diamonds ever existed, Horace Kingsley died of tuberculosis in a charity ward in Savannah. However, a secret place presumably exists as island lore recounts that the Michael McKays, who owned the house in the nineteen forties, enjoyed showing their friends the

cleverly concealed hiding place. At one time, Miss Letitia Prescott, the last owner, stitched in needlework on a cushion a rhyme which pointed the way.

Annie grabbed the phone. She called the police department, frowned when she got voice mail. Where was everybody? Probably in Beaufort or, with Ben Grant in jail, enjoying time off. That no one was on the dispatcher's desk on Saturday morning wasn't a big surprise since they were shorthanded and had been working extra hours. The recorded message began: "In case of emergency dial nine-one-one. The police department is open . . ." She wriggled with impatience. Finally she was offered a menu. She entered Harrison's extension. "Officer Harrison, this is Annie Darling. I may have found directions to the hiding place in the Franklin house. I'm on my way there now." Annie glanced at her watch. "It's a quarter to ten. If I find anything, I'll call nine-one-one." Until she looked, she didn't know if it were important enough to roust an officer from off duty. She clicked end, punched Max's number. She willed him to answer. He didn't and the call was directed to voice mail. Would he ever, ever, ever start carrying his cell instead of leaving it in the glove compartment of his car? Well, it served him right if he missed out on the excitement of finding the Double Eagles. As she walked toward the front door, she left her message. "Max, I've got directions to the hiding place . . ."

Once again the Corvette nosed behind the Toyota on the ferry. Max put down the windows and breathed in the salty scent of the sea with a dash of diesel fuel. As the *Miss Jolene* chugged toward the island, laughing gulls gave their distinctive cry. Max usually enjoyed the twenty-minute crossing, but today he felt edgy and uncertain.

The smear of blood in the well of Ben Grant's MGB without doubt would match Denise Cramer's. A charge of murder would promptly follow, murder in the first degree. No one goes calling with a baseball bat without premeditation.

Max's eyes narrowed. Could Ben, if he were guilty, have ended up with bloody hands? Yes. Why not throw the cloth behind the nearest bush? Possibly the cloth could be linked to him and had to be hidden for later disposal. Was the well in his MGB a good place to stash a stained cloth? Almost. He would have gotten away with it except for the police dog. Could someone else, a shadowy figure who seemed to be able to move unseen leaving death behind, have deliberately smeared a cloth with blood and wiped its grisly dampness in the well and pulled the cloth out again? It was possible.

If so, the murderer planned Denise's murder with care and precision and set out deliberately to create a trail to Ben.

Why Ben?

Ben knocked on Denise's back door. Perhaps it was that simple. Perhaps it might have been any one of the others except that Ben was seen at the cottage.

Was the murderer clever enough to leave a less than apparent smear and trust the police to uncover it? Nothing ventured, nothing gained. If it hadn't been found, no harm done, but the blood was found.

There was one fact that might induce the police to look beyond the obvious. If Ben's car had been unlocked, as cars so often were on the island, it would be possible to argue that the bloodstain had been planted just as the murder weapon had been placed in Robert's trunk. Surely the police would see the parallel. The murderer had already demonstrated a talent for improvisation. The murderer couldn't have known Robert would come to the Grant house Wednesday morning or that Ben would go to the cottage, but in each instance the murderer had taken advantage of circumstances.

Everything hinged on whether Ben kept his car locked. Max opened the glove compartment and picked up his cell. Officer Harrison would know the answer.

He had a message from Annie. Maybe she wanted to meet at Parotti's for lunch. He punched to listen.

Annie flung herself from the car, ran up the back steps of the Franklin house. Her slam-bang arrival was precipitous enough to startle a flock of glossy greenish-blue jackdaws from the roof. They squawked in protest as they rose and wheeled toward the marsh. She hurried to the door, key in one hand, the slim volume in the other.

She was breathing fast when she skidded to a stop in the central hallway. The Palladian window on the landing blazed with color, spilling streaks of red and gold and violet down the steps, emphasizing the richness of the mahogany banister. Annie stared at the decorative carving of a griffin atop the newel post. The griffin was large as a crow, sharp-beaked with the head, wings, and claws of an eagle on the muscular body and hind legs of a lion.

Gri . . . ff

Gwen Jamison had made a last, desperate effort. She forced dying lungs to expel the beginnings of a word: *Gri . . . ff*

Annie took one step forward, another, touched the pointed ears, the stylized representation of feathers. She didn't look again at the page marked by her thumb. She knew the rhyme now, would never forget it:

Griffin stares,
Lambs in pairs.
Look straight,
Count eight.
Jiggle right,
Hold tight.

She lifted a hand until it was level with the griffin's eyes. As high as her shoulder. Now she turned and faced in the direction of the griffin's stare. She felt a surge of triumph. The griffin faced the doors to the drawing room. The doors were wide open and across the expanse of the huge room was the fireplace, the old and beautiful fireplace with its pattern of blue-and-white Delft tiles.

At the fireplace, Annie forced herself to be patient. She looked back at the griffin and positioned herself in a straight line with him. Up to her shoulder . . . Her hand touched the fireplace at that level. Two blue lambs frolicked forever on the creamy tile. She counted down eight bricks. Kneeling, she bent near. Was the join without any mortar? She moved her fingers to the right end of the brick and pushed hard.

The brick didn't move.

Jiggle right. . .

Annie stiffened her fingers, gave the brick three sharp taps at its right end. As if she'd turned a key, the brick slid away from her fingertips, pivoting into the fireplace. The left side swung out over the hearth. With it came a musty scent. As quickly as the small space opened, it began to close, the aperture vanishing with eel-like swiftness.

Annie gripped the open end.

Hold tight.

A system of pulleys or springs apparently controlled the mechanism. She switched hands, her right hand now firmly tucked around the brick. With her left, she gingerly reached into the opening. Her fingers closed on a lumpy package. She felt the slickness of a plastic trash bag and the roughness of duct tape. She was swept by amazement and dread and excitement. In her hand she held—

"I'll take that."

Annie stiffened. The familiar voice was easy and smooth. Still on her hands and knees, clutching the package, no larger than six inches by four, she turned to look up at Hal Porter. Behind her the brick clicked into place, the hiding place no longer exposed.

He stood a few feet away. He didn't cradle the double-barreled shotgun as he had Wednesday morning. He held the shiny weapon straight and true, aimed directly at her. "Don't do anything stupid. Or your pretty face will be in bloody ribbons."

She stared into mocking brown eyes. Hal Porter. Tall, strong, athletic, handsome Hal who had been involved from the first, pretending to be a friend and helper. Emma had been right. "Beware the Trojan Horse." She'd been suspicious of the woman beneath the pier. They should have been suspicious of the oh-so-helpful handyman.

He stood at ease. He was enjoying himself. Annie felt icy

deep inside. Hal was looking forward to killing her. She pushed away the thought, knew she mustn't let fear devour her.

But Hal wasn't a member of the family. Gwen Jamison told her friend she'd seen a member of the family hide a package in her family cemetery.

"You?" Annie's voice was uncertain.

"Me." His grin was satisfied. Chilling. "Me and a friend."

Annie had a swift memory of Denise's bouncy, eager face. No one had mentioned her involvement with a man. Hal Porter was a swaggering, bold, sexy man. Had Gwen seen Denise? That made sense. Denise could easily have broken into the library, taken the coins, hurried to Gwen's family cemetery to hide them. Gwen must have contacted Denise and promised to protect her if the coins were returned. Instead, a gunshot ended Gwen's life. Annie had no doubt whose hand had held that gun.

Now she faced a calculating killer armed with a shotgun. His shotgun, of course. There had been no black teenagers trying to break into the Franklin house late Wednesday night. If—when—she were found maimed and dead from a closeup blast, the search for the imaginary thieves would be intense. Thursday night the watching eyes had been his. She glanced at his shoes. Cowboy boots.

"You had on sneakers Thursday night."

"What a smart little lady." The derisive glitter in his eyes made clear his disdain for women. "If you'd pointed the flashlight at my feet, I'd have had to take you and the dude out then. You bought yourself a little time. Those shoes are at the bottom of a lagoon. I had to go home and get the boots."

Annie found it hard to breathe. Hal was relaxed, a man enjoying sport. When he'd walked toward them Wednesday morning, fresh from his first kill, she had admired his sun-bleached hair, strong features, and athletic build, his aura of insolence, his swagger, the confidence of a man who expected women to notice him. Now she saw the predatory gleam in his eyes.

"Slide the package to me on the floor. Then the book." He was impatient, but the shotgun never wavered.

The fireplace was behind her. Hal stood between her and the hall. She still crouched. The barrels of the shotgun aimed at her face seemed enormous.

Annie placed the slick package on the floor, pushed. The little book skidded close behind.

Hal's half smile and the aim of the shotgun remained steady as he scooped up the package and the book, tucked them inside his partially unzipped leather jacket. The smile slid away. His look was dreamy. He lifted the stock to his shoulder, his left hand slid along the barrel.

Annie stood frozen. All she could think of was the horror for Max. Shotguns did dreadful things. She knew something about them. Hal's was a twelve-gauge pump action, probably loaded with buckshot. If she were found on the floor of the lovely old drawing room, there would be blood and tissue splattered in every direction.

Please, God, don't let Max come to the house, please . . .

At first the sound made no sense to her, a hard rock beat, thump thump double thump.

Hal's eyes blinked. It was as if he came back from a long way. He still held the shotgun high.

Thump thump double thump.

His left hand fell away from the barrels though his eyes never left her face. He pulled out a cell phone, flipped it open.

"Yeah?" He was brusque. He listened. Suddenly he smiled, a huge, triumphant, elated smile. "Blood found in his car? That's great. I was afraid they were too dumb to find it. . . . Sure I put it there. Why not?" His eyes narrowed. "Are you crazy? Who cares what happens to him? Somebody's got to take the fall and it's not going to be us. . . . You don't have a choice." The words were freighted with malignity. He still watched Annie.

Slowly his gaze changed, bloodlust giving way to speculation. His eyes looked bright. His lips curved in a satisfied smile. "I'll tell you what. We'll talk about it. I'm at the Franklin place. Bring your car and we'll go for a little drive." His jaws ridged. "I don't care what you tell anybody. You got to go to the grocery. You got to see about Denise's funeral. Stop sniveling. Get in your car. If you aren't here in five minutes, I'll come after you." His tone was silky. "You wouldn't like that."

Max listened, his smile fading. ". . . to the hiding place in the Franklin house. At least I think I do. Max, there are directions in a wonderful little book. I'd bought it to surprise you, a history of the Franklin house. Rhoda Grant's been hunting for it. She tried to find it at Miss Pinky's and I'm sure that's why she went to Chastain Friday morning. Anyway, I've got it and I'm going to go see what I can find." Her voice was excited. A car door slammed. "I'm on my way there right now. I called and left a message for Harrison. I told her I'd ring nine-one-one if I found anything. I hope Posey listened to Barb and Kerry. Talk to you soon. Love you." The connection ended.

"Annie." His voice was deep in his throat. Annie on her way to the Franklin house. Alone. His chest felt tight. She'd called at a few minutes before ten. It was ten twenty-five. The ferry was due to dock in five minutes. The island loomed ahead of them, a growing green smudge on the horizon. Annie had certainly had time to get to the Franklin house, time to look, time to call him back. She hadn't called.

Quickly he punched her number. Annie always carried her cell. The number rang five times, switched to voice mail.

Maybe she'd left her purse in the kitchen. She often dropped it on a counter when they came in that way. The telephone there was in service in readiness for their move. Quickly Max dialed the new number. Once. Twice. The peals continued until voice mail was activated.

Max punched 911. "I've got to talk to Officer Harrison . . ."

Annie heard the trill of a mockingbird, the industrious rat-a-tat of a pileated woodpecker, smelled the sweet scent of camellias, watched oyster-shell dust plume beneath the wheels of a black Lexus as it pulled up behind her Volvo. She had never been so aware of the feel of the sun on her face.

Rhoda Grant watched as Annie and Hal crossed the uneven humpy ground. Rhoda looked lost and bewildered. The eyes lifted toward Hal were filled with foreboding.

Rhoda, the wife who wanted to fly, who loved fine things, who slept in a separate bedroom, who was seen by Laurel at a gambling club with a possessive man not her husband. How easily had she become involved in an affair with a dominating, sensual, dangerous man? Was the theft his idea or hers? Did they intend to sell the coins and run away together? Or was she a tool chosen by Hal for sex and later for crime?

Hal opened the back door, jabbed the shotgun against Annie's side. "Get in."

She slid into the back seat. Relief almost made her dizzy. Whatever happened, she wasn't in the drawing room. Max wouldn't find her there.

Hal kept the shotgun trained on Annie.

Rhoda looked toward him, her expression terrified. "You didn't tell me she was here. You have a gun on her. Why?" There was a sob in her voice.

"Stop crying." His tone was ugly. "I don't like women who cry. You've cried enough. It came in handy because everybody feels bad for you, the way you've howled over Denise. You're a fool. She saw us walking toward Gwen's house. She had to die. And so does she." His eyes never moved from Annie's face. "Roll the windows down."

The windows whirred down.

Hal slammed the back door shut, spoke to Annie through the open window. "Bend over, face on your knees, hold your ankles."

Annie felt confused. Was he going to shoot her in Rhoda's car? With a sense of inevitability, she bent forward, gripped her ankles.

A car door opened, the car rocked a bit, a door shut.

"You can sit up." Hal's voice came from the front seat. The shotgun poked between the driver's seat and the passenger seat. "Enjoy the ride."

The Corvette jolted to a stop behind Annie's Volvo. A police cruiser was parked beside the Volvo. Max flung out of the car.

Officer Harrison, her pale face troubled, walked toward him.

Max looked past her at the back door to the Franklin house. He couldn't speak.

Harrison's eyes showed pity. "She's not there. I searched the entire house. Her purse is on the kitchen counter."

Max whirled, shouted. "Hal?"

The only answer was the rustle of magnolia leaves in the dancing breeze.

The Lexus jounced in the ruts of the narrow dirt road. "What if somebody sees us?" Rhoda's voice shook.

"It isn't tourist season. If we see another car, we'll go somewhere else." Hal jerked his head toward Annie. "I doubt if she's in any hurry."

Annie looked away from her captor, looked out into dimness, the sunlight blocked by a canopy of live oaks, magnolia, and slash pine. The car eased to a stop next to a yaupon holly shrub. Rhoda turned off the motor. The only sounds were the slap of bird wings as a flock rose from an island in the murky lake, the rustle of pine boughs, the rattle of magnolia leaves.

Annie sat stiff and still. She and Max always came to the rookery in March to see the blue grosbeaks and summer tanagers and ruby-throated hummingbirds and indigo buntings. Last year they brought a picnic with ham and cheese sandwiches on homemade white bread and a bottle of chilled chardonnay. She'd been the first to spot a lemon-yellow parula. She and Max had spread a blanket in a secluded nook. After lunch, she'd lain in his arms and looked through binoculars until Max nuzzled her cheek and said birds were lovely but she was lovelier. She'd pointed out they were in a public place but he pointed out there was no public and he'd carefully chosen their luncheon spot and . . .

"You can't kill her, too!" Rhoda's voice was shrill and desperate.

Annie heard the words, but they didn't penetrate her icy shell. Now it was said, words that could not be taken back.

Hal flicked Rhoda a swift, bright look. "I'm not going to kill her." He sounded amused.

Rhoda sagged against the seat. "Will you tie her up, leave her? You've got a cabin cruiser. We can get away."

"Listen real close, Rhoda." His easy drawl sounded comforting. "I'm not going to kill her. You're going to kill her."

Rhoda leaned away from him, pressing against the door frame.

His face was unyielding, merciless. "Get out. Both of you."

By the time Annie stood on the uneven sandy ground, Hal was around the car, the shotgun trained on her. He didn't look toward Rhoda, who leaned against the car, trembling.

"It's your turn, Rhoda." He pulled her away from the car.

"I can't." The cry came from deep in her throat.

He jerked her upright, slapped the shotgun into her hands.

Annie tensed. Could she run? Should she run? But where? By the time she'd taken a half-dozen steps, he'd grab the shotgun and shoot.

He moved a few feet to one side. "Lift it."

An ashen-faced Rhoda slowly raised the shotgun. "I could have put the coins back. I told Gwen that's what we'd do. But you killed her." Tears spilled down her cheeks.

"You're a fool. How safe did you think you'd be? We didn't have a choice." He looked impatient. "Come on, shoot."

"You said you loved me." Her voice was a scarcely heard whisper.

"Love?" He was derisive. "When I saw that gold, I decided you could get it for me. You were easy. Then you had to screw up, get yourself seen. But I've got the coins and I'm going to keep them."

"What about me?" The shotgun wavered in her hands.

He shrugged. "What about you?" His tone was dismissive. "Stop wasting time. Aim."

The shotgun was level with Annie's chest.

Annie whirled and began to run.

"Shoot, damn you. Shoot."

The shotgun roared.

Officer Harrison looked tough and angry, her freckled face stern. "Where is Mrs. Grant?" The family stood by the side of the Grant house, Geoff, Justin and Margaret, Kerry and Barb. Missing were Ben and Rhoda. All of the family cars were there except for Ben's MGB and Rhoda's Lexus. Hal's pickup was parked a little to one side.

A shaken Geoff stared at Harrison in silence.

Max struggled to keep his fury and fear leashed. Harrison was doing her best. But Annie was gone. What if no one knew? What if no one answered? The minutes hurtled past and Annie was gone.

Geoff hunched against the cool breeze. He looked older and

smaller. Justin stood with his arm around Margaret. Kerry's violet eyes were huge and frightened. Barb trembled.

Sunlight turned Justin's hair and mustache to flame, but his face was pale. "Rhoda left in her car around twenty minutes ago. I was looking out the window of my room."

Geoff's voice was thin. "Why are you looking for Rhoda?"

"Information received. She was identified as the person who buried the stolen coins in Gwen Jamison's family cemetery." Harrison looked grim. "However, she was off island when Denise Cramer was killed. I told the circuit solicitor we needed to look for someone linked to her. Instead, he—" Harrison broke off. "I disagreed when Ben Grant was taken into custody. I asked our former police chief to investigate, see if there was any island gossip. We have no substantiation as yet but Rhoda Grant was observed at a Holiday Inn on the mainland with Hal Porter."

Geoff turned away.

Max wanted to smash the world. He balled his hands into fists. Hal Porter. Hal and Rhoda were gone and they'd taken Annie.

The sound came first, wheels crunching oyster shells. As the black Lexus came around the curve, no one moved or spoke. A woman slumped in the passenger seat. The car jolted to a stop a few feet behind the black truck. The driver's door opened and Annie scrambled out. Pale and unsteady, she ran toward Max, her arms open wide. "Rhoda saved my life. He told her to shoot me, but she shot him instead."

Harrison strode toward the Lexus, revolver in hand.

Annie reached the safe embrace of Max's arms. Only then did tears come.

Chapter 18

Annie pulled Saran Wrap from a tray of Max's finest appetizers, crisp rye crackers topped with Swiss cheese and carraway spread or feta and red pepper spread, celery loaded with cheddar and dried-apple spread. She'd declined his offer of coconut fried frog legs, but happily accepted marinated salmon strips on toast points.

Max poured chardonnay into delicate crystal glasses.

Flames flickered cheerfully as the logs shifted and settled in the fireplace.

Annie looked around in gratitude. Death on Demand had never looked lovelier. She would be forever indebted to Rhoda Grant, who had been unfaithful and willing to steal but had never envisioned murder.

The front bell announced the arrival of their guests. Emma Clyde moved down the central aisle, her blue-and-gold caftan billowing. Her square face was ruddy from sun at sea, her spiky hair a deep bronze. Henny Brawley, eyes shining with tears of happiness, rushed past Emma to envelop Annie in a hug. Laurel, a glorious vision of blond beauty in a swirl of soft violet silk, clasped her hands prayerfully. "My dear, such a terrible experience."

Surrounded, Annie reached out to them, welcomed their love and caring. She'd planned this party for the return of the traveling trio long before she'd come so near to death. How special it was to celebrate their return and her deliverance.

Laurel perched on one of the tall stools at the coffee bar. "Now." Her breathy voice was intense. "Tell us everything . . ."

Annie and Max took turns, but it was Annie who concluded. "He told her to shoot me. That's when I ran. I stumbled over a branch and fell. I heard the gun go off. I thought she'd missed and then I heard her scream. I looked back and he was lying on the ground."

Emma cleared her throat. "I warned you of collusion. As I told you, Marigold is always suspicious of an apparently peripheral witness who purports to offer clinching evidence. Clearly, you should immediately have been suspicious of the ubiquitous handyman."

Laurel's tone was gently chiding. "I do feel that I first offered the solution. As I said, my dear, look to passion. Passion is always involved."

Henny grinned at Annie, gave her the slightest flutter of a wink. "I recall emphasizing character. That turned out to be right, but I didn't have Rhoda in mind." Henny beamed at Annie. "In any event, you're safe and sound and"—her voice lilted with pleasure—"I see that no one has yet identified this month's paintings. I hoped I'd get home in time."

Annie knew what was coming. Would anyone ever match Henny's record for identifying the books and authors in the monthly watercolors?

Dark eyes sparkling, Henny pointed at each picture in turn. "*The Body in the Snowdrift* by Katherine Hall Page, *Murder on Monday* by Ann Purser, *Hornswoggled* by Donis Casey, *The Chocolate Bridal Bash* by JoAnna Carl, and *Dead Man Docking* by Mary Daheim."

Epilogue

Sculptures shimmered as raindrops slanted in a thin line. Despite the rain, the sun was shining, an odd weather pattern Felix Fogg had rarely seen. Interesting country, America. In Singapore, sodden black clouds kept the sun at bay when rain streamed against the windows, the hot air heavy and wet. Fogg made a final circle of the Wieland Pavilion. His hooded dark eyes scanned the surroundings. He was alone in the sculpture garden. He'd waited half an hour. He would wait no longer.

He was unemotional as he hailed a cab in front of the museum. Something had gone wrong. As the cab sped toward the airport, Fogg wondered what had happened. Had the coins not been available? Had the seller changed his mind?

No matter. There was always another contact to be made . . .